P9-APQ-260

"Keep *you* awake?" Sebastian repeated. His temper had been simmering when first he had entered the house. Now it rose slightly in degree. "My dear young woman, it is you who keeps me awake at night. I have called here today to express to you, in no uncertain terms, that your behavior is unacceptable. I cannot imagine what sort of activity you are engaged in that should kick up such a riot and rumpus every evening, but I should hazard a guess it is not of the educational variety."

Amelia felt a hot flush of anger mantle her cheeks as she started to descend the remaining stairs. She intended to ask that he leave. No, she intended to *demand* that he leave.

She had very nearly completed her descent when her kitten appeared and chose that very moment in which to express its affection for her. Jelly tangled her body and tail about Amelia's booted ankles just as she gained the bottom of the stair.

Amelia tried to avoid treading upon her kitten and that proved her undoing. One of her booted feet slipped from the step as she rose up on the toes of her other foot to a precarious height. For a moment she teetered on the brink of catastrophe, balancing uncertainly upon the step, the linens still clutched in her arms.

Vainly did she struggle to maintain her dignity and her balance. In the end, the linens went flying, the kitten let out a yowl and streaked back up the stair, and Amelia pitched forward . . . straight into the arms of Lord Byefield.

He caught her securely against him. His arms slipped about her shoulders and waist and she flung her hands about his neck and held on. How long she remained in such a position, she had no idea, but she rather thought she might have been content to stay in his arms forever. . . .

—from "A Bewitching Minx" by Nancy Lawrence

BOOK YOUR PLACE ON OUR WEBSITE
AND MAKE THE
READING CONNECTION!

We've created a customized website just for our very special readers, where you can get the inside scoop on everything that's going on with Zebra, Pinnacle and Kensington books.

When you come online, you'll have the exciting opportunity to:

- View covers of upcoming books

- Read sample chapters

- Learn about our future publishing schedule (listed by publication month *and author*)

- Find out when your favorite authors will be visiting a city near you

- Search for and order backlist books from our online catalog

- Check out author bios and background information

- Send e-mail to your favorite authors

- Meet the Kensington staff online

- Join us in weekly chats with authors, readers and other guests

- Get writing guidelines

- AND MUCH MORE!

Visit our website at
http://www.zebrabooks.com

ENCHANTING KITTENS

Cindy Holbrook
Nancy Lawrence
Hayley Ann Solomon

Zebra Books
Kensington Publishing Corp.
http://www.zebrabooks.com

ZEBRA BOOKS are published by

Kensington Publishing Corp.
850 Third Avenue
New York, NY 10022

First Printing: October, 1999
10 9 8 7 6 5 4 3 2 1

Printed in the United States of America

CONTENTS

CONTENTS

A FAIRY TAIL

by

Cindy Holbrook

ONE

Creighton Farewell, yawning widely, threw back the mound of velvet down-filled blankets covering him and slowly rose from his bed. He picked up his morning chocolate and the London daily from the bedside table, where his servant had left it in expectation of his awakening. Smoothing his midnight blue nightgown and straightening the matching cap, he padded across his large, palatial bedroom and lowered himself onto a huge, ornately carved wing chair set before an even larger and more ornately carved table. With a deft turn of the wrist, he pulled a deep blue velvet drape from an object centered upon that table. A goodly sized crystal, sheered and smoothed upon the side facing him, was revealed.

"Good morning," Creighton said. He proceeded to mumble a litany of Latin while snapping open the newspaper. His last words were finished around a hearty mouthful of hot chocolate. The crystal glowed blue and images appeared within its depth.

Creighton settled back, casting a half a glance to the crystal, as it revealed scene after scene, and the other half to the newspaper. He sighed. "Nothing of interest anywhere, heh?"

He shook his gray head and took another swallow of chocolate. Then he froze as the crystal flashed an image of a girl in her bath, her back displayed to him. Creighton stared a moment. Sputtering out his chocolate, he grabbed

for his spectacles and almost poked his eye out as he hastily
donned them. Blinking, he leaned forward until his face
was an inch from the crystal. His expression was not that
of a man viewing the delicious sight of a lass in her bath;
rather it was that of sheer consternation as he focused his
attention on the girl's left shoulder.

"It is not possible." He fell back into the chair as if
someone had just punched him in the stomach. The crystal rumbled upon the table. "Very well, blast it. I see the
mark. I see it." He gasped, horror blanching his face anew.
"Bedamn, what day is it?"

He snapped his fingers. A large book resting upon a
shelf across the room levitated up and flew to settle upon
his lap. He paged through it and read it swiftly. "It will be
this Hallow's Eve!"

He scrambled from the chair and stalked to the center
of the room. He spread his arms out wide. Wind whirled
about him and he bellowed over the roar of it. "Son, come
to me. Stop whatever you are doing and come to me immediately!"

Blake Farewell, the Duke of Trenton, strolled into his
father's bedroom a bare few minutes before noon. He was
dressed in buff unmentionables, a blue jacket with a fit
only Weston could tailor, and Hessians polished to a shine
only a blacking mixed of champagne could create. He
raised a fine dark brow as he studied his father. "Still in
nightgown and cap, Father? My, what a slugabed."

Creighton Farewell, standing knee-deep in charts and
scrolls, glared thunder at his son. "Where have you been?
I told you to come immediately."

"I could not," Blake said, smiling. "To . . . er . . . depart
at the moment would have been . . . err . . . highly indeli-
cate, not to mention frustrating to both me and the lady
involved."

"Eh, you were with that Trillion witch?" Creighton
asked, diverted for a moment.

"No," Blake said coolly, moving to lower his large frame into a chair. "I cast her off well nigh over a week ago. This was but a lady for the night."

"You cast Trillion off?" Creighton asked, his eyes narrowed. "How did she take it?"

"What does it matter?" Blake asked, raising his eyebrow in amusement. "There is naught she can do. When a relationship is over for me, it is over."

"Hmm," Creighton said, rubbing his chin. "Well, can't say that I'm not glad. Something about that witch unsettled me."

"Impossible," Blake said, staring at his father. Then he laughed. "Unless it was her lack of powers which unnerved you."

"No, no," Creighton said, waving a dismissive hand. "But enough. There are far more important matters to attend."

"Yes?" Blake asked, with only the mildest of interest. "And what might they be?"

A flush actually rose to Creighton's face. "Er, this is going to come as a surprise to you. I suppose I should have told you before, but . . . I simply never believed it."

"Believed what?" Blake asked.

"The legend," Creighton said, sighing. He waded through the charts and came to sit down across from Blake. "The family legend."

"We have a family legend?" Blake said, smiling. "How droll."

"You won't think so when you find out what you must do," Creighton said, his tone dark.

"I must do?" Blake asked, less amused. "There is something I must do in this legend?"

"Er, yes," Creighton said. He shifted in clear discomfort. "And soon. I fear I never was one for calculations, and it has been decades after all. It isn't as if keeping a tally of each All Hallow's Eve's moon is something easily done through all this time. The years do run on."

Blake shook his head. "Just what are you meandering about?"

"I'm not meandering," Creighton growled.

"Then tell me what you are talking about," Blake sighed, impatiently.

"Well . . . you see . . . ah . . ." The large crystal shook upon the table. "I'm getting to it," Creighton said, glaring at the crystal. He drew in a deep breath. "You must seek out the girl with the mark of the snowflake and gain both her love and her hand in marriage. You must do so before the end of this All Hallow's Eve—else you and I, and anyone baring Farewell blood, will become slaves of the fairies in their land . . . for eternity."

"Just what potion have you been drinking, Father?" Blake asked, staring. He shook his head. "And so early in the morning yet. For shame."

"I didn't drink any potion," Creighton snapped.

"Just a little of the homebrew then?" Blake asked dryly.

"None, I tell you," Creighton exclaimed. He jabbed his finger at the crystal. "It showed me the chit this very morning. . . ."

"The girl with the mark of the snowflake?" Blake hazarded.

"Yes, that one." Creighton nodded vigorously.

Blake frowned. "Why a snowflake?"

"How the devil should I know?" Creighton said, his tone sharp. "The infernal fairy chose it as the sign, not me. And fairies never make any bloody sense. You know that."

"No, I don't know that," Blake retorted, exasperated. "I've had no real experience with fairies."

"Be grateful you haven't," Creighton said. "A capricious, difficult lot if there ever was one. Pretty things and all, but mean-spirited when it comes down to it. They don't have souls is what their problem is. They are all magic and nothing else. Don't see them in the modern world much, thank God. Not enough magic for them, but there are still places, and they will always exist." He grimaced. "Just hope *we* don't have to exist with them as their servants."

"If you would care to explain," Blake said, attempting

to reign in his temper, "we would not have to be their servants."

"I *am* explaining," Creighton stormed, indignation crossing his face. "You and I, and all of our line, did not come into warlock powers naturally. We received them in a rather odd fashion."

"Don't tell me," Blake said with a snort. "The fairies gave them to us."

"Smart boy," Creighton said, smiling. "But it was only one—a princess of the fairies. She gave them to our great-great . . . Bah, anyway, the first Farewell—a Jack Farewell—in return for a favor he had rendered her. And don't ask me what the blasted favor was because that portion of the story is very murky. He was a mere peasant, though—that I can remember. Nevertheless, the princess grew enamored of him . . ."

"Of course," Blake said, rolling his eyes.

"Now you can see why I never believed in the legend," Creighton said. "I always figured our ancestor Jack was just puffing off his own consequence. Anyway, she became enamored of him, and just like a fairy, she offered him a reward and then immediately turned it to her advantage. She invited him to become her consort. Thank the powers, old Jack wasn't such a fool. He turned her down flat. Said he would prefer warlock powers for his reward."

"You say he was a peasant?" Blake asked, intrigued despite himself.

"Yes, yes," Creighton said. "However, back then even a peasant knew of magic and its powers. Old Jack turned the tables on the princess, and she was forced to give him the powers." He paused. "However, spiteful creature that she was, she proclaimed he had chosen the power over love and therefor—as if she knew of love; fairies only know of want and desire—but anyway, I digress. She said she would give him the powers if he accepted that there would come a time when a descendant of his would be demanded to win the love and hand of the girl with the snowflake mark. This would be a girl with fairy blood in her veins. Else, the princess would come and take all his offspring to her land and enslave them."

"Good Lord," Blake muttered in disgust.

Creighton's eyes turned agate hard. "Think what you will, son, but make no mistake: The crystal shows that the girl is alive. I've studied the blasted charts and the confounded moons. It is occurring now. You are the chosen descendent."

"Fortunate me," Blake said dryly, "to be so honored."

"We are powerful warlocks," Creighton said. "But our powers will not be a match against the fairies, since our powers are derived from them. And this princess was one of the most powerful. Our powers have grown over the ages, but I don't like to think about hers. Nor will I be able to help you either. It will not be permitted."

"The princess even thought to demand that?" Blake asked.

"They always stack the deck," Creighton said. "Rather than merely one Farewell as a consort, she gave him powers and permitted his line to grow. He was a prolific breeder as the family tree shows. If this princess wins, she will have many Farewells to serve her rather than just one."

Blake stared at his father, his eyes narrowed. He shrugged his broad shoulders. "I can think of some of our branches which I'd gladly turn over to the old gal. Oh, very well. I shall marry this girl with the mark of the snowflake, if I must."

"You must," Creighton said. His own eyes narrowed. "Do not take this lightly. It may not be an easy task."

"Why? Is she hunchbacked or disfigured?" Blake asked dryly.

"No, no," Creighton said. "She is fetching enough."

"Then there will be no problem. It would be daunting if I was forced to take a hunchback to wife, but if she is even passable in looks, we shall be married, and well before midnight of All Hallows' Eve." Blake rose. "Show me this girl, and I will be off."

"Very well," Creighton said and moved to his crystal.

Even before he finished his litany, the crystal flared to life with images, as if eager to impart its knowledge. "I have watched the girl this morning. Her name is Alwayna."

Blake gazed at the girl within the crystal's sheen. She had wild curls the color of fire. Her skin was the rarest amongst redheads, clear and creamy without freckles. With a delicate pointed chin and green eyes that slanted up slightly, she was more than fetching. If such looks came from fairy blood, Blake welcomed it. Indeed, something deep inside wrenched within him. An odd, longing need rose within him. He shook himself. He had not known he could desire so swiftly, for surely that was what it was. "She is more than acceptable. I shall marry her within the week."

"You sound positive," Creighton said.

"Why should I not be?" Blake murmured, his gaze steady upon the girl. She appeared to be in a small cottage kitchen with two older women. They looked to be cooking. "I am reasonably handsome, I am rich, and I have the powers. Do you say this peasant girl will deny me when no other woman has?" He frowned. "Just what in blazes are they cooking?"

"They aren't," Creighton said. "They are trying to concoct a spell."

"What?" Blake asked.

"It has been very painful to watch," Creighton said, sighing. "They've been at it all morning. It appears she is a novice witch, and these two old biddies are attempting to teach her. None of them have a clue whatsoever. I've requested the crystal to remain mute. Their notion of Latin is bloodcurdling." He sighed. "You may have the powers, but it is clear she does not. I fear she is an easy pigeon for the plucking if the fairies wish to play off their games. That is why I warn you not to be overconfident."

Blake laughed. Despite his father's warning, his confidence flared high within him. He felt his powers surge like the crashing tide. He would own this girl in the crystal. She would be his. "Trust in me, Father. Just sit back and enjoy. Else I'll be forced to call you a fretsome old man."

"I *am* an old man," Creighton retorted. "Too damn old to be a servant of the fairies, I assure you."

Blake sat, relaxed, against the plush squabs of his coach. With his fastest team of cattle, he was making excellent time. The roads into the small village of Chancellorville had been certainly rough, but his coach was well sprung and he barely noticed any discomfort. Now they were upon the lane that would lead to the cottage where Alwayna resided with those incompetent witches, two sisters of the Goodfellow.

A smile of anticipation curled his lips. He had not come unprepared. Trunks with baubles and gifts and a fully prepared bridal trousseau were tied to the coach. Fate might have made the selection, but he looked forward to overwhelming the girl. He looked forward to her worship and adoration.

Strange, such was not a common requisite of his in relationships. He needed no woman's approval to build his self-worth, nor the fawning of any man to puff off his consequence. Granted, he received it generally, but he did not ask for it. Yet in this instance, he looked forward to seeing the awe in the face of the girl with the green eyes and the mark of the snowflake. Perhaps it was due to the fact that he must marry her. She would be his either way, but adoration would be a useful thing in a marriage.

The coach jerked to an abrupt stop. Frowning, Blake peered out the window. A curse escaped his lips and irritation welled within him. He swung open the door and alighted.

The cause of the coach's stop was evident. Another carriage sat drawn across the road. A willowy blond woman, dressed in the highest kick of fashion, stood before it.

"I'm sorry, Yer Grace," Randell said from the coach's box. "But . . ."

"It's not your fault," Blake said as he strode over to the woman. "What the devil are you doing here, Trillion?"

Trillion smiled, her blue eyes widening in feigned innocence. "What do you think I am doing here?"

"I told you a week ago that it was over between us," Blake said, his voice testy. "I do not know why you followed me here, but I warn you, I do not respond well to tantrums or fits."

"Oh, I do not intend to throw a tantrum," Trillion said, her tone dulcet.

"You do not?" Blake asked suspiciously.

"No," Trillion said. "Nor will I subject you to tears and reproaches."

"Thank God," Blake said.

"No, you are far, far too accustomed to that, *Your Grace.*" Her eyes almost glowed.

Blake remained silent. He could not deny it. He *was* far too accustomed to it and it always proved to bore him.

"No," Trillion said, tapping her finger to her chin in a meditative gesture. "I am here, rather, to—let us say—assist womankind, my sisterhood as it were, against you." Blake stiffened, narrowing his eyes. Trillion laughed. "Yes, I know your story and your purpose in coming to this charming little village of Chancellorville. This dear little village where they have not forgotten magic. In truth, I know it *very* well."

Blake shrugged. "So you've read your crystal ball correctly for once?"

"Ah, there it is," Trillion said. She shook her head. "That tone of yours. The great warlock condescending to the poor weakling witch. Just as you intend to condescend to that peasant girl, do you not?"

"What I intend is none of your business," Blake said, surprisingly nettled.

Trillion gave a silver laugh. "Mmm, but you are confused. It *is* my business. Your arrogance and conceit are far too overweening. I suppose it cannot be helped. You are a man of power after all. Indeed, you come from a line of powerful men. Men who choose power over everything else, in fact. Most certainly over love."

"Do not talk to me of love," Blake said, exasperated. "You do not love me."

"No," Trillion said, a feline smile upon her lips. "Alas, it is not in my nature. I only know of want and desire." An odd twinge passed through Blake. "But then, it is not in your nature to love either."

"I suppose you cannot refrain from being a cat," Blake said, feigning a bored tone. "Do tell me when you have flexed your claws enough."

"Cat?" Trillion stared at him, stunned. She laughed. "Why, that is perfect. You do not think much of me as a witch, and I admit I am not . . . much of a witch. Yet I have decided that you are far too accustomed to being powerful. That must change, I think."

Blake laughed, even as he marshaled his powers. If she wished for spell play, he would oblige her. "Do you?"

"A cat as a witch's familiar is a creature whose position is to serve." Trillion clasped her hands together. "I like that notion, too."

"Do not become overly fond of it," Blake said, debating what he intended to do with Trillion.

"Oh, but I am," Trillion said. She held out her pale hand. "You should not have called me a cat, for I am not a cat . . . but you are."

Blake opened his mouth to retort. The strangest sound came out. The power he had been funneling dispersed to the four winds, even as he felt his body diminish. An excruciating roar sounded in his ears. A sharp white light blinded him.

Then he could see again. He was unaccountably gazing up at Trillion . . . a long way up.

"Well, not exactly a cat," Trillion giggled. "Just a kitten. Consider this training for your future as one of the least, rather than as one of the greatest."

Blake heard Randell exclaim from the coachman's box, even as he looked at what should have been his arms. They were furred, pawed, and clawed.

Trillion glanced in speculation at the coachman. "Oh,

yes. What shall we do with your faithful and loyal servant?"
She laughed. She waved her hand. Randall bellowed in
fright. His bellow wheezed into a squeak as his large frame
shrunk into the body of a mouse.

"You'll gain no assistance from him, I think," Trillion
said, smiling. Her eyes glittered. "And what about your carriage, and all those lovely gifts you brought—all meant to
sway a poor unsuspecting peasant girl's heart? Hmm, yes!"
She snapped her fingers. Where once a carriage had stood,
now resided a gargantuan pile of brambles. Randall the
coachman scampered from beneath the briars. Squeaking,
he scurried down the lane.

Blake cursed. It came out as a hiss.

"Tsk, tsk," Trillion said. "Is that any way to act toward
your past lover? And your future mistress? Who knows? If
you learn your place well enough, you just might become
my lover again." The hair on Blake stood up and his back
arched upon its own accord. "Until we meet again . . .
which I believe will be midnight on All Hallow's Eve."

Blake stared as Trillion's image shimmered and shifted.
He saw supernaturally brilliant blue eyes slanted in a pointed,
translucent face, a diminutive body in flowing, gossamer silver, and the flutter of wings before she disappeared.

He groaned, for he now knew her for what she was.

Blake picked his way along the winding path, attempting
to grow accustomed to his new form, feeling the different
muscles as he worked them. Trillion had certainly offered
him obstacles, but Blake refused to turn tail. He winced at
his own unfortunate use of words, whipping that recently
acquired appendage in anger. He did not know how or what
he was going to do, but he was certain he would find a way
back to his human shape. Then he would show Trillion his
worth. He'd not be her servant. She'd not win.

So deep was he in his vengeful thoughts that he did not
take due note of the two large dogs padding down the

path. Neither appeared exceptionally ferocious, they were merely two hounds out for sport.

Blake's hairs rose when the two hounds spotted him and bayed in unison. He had forgotten that he was now in the category of "sport" for them. The two beasts charged. Blake, accustomed to meeting all head-on, lowered himself into a fighting crouch. He spat and clawed at the two hounds as they descended.

His fierce snarls and scratches fazed neither brute, and he discovered himself springing desperately before snapping teeth and slobbering dog breath. He rolled beneath the one hound, as the other lunged at him and rammed into his companion instead. Both dogs became a muddle of legs as they strove to untangle themselves and seize Blake.

Blake dug his claws into the one, but it garnered little effect. This from a man who had once floored Gentleman Jackson, and that without magic! Acknowledging that he could not damage the two large hounds, and not wishing to become their chew toy, Blake scampered from under their feet and pelted toward the nearest tree. He was up it before he realized that it was but a sapling. The two heavy-bodied hounds yapped in sheer triumph and charged the slight tree. It bent and swayed with their weight. Blake was forced to climb to its fragile tip, clinging to it for dear life. It did not stop him from cursing the hellhounds with every invective in his vocabulary. Unfortunately, his words came out as mewling howls.

"Oh, dear," a female voice exclaimed. "Brutus and Maximilion, stop this instant! Leave that poor kitten alone."

Blake had but one moment to glance at the source of such sound advice. He howled again. It was the girl with the mark of the snowflake. The girl he had come to overwhelm with his charm and wed within the week. She hastened forward, her green eyes full of righteous anger, her red curls wild in the fresh breeze. The wildest feeling passed through Blake at the sight of her—it was so overpowering he almost lost his hold.

Apparently Brutus and Maximilion experienced no such

gripping emotion, for they ignored her orders and yapped eagerly, pounding and pawing upon the sapling.

"Stop it, you bad dogs," Alwayna cried. She reached down and swatted both dogs. Her force appeared no stronger then Blake's own swats and he rolled his eyes. However, both dogs, upon receiving those mere taps, ceased and hunkered down upon their haunches.

"You two ought to be ashamed of yourselves," Alwayna said, her hands upon her hips and her tone scolding. The two dogs lolled out their tongues, even as they cast longing glances at Blake. "No, do not even think of it. Now go home. Squire Petersham is going to be angry enough at you two as it is." She flapped her hands. "Now shoo! Go! Be gone!"

Brutus and Maximilion looked sheepish, then good-naturally obeyed Alwayna, padding away.

"Hello, little fellow," Alwayna said, turning sympathetic green eyes upon Blake. Her voice was a coo, the type women employed upon puling infants. She reached toward him. "Those nasty dogs are gone. Now don't be afraid."

Blake hissed and spat. He wasn't frightened. He was furious. Furious that he had been forced to flee two hounds. Furious that he had been discovered in such a helpless, ridiculous position, clinging to a branch for dear life. Furious that Alwayna, a girl, had rescued him with a mere order and slap of her hand. And furious, most of all, because she called him little fellow!

He raised up a staying hand, or paw, and hissed again. Determined to regain his dignity and show Alwayna he required no assistance, he attempted to back down the sapling. He had always thought cats that climbed trees and could not come back down were weak creatures. He now realized the difficulty when one clung upon the very last twig.

"Let me help you," Alwayna said soothingly.

Blake hissed and glared at her.

"Very well, have it your way," Alwayna said with a sigh. Blake misplaced a paw into thin air rather then branch. "Oh, do watch out!"

Blake watched out to no avail. He lost his purchase and

fell to the ground. Fortunately he discovered a new talent. He landed upon his feet, though even that short distance jarred him and left him disoriented.

"Are you all right?" Alwayna cried, bending down to Blake.

"Of course I'm all right," Blake roared. It translated into an uninviting yowl.

"Gracious, you are a feisty little fellow," Alwayna murmured, settling back upon her heels, her gaze a mixture of both perplexity and amusement. Blake dug his claws into the dirt and managed a low growl in retort to her amusement.

"Just what are we to do with you?" Alwayna sighed. She reached out a gentle hand.

Blake, still furious, swatted at it before he realized what he was doing.

"Ouch!" Alwayna jerked her hand back. There was a definite scratch, reddened slightly with blood. She shook her head and frowned at him. "Very well. It is clear you wish to be left to yourself. Do take care." She rose. Then she turned and actually began walking away from Blake.

"Come back here!" Blake ordered, stunned that she was indeed leaving him.

The sound was a very indignant meow.

"No," Alwayna called without halting. "I tried to help you and you scratched me."

"Meow!" Blake cried again.

The blasted chit continued walking.

Blake blinked and blinked again in befuddlement. Women did not walk away from him! At least they never had before. He clawed the ground in frustration. He refused to go chasing after a woman. He simply refused. "Meow!"

"Good-bye," Alwayna said, her voice drifting back. She would be gone from sight soon.

Despising the moment, Blake meowed again and, for the first time in his life, ran after a woman as fast as his four little paws could carry him.

TWO

Alwayna forced herself to walk onward, even as she heard the infuriated meows from behind. She understood cats very well. It was often necessary to show them you cared not one whit before they would deign to befriend you. Surely it was an odd quirk to their nature, but quirk it was. It was as if responding openly to kindness would prove it was not their decision to be friendly and with cats it always must be their decision.

She knew it should not matter if a kitten befriended her, but indeed it did. The thought of leaving the kitten out in the wilds to fend for itself wrenched at her heart.

She heard another yowl, this time close behind her. Hiding her smile, she turned. The small kitten, the oddest blend of raven black and silver hair, stood stiff legged. He glared up at her with golden cat eyes. "Yes. Did you want something?"

The kitten's recalcitrant look was almost human, far too human. Alwayna shook herself. People had called her odd her entire life. The villagers of Chancellorville, with their acceptance of superstitions, merely called her fey. Sometimes she was forced to admit that perhaps they were right. Like now. After all, she was talking to a small kitten, feeling as if it were a human. Regardless, the kitten's look told Alwayna that she was still being measured.

"I guess not," she said in determination, turning slowly. "Meow."

Alwayna turned back. There was a far more conciliatory tone to the meow. She smiled, despite herself. "Very well, you are forgiven." Unable to resist, she reached down and scooped the small fur ball up into her arms. She felt a sudden jolt. The kitten blinked its eyes as if it too were shocked. Alwayna shook her head once more. "Fey, I am."

The kitten's eyes seemed to darken and draw her. She laughed. "Do come along. Let me take you to Bathsheba and Dorinda's." She absently stroked the kitten and started walking. "You will like the two dears. They are . . . are very sweet. I'm sure they will be glad to give you a bowl of milk. They are very kind to orphans like us." The kitten growled slightly. Alwayna flushed. "Forgive me. Perhaps I presume too much. You . . . you may not be orphaned as I am." Suddenly she felt lonely and foolish for feeling so. Even more so for talking to a kitten about it.

She pushed all such thoughts to the back of her mind. She was generally of a buoyant personality, having learned early in life to accept gladly when kindness was given to her and to overlook those wounds and offenses tendered. As a child with neither known mother nor father, and no last name, Alwayna had decided it best not to ask too much, nor did she expect too much.

Yet in the last few days an unsettling feeling had haunted her. It was an almost breathless feeling that something important was about to happen to her. As if she herself were important!

"Silly," Alwayna sighed. She hugged the kitten close as they approached the cottage of the Goodfellow sisters. "You know, kitten, that is what I am. Terribly silly."

She reached to open the back door of the cottage. She clasped the handle with one hand, holding kitten near with the other. As she opened the door, kitten let up a hiss and howl. "Shhh, don't be rude."

She swung wide the door and stepped directly into the room. She directly skittered to a halt. She was forced to do so, for a huge ivy vine serpentined its way toward her. Kitten meowed and dug his claws into her.

"Oh, hello, dear," Bathsheba Goodfellow, the younger of the two sisters, gasped. Then she hiked her skirts up, displaying stockings and sturdy, dimpled knees as she successfully jumped over a waggling, searching vine. "We . . . we are suffering a minor mishap."

"Humph," Dorinda Goodfellow said, her tall, Spartan body stiff with outrage as she sidestepped an intrusive, pronged leaf. "I told you *vigorous* was the wrong word to use."

"Yowl," Tomolina, their large black cat, howled as it clambered up the rough-hewn kitchen shelves, mere inches ahead of a thick horticultural rope snaking its way after her.

"Grrrr . . . yowl," the small kitten in Alwayna's arms echoed.

"D-don't be fr-fr-frightened," Alwayna murmured, wide-eyed. The entire kitchen was writhing with vines stemming from one meager clay pot upon the kitchen table. They shot along the wooden floor, they popped the hanging pot from the fireplace hook, and they engulfed the curtains and window, shutting out the light.

"I-I only meant to . . . to p-perk up the poor little ivy," Bathsheba cried as a lecherous vine wrapped itself around her plump ankle. She batted at it ineffectively. "It was—was appearing somewhat p-peaked."

"You've done that," Dorinda said, stomping on a vine with vengeance. "Now what?"

Kitten hissed in Alwayna's arms. She clutched the tiny creature to her. An amazing feeling of strength flowed into her. Perhaps this was why she had been feeling unsettled this past week. This could be her moment! She had not performed one jot of magic to date, no matter how hard she had tried, yet a voice whispered inside that this would be the time. She nuzzled the tiny, defenseless kitten. "I'll . . . I'll take care of this."

The kitten blurted out a meow that sounded positively negative.

Alwayna scrunched her eyes shut. Determined to do it

up to the hilt, she chanted in Latin. As she spoke, an alien feeling of power entered her and she added a few extra lines on for double measure, even as she heard something like children's laughter in her head. The kitten squirmed and yowled in her arms as she completed the verse.

Alwayna opened her eyes eagerly.

"Oh, dear," Bathsheba sighed.

"That was . . ." Dorinda breathed.

The vine's tendrils, all fifty of them, boinged back into the pot. Alwayna's heart jumped in triumph. Only then, they roiled together, braiding into one massive stalk. It shot heavenward, spearing through the thatched roof. Timber and rushes crashed down.

"Not the correct spell," Dorinda finished, peering up.

"Wh-what did I say wrong?" Alwayna asked, bewildered and embarrassed. The small kitten in her arms let out a staccato of hisses, meows, and burrs.

"Well, dear . . . let me make certain," Bathsheba said. She picked up her skirts and, nimbly skittering over the rubble, darted across the room and out the door, knocking Alwayna aside.

"What is she doing?" Alwayna asked nervously.

"Wait," Dorinda said, her tone tense. "I was not sure of the last words you spoke."

"I'm sorry. I-I got carried away," Alwayna admitted. "The words just . . . just came to me."

"Hurry, it's already through the clouds," Bathsheba cried, charging through the door, red cheeked and puffing. Her mild blue eyes were wide as saucers and shockingly she wielded an ax. Granted, it was rusty and had resided against the cottage more as a fixture than anything else, but it still was threatening.

"F-f-forgive me," Alwayna pleaded, cringing back.

Bathsheba raised the tarnished weapon, appearing an angelic Viking. "We must chop it down!"

"I was afraid of that," Dorinda said. Her brown eyes snapped with a feverish light. She dashed over to the kitchen drawer and pulled out a large butcher knife. "There is no time to waste."

Bathsheba charged at the stalk, her ax swinging. Dorinda attacked, hacking at it as if it were a tough side of beef. Even Tomolina scrambled from her purchase upon the shelves and leapt upon the stalk at a higher level, scratching and gnawing at it with her teeth.

Kitten within Alwayna's arms, its eyes closed, growled lowly in what seemed to her a catatonic trance.

"I must leave you, little one," she said and set the rigid cat upon the floor. She rushed over, grabbed up a cast-iron skillet, dived in, and thwacked steadily at the stalk.

The three warrior women quickly fell into a synchronized pattern. Knife—frying pan—ax. Knife—frying pan—ax. Tomolina gnawed and sharpened her claws in a groove above them. Soon they had chopped three-fourths of the way through. Yet the stalk began to rumble and tremble and shake, not from its roots but rather from above.

"We must," Dorinda cried.

"Oh, yes, it's coming! Hurry!" Bathsheba wheezed, sweat dripping down her round face. She buried the ax into the stalk with a viciousness.

"What is coming?" Alwayna panted, pounding her skillet against the stalk, crushing its fiber to pulp.

"You . . . don't . . . want . . . to . . . know," Dorinda said, slashing with her knife in extreme punctuation.

The stalk cracked in two.

"We have it," Dorinda exclaimed. "Step back! Step back!"

The ladies scattered. Tomolina sprang clear with feline grace. The kitchen fell silent as the stalk caved in upon itself. It was like a rope coiling in reverse. Vines, length after length, descended through the roofs opening, growing into a heap.

"We've killed it," Alwayna cried, exhilaration bursting through the pain in her chest.

"Shh," Bathsheba whispered.

The Goodfellow sister remained still, clearly not breathing.

Finally Dorinda moved. She walked over to peer up through the gaping whole in the roof. "It didn't make it. Praise the Almighty."

Bathsheba approached and gazed up in awe. "Where do you think *It* is?"

A wicked grin cracked across Dorinda's face. "*It* most likely caught on to some different cloud, some different plane."

"What is *It?*" Alwayna asked hesitantly. The sisters peered at her. Tomolina stared, unblinking. Even the kitten looked at her. If a feline could shake its head, it did. Alwayna swallowed, her mouth dry. "Pl-please tell me."

"The giant of course," Dorinda said, a frown marking her brow. "Everyone knows if you send a stalk up that high, it's an invitation for them to come back down to earth. They simply can't resist."

Alwayna groaned. "R-really?"

"Ahh, I bet you thought that it must be a beanstalk, didn't you?" Bathsheba said, nodding her head sympathetically.

Alwayna gaped at her. The dear woman was offering her an excuse on a silver platter. She swallowed. She could not lie, not when she had endangered them all. "I—I didn't know any of that. I fear I made a mistake. I—I simply made a mistake."

"Oh," Bathsheba said, her mouth in a perfect circle.

Alwayna glanced at the heap of vine and the gaping hole in the roof. Her heart sank. She had so desperately wanted to finally do something good, something special. She bit her lip. "I—I will begin packing."

"Packing?" Bathsheba asked, frowning. "Why?"

Dorinda studied her. Then she grunted. "Humph, that's a tottyheaded thing to do. Won't help clear up this mess one whit. We've got some work on our hands."

The slightest bud of hope bloomed in Alwayna. She suffocated it. "N-no. I—I know you must wish for m-me to leave." She'd been thrown out of a house before for accidentally breaking the best china. That was small compared to inviting a giant down from the higher spheres. "It—it will not take me long."

"Leave? Why ever should you leave?" Bathsheba cried. "We all make mistakes, dear. Gracious, you've witnessed some of ours."

"Magic is unpredictable," Dorinda said staunchly. "Our niece Sarabeth says if magic were predictable it wouldn't be as interesting, now would it?"

"I—I suppose not," Alwayna said, hope flaring. She had never felt more at home than with the Goodfellow sisters here in Chancellorville. "Y-you are right."

"And you know she is married to a great warlock," Bathsheba nodded. "Therefore, she can't be wrong."

A weak meow permeated the air.

The three ladies looked to its source. The kitten lay upon the floor. His tiny paws covered his eyes. He meowed and he shook his head.

"Why, what a dear, enchanting little fellow," Bathsheba exclaimed. "Where did he come from?"

"I found him in the woods," Alwayna said quickly. "Brutus and Maximilion were attacking him."

"For shame," Bathsheba said. "What bad doggies they are."

"I thought the same." Alwayna hurried over and scooped the kitten up. "I—I think he needs a home."

"But of course he does," Bathsheba said quickly.

"He has one now," Dorinda said, nodding her head.

"Grr . . . burr," Tomolina yowled.

Dorinda looked sternly at the large cat. "You will be hospitable and accept the little one, Tomolina."

"Yes indeed, dear," Bathsheba said, her tone gentle with reproach. "You should always be kind to those less fortunate."

"Then h-he can stay?" Alwayna asked in relief. "And—and I—I can stay."

"Of course, dear. You only made a mistake," Bathsheba

said. Then her eyes widened. "Heavens, Alwayna, do you realize you performed your first magic?"

"Sister, you are right," Dorinda exclaimed. "It was wide of the mark, but you did it!"

Blake rested upon the parlor rug at Alwayna's feet. He might be just a kitten at the moment, but he intended to trail Alwayna constantly. Her mistaken charm cast yesterday had him on tenterhooks. He would lay odds that her sudden new ability to perform magic—magic that invited giants—had something to do with Trillion. It was the kind of prank a fairy would do for amusement.

A stack of clothes was piled beside Alwayna; she was steadily mending her way through it. Blake acknowledged that it should be a safe enough occupation for her. The two sisters were out in the garden picking herbs. Also, a safe occupation for them, he hoped.

Blake sighed. Now if the hazardous trio would stay put, he might, just might, accomplish something. The magic emanating within the house was astonishingly strong. No doubt it was built-up magic left over from a long string of spells that had "gone wide of the mark," as Dorinda would say.

He purred. Trillion's sudden attack and her strength might have successfully overpowered him. If he had been prepared, he might have protected himself from her, stopping her from casting her wretched spell, but there was no use in regret. With the stunning amount of magic here at his disposal, he should be able to rectify the matter. He promised himself he would be a man within the next hour. And when once again a man, he could then take Alwayna in hand and settle everything completely.

He began to focus his mental powers, opening himself to the magic. Soon he was submerged in strains and twines of magic flowing around him and in him. The power was building and building. Soon, soon, he could speak the words.

"Drat, I have the wrong thread," Alwayna murmured. She stood and left the room.

Blake did not follow. Drawing the last measure of power into him was too important.

"Brrr, howl!" A cat's cry interrupted Blake's meditation.

Offset, Blake glanced quickly about the parlor. Tomolina had entered. The large cat's fur stood on end. No doubt the familiar knew that something was afoot. Blake turned his attention back to his work. Just a little more power needed . . .

"Me—me—ow," Tomolina said, stalking over to Blake. The cat stared at him with intent yellow eyes.

"Depart," Blake meowed back, irritated but determined.

"Growl!" Tomolina returned.

Blake didn't know if she understood him, but he certainly didn't understand her. He had never cared to communicate with animals, especially cats. He meowed. "Go find a mouse and leave me alone."

Tomolina's eyes narrowed. Her paw flashed out like lightning and swatted Blake.

Blake, by far the smaller one, tumbled feet over tail. *Famous,* he thought. That language he very well understood. Tomolina had come to put him in his place and claim her superior position in the house. Blast it if he'd submit to her. Enraged, Blake did not wait a second more. He spoke the words.

Exhilaration shot through him as he saw the blinding white light, felt his form change.

"Ha!" he shouted, once again standing tall as a man.

"Y-yowl!" Tomolina squeaked more like a mouse than a cat. She crouched back.

Blake stalked toward her with menace. "Now try to put me in my place, cat. Swat little kittens about will you?"

"How-w-l-l," Tomolina screeched loudly, scurrying backward. "Meow-ww!"

"Tomolina?" Alwayna's voice called from outside the door.

Blake halted his attack. In fact, he stopped dead in his tracks as he realized two monumental things. First, he was about to see Alwayna for the first time when he was in the shape of a man. Second, now that he could take clear note of everything, he realized his magic hadn't been as well served as he expected. Indeed, he had turned himself back into a man as intended, but his clothes hadn't materialized with him.

"Howl, brr, yowl!" Tomolina shrieked out.

"Be quiet," Blake hissed, looking desperately about. "This is all your fault. You distracted me!"

"Tomolina!" Alwayna's worried voice called once again, closer this time.

"Meow, meow, meow, meow!"

"Fiend seize you, you cat of Satan," Blake muttered, diving for the stack of clothing on the settee. He grabbed the first piece he could. It was a petticoat! Cursing even more, Blake stepped into it, drawing it up to his waist, just as Alwayna entered the room.

"What is the mat—" Alwayna halted as she spied Blake.

For the first time in his life Blake blushed. He clutched the petticoat to his waist. It must be Bathsheba's, for it was ridiculously short and scandalously wide at the waist. "Er . . . hello."

"Wh-what . . . who . . . who are you?" Alwayna stammered.

Blake straightened up, throwing off his embarrassment. "I am Blake Farewell, the Duke of Trenton."

"Y-you are a Duke?" Alwayna asked, swallowing. Her eyes were wide in apparent awe.

Ah! This was better! Much better. Blake smiled gently, only a touch of condescension in his voice. "Yes, I am the Duke of Trenton. But you need not be frightened."

"I—I am s-so glad to know that," Alwayna said. Her gaze lowered delicately and her voice was appropriately meek. "I—I am honored to meet you, er, Duke."

"And I you," Blake smiled, bowing with as much aplomb as a man in a petticoat could.

"However, I—I have much to do. If you c-could please leave . . ." Her gaze rose. There was no awe there—only nervous appeasement. "I mean, you surely have many er . . . dukely duties . . ."

"Dukely?" Blake asked, stunned.

"Or dukeish . . . yes, dukeish duties to attend," Alwayna said swiftly. "And . . . and do not hesitate to keep the petticoat, if you like. And . . . any other thing you might need."

Blake stiffened, thunderstruck. "You think I am a thief!"

"No," Alwayna said, her voice strong. "No. I am sure you are just borrowing it. Which I completely understand. I assure you, I do. All of us at one time or another falls on hard times. I know I have. Not to the point that I have no clothes . . . but . . . but I have been fortunate, I see."

Once again that unfamiliar feeling of embarrassment gnawed at Blake. "I have not fallen on hard times! Very well, I have suffered setbacks . . . but I am not a *thief* or . . . or a vagrant gypsy."

"I—I don't know if we have a blouse—I mean, a shirt— for you. This is a ladies' household," Alwayna continued, a fretsome frown marking her brow. She brightened. "I know! We should be able to spell one up for you."

"No!" Blake yelped. Tomolina yowled in agreement. "Whatever you do, do not do that! I assure you, I can do that for myself!"

"Oh, that's right," Alwayna said nodding, a sympathetic look to her gaze. "You are a duke. Dukes can do anything."

"Blast it, I am a duke!" Blake exclaimed, frustrated and enraged. He stalked toward her. "And I am here because . . . I am here to protect you, damn it!"

Alwayna skittered back. Tomolina, clearly misunderstanding Blake's good intentions, growled. She sprung at his skirt, snagging her claws into it.

Blake, clutching his dragging skirts with one hand, turned to fend the feline off with the other. "Let go, confound it!"

"Don't hurt her," Alwayna cried. She leapt forward, slapping ineffectually at his shoulders and chest.

Beleaguered on both sides by angry felines, Blake used his one free arm to clamp Alwayna to him, confining her swinging range. He jerked up on the petticoat with the other. The sound of overstressed material ripped through the air. "Stop it!"

A loud thump sounded as Tomolina and torn cloth hit the floor. Blake didn't notice, for his own heart thumped more loudly. His head pounded as he gazed down at Alwayna. Her green eyes were wide and arrested. He grew dizzy, lost in the depths of them. His arms tightened around her more surely. Never had a woman's body felt so perfectly right against his. Never had desire filled him so completely. He had felt lust often, but this desire was different, sweet and strong. He forced himself to think. "Y-you must listen to me. You are in danger."

"I-I know," Alwayna said breathlessly.

"You do?" Blake asked. "How?"

"Pl-please just release me," Alwayna asked, her tone nervous.

"No. I'm not the danger!" Blake said, astonished at her misunderstanding. "I am here to save you, Alwayna. Truly, I am."

"Sir—I—I mean Duke," she amended, a flush rising to her cheeks. "I thank you, but I do not wish for the k-kind of saving you are talking about."

"The kind of saving . . . ?" Blake asked. "Just what are *you* talking about?"

Alwayna stared at him with what could only be a brave expression. "Duke, you have dropped your petticoat."

"I have?" Blake exclaimed. Her nervous, little nod let him know she did not lie. "Confound it! Excuse me."

Blake released her and bent to retrieve his petticoat. The moment he did, Alwayna dashed from the room. Blake drew up the petticoat. "Alwayna, come back!"

He stepped forward and then froze. An immobilizing pain ripped through him and a blinding white light seared his eyes. He moaned as he felt his body change. When his vision cleared, he was once again a kitten.

Dazed and winded, he looked at Tomolina. The big cat stared at him with unblinking eyes. She neither moved nor attacked. Her reaction only disheartened Blake all the more. To receive such sympathy from a cat was mortifying.

A babble of voices arose. Alwayna, flanked by Bathsheba and Dorinda, dashed into the room. Bathsheba waved a wicked garden sheers while Dorinda clutched a sharp trowel as they peered about with righteous fervor.

Alwayna halted, blinking. "He—he's gone!"

"So he is," Bathsheba said, lowering her garden sheers. Her face showed severe disappointment. "What a shame."

"Shame?" Dorinda asked, frowning.

"Dear me, I'm sorry. I fear I wasn't thinking," Bathsheba said, flushing. "Only . . . well, one doesn't meet a duke in a petticoat every day. And from Alwayna's description he sounded terribly handsome. He was handsome, was he not?"

"Y-yes," Alwayna said. "Y-you could say that."

"Don't be a twit, Bathsheba," Dorinda said tersely. "The man wasn't a duke. And handsome or not, he was nothing but a thief, and a lecherous one at that."

"But he said he was here to save Alwayna," Bathsheba said.

"Very well," Dorinda sniffed. "He was a *crazy*, lecherous thief. That is if he was here at all."

Alwayna paled. "Wh-what do you mean?"

"You worked your first spell yesterday," Dorinda said. "That can unsettle a person."

"Yes," Bathsheba said. "Why didn't I think of that? That would explain it."

"You—you think I imagined him?" Alwayna gasped.

"Well, dear," Bathsheba said. "It was confusing me. I mean, Damian, Sarabeth's husband, is a duke, and I assure you, he would never behave in such a manner."

"Also the man just appeared in the house," Dorinda said. "We can see anyone approaching from the garden. And then he disappears before we come back?"

"True," Bathsheba nodded. She patted Alwayna upon

the shoulder. "It might have been your imagination dear. A duke in petticoats is slightly far-fetched."

"And if he was a thief he would have wanted to take more than just a petticoat," Dorinda said. She nodded to the floor. "And he didn't even take that."

"I—I didn't imagine him," Alwayna said.

"Perhaps," Dorinda said. "But whoever he was, he's gone now."

"Yes," Bathsheba said. "Why don't you rest awhile, dear?"

"Yes, yes, I will," Alwayna said, her face turning deep red. She walked over and sat quickly upon the settee.

"Will you be all right?" Bathsheba asked, her voice concerned. "We can stay with you, if you like. Only the next coven meeting is tomorrow, you know, and we must have those herbs."

Blake shivered. Faith, what were the biddies planning to do now? He was too drained of power to be of any service.

"You know my pies aren't special without them," Dorinda said. She cracked a smile. "No one ever guesses my secret."

Blake breathed a sigh of relief.

"No, no," Alwayna said, her voice soft. "I—I will be fine. D-do forgive my silliness."

"Merely shout if the petticoat man appears again," Bathsheba said, turning to leave the room.

"Yes." Dorinda nodded and followed her sister.

Blake watched Alwayna. Her expression showed a frustration that matched his own. Unaccountably, he desired to comfort her. He leapt onto her lap.

"Oh, Kitten," Alwayna sighed. She picked him up and cuddled him against her chest. "I thought *he* was crazy. And now they think *I* am crazy!"

Blake meowed glumly. They only thought she was crazy. If they ever accepted his existence he would not only be considered crazy, but a crazy, lecherous thief at that!

Still, a ray of hope flared within him. His confidence

bounded back. Alwayna *had* thought him handsome. The next time he would do better. Indeed, the next time he would not waste a second of his time frightening her with the truth. Since he now knew he did not possess enough power to remain human for long he must woo and win her as swiftly as possible.

THREE

Alwayna paced the small kitchen, desperation gnawing at her. In a few more hours Dorinda and Bathsheba would return. That did not give her much time to try to learn the spell. Learn it. Ha! Learning it was not the difficulty; performing it was the rub.

She spun and glared at the red rose on the table. "Turn blue, drat it! Turn blue!"

"Meow," Kitten said, his eyes appearing reproachful.

"Yes, I know. That wasn't very professional," Alwayna sighed, crossing to plop herself into the kitchen chair. "But the Latin did no better, you must admit."

"Grrr . . . brr," Kitten said. His fur rose and he cringed.

"I didn't think it was that bad," Alwayna said, hurt. He gazed at her, unflinching. "Very well, I suppose it was. One of the most simple spells in the witch's primer and I cannot even get that right." She sank her head onto her arms. "I made a whole stalk grow, but I can't turn a rose blue. And the coven meets tonight. I'll have nothing to show them. Again!"

"Meow?"

Alwayna gazed at the kitten, only her mind drifted. She envisioned the man she had seen the day before. Tall, hair as raven dark as that of Kitten's, eyes verging on black, and a glorious body, which even a petticoat could not belittle. She shook her head to clear it as she once again felt the dizziness and shattering breathlessness she had known upon seeing him.

The sisters must be right. Such a man could only be a fabrication of her wishful imagination. Yet would she have dreamed up a man who so fully attracted her and frightened her at the same time? She stiffened, taking herself to task. "I'm crazy. I must forget him."

Kitten sat up. His tail whipped in interest. "Meow?"

"No, I am not going to discuss it. I—I refuse to think about him," Alwayna said firmly. "Whether he was real or not is not important. What is important is that I must not be not distracted right now." Kitten let out the oddest *brrr*, as if the tiny creature was laughing. "Oh, do go away. I need to learn this spell."

Kitten meowed. Rising, he padded from the room. Alwayna sighed. No doubt she had offended him.

She refocused her wandering attention back on the rose. Knowing herself to be alone, she leaned close and whispered, "Please just turn blue for me. I've said all the correct words a dozen times. I am really trying. Cannot that be enough for you? I mean, blue is a nice color. Wouldn't you like to try it for just a while? You'd be the envy of all the other roses. Please, oh please, turn blue."

"You do not ask," a deep, modulated voice said from the door. "You merely bend it to your will. You bend the magic to your will."

Alwayna squeaked and looked up. Her jaw dropped. It was the man again, a figment wished into form and definition by her spurious imagination. Only this time he wore no petticoat. He was dressed in the most stunning of jackets and pantaloons. Her imagination was definitely becoming more skilled. In fact, she was uncertain this was of her making for she had never beheld such perfect attire; this time the man looked like a prince.

"Blake Farewell," the man said, grinning. He offered her a bow. "The Duke of Trenton."

"Y-you are real?" Alwayna stammered. "Aren't you?"

He strode over and held out his hand. A teasing, wicked look entered his eyes. "Touch me and see if I am not."

Alwayna automatically lifted her hand to him. Then she halted. She remembered the confusing, frightening emotions she had felt before when he had held her. She pulled her hand back. "I'll believe you."

"Do, Alwayna," Blake said softly.

"You know my name?" she exclaimed.

"Yes," Blake said. His eyes darkened. "A thousand pardons for our first unfortunate meeting. But I assure you, Alwayna, you are not crazy. Neither am I."

"Then why . . . why?" Alwayna shook her head.

"Why what?" Blake said.

She blinked. There were simply too many questions. "Why . . . why everything? Why did you appear and then disappear? Why were you in a petticoat? How can you be here now? Where did you come from? What do you—"

"Enough, enough," Blake said, holding up a staying hand as his laugh rumbled through the small kitchen. He flashed her the most stunning of smiles. "Let us forget the many whys for the nonce. You will only think me crazy and I am taking great pains to retrieve my tattered reputation from yesterday." He sat down and after reaching over, clasped her hand with his large one. Alwayna's entire limb tingled from fingertip to shoulder at his touch. "What matters is that I think you the most beautiful woman I have ever seen."

Alwayna jerked her hand away. She glanced down at herself. The dress she wore was one of her oldest and most faded. She lifted her gaze to him with suspicion. "Now I know you *are* crazy."

"No," Blake said, a smile hovering upon his perfectly molded lips. "I am not crazy. I think you are the most beautiful woman, Alwayna. Do not fret over inconsequential questions. Only know that we are destined for each other."

His voice hypnotized Alwayna. His dark eyes compelled her. She sighed. "W-we are?"

He brushed her cheek gently with long, tapered fingers.

Alwayna's head bent on its own accord, seeking his touch. It enchanted her, even as his voice lowered. "Yes, we are. You are destined to love me."

"I am?" Alwayna murmured.

"Yes, Alwayna," Blake said. "I will give you everything in the world, my sweet. I am rich. I will dress you like a queen. You shall have all the clothes and jewels you could desire. Every comfort imaginable. Servants will wait upon you hand and foot."

They w-will?" Alwayna breathed. She could not help herself. She swayed toward him. The words did not matter. His eyes and his touch melted her very insides.

"You will make a beautiful duchess," Blake whispered, leaning close.

"Duchess?" Alwayna asked.

"Yes," Blake said. His lips hovered tantalizingly close to hers. "My wife."

"Wife!" Alwayna sprang back so suddenly she almost rocked off the old chair.

"Yes, wife," Blake said. His perfect smile twitched with condescension. "Would you like that?"

"Would I like that?" Alwayna leapt from her chair and hastily placed the kitchen between them. Her heart sank as reality overtook fantasy. She laughed bitterly. "You must be a duke after all."

"I am." Blake stood. He lifted his head. "I do not lie to you."

"Not about being a duke perhaps," Alwayna said.

His dark brows snapped down. "What do you mean?"

"Do you do this with all the peasant girls you meet?" Alwayna asked. "How many have believed you? How many have you lead into sin with the simple promise of marrying them?"

"None," Blake said, his voice curt. "I do not dally with peasant girls."

Alwayna stiffened. "Then why do you dally with me? Is this a new sport for you?"

"Blast it," Blake said, bewilderment tingeing his face.

"I did not mean it that way. I told you that you are the most beautiful woman in the world. I offered you all my wealth and position. I offered you my name. It is not intended to be an insult."

"It is to me," Alwayna said.

"Why?" Blake asked, frowning even more severely.

"Because . . . because . . ." Alwayna sputtered, her roiling emotions difficult to articulate. She drew in a deep breath. "I know you do not love me and I do not love you. We just met yesterday. I know nothing about you and you know nothing about me."

"I told you," Blake said, his voice rather irritated. "We are destined to be together."

"Forgive me, Your Grace," Alwayna said, her tone dry, "if I do not take your word for it."

"Just what is it you want?" Blake suddenly asked, his eyes narrowing.

Alwayna's eyes widened. "I-I do not want anything."

"Everybody wants something," Blake said, his voice firm. "What do you want, Alwayna? In the very depths of your heart, what is it you want?"

Alwayna's breath caught in her throat. No one had ever asked her that question. She thought a moment. The need and the words to suit it rose within her, a lonesome cry. "I-I want to belong."

He stared at her. "I offered you to become my wife. Would not that mean you would belong?"

"N-no," Alwayna said, twisting her hands. "Indeed, if you *are* a duke, I would never belong."

"You make no sense," Blake said. "None whatsoever."

"I—I have lived with many different people," Alwayna said. "Some have been kind, and some have not been. But . . . but I am always a visitor. I—I am not family. They may care, but it will not last for long. I—I know I am different. I don't know why I am. I try not to be, but I am. And . . . and people do not trust people they cannot understand. And perhaps they have the right. I—I never seem to do things right. They cannot depend upon me. . . ."

"Nor can you depend upon them," Blake said in an odd tone. He walked slowly over to her. Alwayna could not move. The understanding in his eyes was balm to her spirit. He placed two comforting hands to her shoulders. "You can depend upon me, Alwayna."

"Can I?" Alwayna asked.

A sudden sharp pain flashed in Blake's eyes. "Only I—I must leave you now."

"What?" Alwayna said, blinking.

"Forgive me," Blake said, his voice strained. "I must leave. Please do not follow."

He turned and walked from the room.

Alwayna obeyed his order, simply because astonishment immobilized her. The man had just said she could depend upon him and then he had walked out. She felt lonely and lost. More lonely and lost than ever before.

She had denied his words. Any reasoning woman must. Yet her heart whispered that she had never depended upon logic too much before and that whether she wanted to believe him or not did not matter. Her heart wanted to believe him. *It* already missed him. *It* was already dreaming of when he would appear again.

Blake hid under the table of Letty Doblin, the hosting witch for the coven's gathering that evening. He had been determined to follow Alwayna to the mighty function. She had told him that he could not come, that it was not permitted, which rankled, for Tomolina had been permitted to go with Dorinda. After a few abortive attempts at accompanying them, he had merely waited until they left and then followed. He felt driven to follow. He was not certain why, but it had something to do with their conversation at noon.

Strange, he had always prided himself upon being different from the other poor, powerless human beings. Being different gave him power. Yet Alwayna, the girl with the snowflake mark, wanted nothing more than to be like them. She wanted to belong. She wanted to be able to depend upon people and to have them depend upon her.

Something lurched inside Blake. He had never needed to depend upon anyone before. Something cruel also whispered that no one had ever depended upon him. He thought of the trail of women in his life—women he had met, conquered, and discarded. No, Alwayna was different. She knew better than to depend upon him.

"I have discovered if you add a pinch of witch hazel to the ointment," an ancient known only as Great Granny was saying, holding a quivering piece of paper in hand, "it will cause warts to disappear lickety-split."

"And a dollop of cream to sweeten the pie," another matronly witch enthused.

Blake shook his head and dug his nails into the floor. As a warlock, he could not help but watch with disgust. This coven gathering was a farce. They all sat upon chairs in a semicircle, some with their cats sitting beside them, some with ravens. Old Great Granny's familiar was a white owl, which perched upon her shoulder. The witches were taking turns in presenting their discoveries, sharing their spells and potions (something you would never catch any self-respecting warlock doing—one kept all power and secrets to oneself).

In between, the ladies shared recipes for cooking as well. If Blake had not been so appalled, he might have laughed when one witch had read out a potion that called for bat wings, newt tails, arsenic, and a pound of sweet butter. She had requested them to strike the sweet butter. That was meant for the other card she was passing along, one for cherry tarts.

Nor could he laugh as he watched Alwayna within the semicircle. The formal presentations had disintegrated into an open forum, with ladies passing cards back and forth and chattering like hens in a henhouse. Alwayna did not enter into the bedlam. She sat quietly, a forced smile upon her lips, as the conversation and the cards flowed about her. For some reason, the spells and recipes being passed along were never offered to her.

He watched, his anger mounting. At last the blond girl upon Alwayna's right handed Alwayna a card. Blake purred in satisfaction. Granted, the girl was talking to someone else at the time, but hand Alwayna the card she did. Alwayna took it, a heart-wrenching look of surprise and pleasure upon her face.

Suddenly, the girl on Alwayna's left, a sassy-looking brunette, shrieked and ripped the card from Alwayna's fingers. The silly chit shrieked once more upon a grander scale. The cackling died down and witches and familiars alike stared at Alwayna.

Alwayna's face deepened to a crimson red.

"Do forgive me," the brunette tittered, waving the card. She cast a vicious eye to the blond girl. "Rebecca passed Alwayna a spell for rainmaking."

The blond Rebecca turned as red faced as Alwayna. "I'm sorry. I—I wasn't watching."

"Then do, gal," Great Granny said, her tone cantankerous. "You know Alwayna cannot touch the cards until she's performed her first spell."

"Oh, but I heard that she has," the brunette said slyly.

"What?" Great Granny boomed. She leveled a rheumy gaze upon Dorinda and Bathsheba. "What is this Betsy is talking about?"

"Oh, dear," Bathsheba said. "Well . . ."

"I think Miss Long Ears overheard a conversation that was not meant for her," Dorinda said, narrowing her own gaze upon Betsy.

"Betsy," a plump lady said from the right. "That was a private discussion not meant for your ears."

"Yes, Mama," Betsy said, widening her eyes. "And I wouldn't have ever disclosed it, but all things considered, it could be dangerous for Alwayna to touch anything."

"Poppycock," Dorinda said. "I remember, Miss Smart Breeches, when you turned your father's prize hog into a rock and couldn't turn it back. Your mama never went touting that tale about, I assure you, and you went without bacon that winter."

Betsy stiffened. "Yes, but *I* never sent a beanstalk up into the clouds."

All in the room gasped in one great concerted breath.

"It wasn't a beanstalk," Bathsheba cried. She flushed. "It was ivy."

"Is this true, Alwayna?" Great Granny asked, pinning the girl with a gimlet eye.

"I—I am sorry," she said. "I—I . . ."

"We did not mention it because . . . because . . ." Bathsheba said. "Well, we cannot be certain it was Alwayna. Dorinda and I were experimenting and I fear a spell of ours grew—I mean, got slightly out of hand. Alwayna walked in at that particular moment and attempted to help. It might not have been her fault. Perhaps it was mine."

"Or mine," Dorinda said staunchly. "And we chopped the stalk down before there was any harm. We also took all precautions afterward."

"We all should have been notified of this," Great Granny said severely.

"Why?" Dorinda said, a defiant glint in her eyes. "There was no harm done, and we will notify you when we are *sure* that Alwayna performed the spell and it was not something else. It was all a tempest in a teapot and nothing more." She cast Betsy a steely look. "It is a story that should remain amongst the coven and not be disclosed to anyone else."

"Of course not," Betsy said. She giggled. "We wouldn't want Alwayna to be the laughing *stalk* of the village."

The younger ones of the group tittered and laughed.

Blake had tolerated more then enough. He yowled his rage and strode out from beneath the table, his tale whipping about, an angry snake.

He progressed no farther, however. His appearance incited pandemonium. Every creature—cat, raven, or owl—converged upon him. The witches shrieked and howled.

"Kitten!" Alwayna cried, springing up.

Blake had no moment to assure her of his safety. He was ducking, rolling, and cursing, fending off the attack from ground and air. Alwayna promptly added the only human element, diving into the muddle of fur and feathers. Blake was jerked up by the scruff of the neck. He wheezed as he was slammed up tightly to Alwayna's chest.

"Stop them!" Alwayna shouted, covering Blake as the birds circled. "Stop them now!"

Various names were called out by the witches. Finally the familiars returned to their respective mistresses.

Alwayna stood alone, panting and squeezing the very breath from Blake's meager lungs.

"Alwayna," Great Granny intoned in a thunderous voice, "is that your kitten?"

"Yes, yes, he is!" she said, her chin jutting out.

"Gel, what is the matter with you?" Great Granny asked, shaking her head. "You know the rules. You are not permitted to bring an unsanctioned animal into the coven meetings. Such things cause an imbalance in the powers."

"She brought her pet," Betsy said, giggling. "Imagine. She brought her pet."

"H-he is not my pet," Alwayna refuted. Blake could feel her tremble. "He is my familiar, and as my familiar, he is permitted."

"You've got to be a witch," Betsy said nastily, "before you can have a familiar."

"I—I performed that spell with the stalk," Alwayna said.

"Not something to brag about . . ." Betsy said.

"Enough!" Great Granny said. Her eyes were narrowed in judgment. "Alwayna, you have broken coven rules by bringing your pet with you."

"I did not break a rule," Alwayna said. Her voice quavered but slightly. "He is my familiar."

"Do not persist in this, child," Great Granny said. "You will only cause more trouble for you and your pet."

"Alwayna," Bathsheba cried, rushing forward. She leaned over and whispered into Alwayna's ear. "Do be careful. She could order Kitten to be killed since he is unsanctioned. And you could be cast out of the coven."

"I heard that, Bathsheba," Great Granny snapped. "And that is exactly what I'm going to do if she does not prove to me that he's her familiar. We cannot have such insubordination."

"Oh, oh, dear," Bathsheba said, wringing her hands. "I am sure she didn't mean to be insubordinate."

"Do not be so stern with her, Great Granny," Dorinda said. "Our coven is of the good. Such rules are old and archaic. They should not be used in this enlightened day."

"They are the rules," Great Granny said.

"And . . . and I will obey them," Alwayna said, lifting her chin. "I will show you I am—am a witch and . . . and Kitten here is my familiar."

"Kitten?" Betsy whispered loud enough for the dead. "Whoever heard of a familiar named Kitten?"

Blake meowed and narrowed his eyes upon the girl. She was no witch—just a bitch.

"Then show us," Great Granny said.

"V-very well," Alwayna stammered. "I—I will turn a red rose blue."

"Simple enough," Great Granny said, her lined face cracking into a wicked smile. She lifted one gnarled finger and pointed to the table. A red rose in a vase appeared. "Turn it blue, gel."

Blake purred in delight. Great Granny's magic was quick, true, and strong. It was also not sealed with a ward against intervention. He grasped hold of the still open vein of it.

"Simple enough," Alwayna murmured, slowly walking over to the table. She stared at the rose. Blake, excited, meowed. He placed his paw to Alwayna's heart. Her gaze turned to him. Fright and determination warred within the depths of her green eyes.

He willed her to open her mind to his. The slightest smile touched Alwayna's lips and Blake shivered. She *had* opened her mind to his. He could feel her drawing from

him—except what Alwayna drew from him was emotion.
He could feel her courage growing and building. "They'll
not hurt you, Kitten. I won't let that happen. You can depend on me." She was drawing his strength. "I must not
ask magic. I must bend it to my will."

Blake meowed. He wasn't certain now if Alwayna was
drawing from him or trying to give to him. He forced himself to open to those emotions, knowing that they must
share and meld as one if he were to channel his magic
through her.

Alwayna returned her gaze to the red rose. Slowly, she
spoke the words she had practiced that morning. Blake
focused all his power on funneling the magic into her.
Alwayna stiffened as if shocked. The rose remained red.

"She can't do it," Betsy cried.

Alwayna repeated the words again, her gaze riveted
upon the rose. Blake realized she had felt the magic, but
had recoiled from its force. He quickly drew it back, merely
offering her the magic rather than trying to funnel it
through her.

He felt her body relax and take it in. He breathed a sigh
of relief. Then he felt the whirl of Alwayna and the magic.

The rose blossomed into the richest midnight blue.

"We did it, Kitten," Alwayna breathed.

Blake meowed, stunned. In the offering and melding of
minds and magic, he had felt Alwayna's spirit. There was
a loneliness, a separateness. There was, also, a natural joy—
the joy of fairies dancing in the moonlight. And there was
so much more. Yet the warmth and sheer pleasure of her
accomplishment overpowered him the most.

Alwayna held Blake aloft to look him in the eyes. "We
did it!"

"Meow!" Blake said, feeling a love of life he had never
felt before. It was Alwayna's. Caught up in it, he could feel
her power abounding, too ecstatic to remain leashed.

Blue roses rained down everywhere.

"How lovely," Bathsheba exclaimed.

"Enough! Enough!" Great Granny shouted, holding up her hands as roses plummeted upon her.

"Oh, I'm sorry," Alwayna said, blinking. The raining roses ceased.

Great Granny cackled. "A little too enthusiastic there, child."

"Yes," Alwayna said, grinning.

"Well, nothing wrong with that, upon occasion," Great Granny gruffed. She nodded her gray head. "You and your familiar must remember not to overdo like that in the future."

"Bravo!" Dorinda said. The coven of witches applauded.

"How embarrassing," Betsy was heard to say. "To have a silly little kitten as a familiar."

The room silenced at the insult. Alwayna leveled a direct look at the pouting girl. Blake jumped as he felt the magic being pulled from him without permission.

Suddenly Betsy's face turned blue—deep, indigo blue.

The witches as one began laughing.

Betsy looked confounded. "What—what is so funny?"

"Your face is blue, daughter," Betsy's mother said, laughing herself. "Just like the roses."

"What!" Betsy screeched. She glared at Alwayna. "Turn it back."

"I don't know," Alwayna said in an innocent tone. "I—I might not be able to do so. Like when you couldn't turn that rock back into a pig."

"Oh!" Betsy cried, stomping her foot.

"But I'll work on it," Alwayna said, grinning. "I might figure out how to do it in a week or two."

Blake purred to himself. Alwayna might not know her origins, but it was clear to him, she indeed had fairy blood within her. Her prank, and her sheer amusement over it, proved it.

He found himself enchanted with her. He found himself in love with her.

* * *

Alwayna strolled through the woods. She had just come from the village of Chancellorville. She laughed aloud. Kitten, who was perched upon her shoulder, meowed in question.

"Kitten, I am just so happy," Alwayna said. She reached up and scratched him. "And I owe it all to you." He meowed. "Yes, I do. I cannot believe it all. Last week I could not perform one spell. This week we have done so many. I liked how we could make that dreadful rash on little Tommy Haversham go away." She giggled. "Now I know we couldn't do anything for Tabatha Florish and her request for a love potion. After all, Dorinda and Bathsheba have already warned me that good witches never attempt love spells. Love is from the Almighty and must never be tampered with whatsoever. But I don't think she needs a spell. All she needed was encouragement in letting her beau know of her feelings. Imagine it. She told me she thinks he will propose, even before Halloween." She literally skipped, causing Kitten to dig his claws into her shoulder and growl. "I'm sorry. But I am so looking forward to Halloween this year. You will enjoy the celebrations. Chancellorville celebrates it greatly. They have a dance and a bonfire in the square. Only think. More than one of the townsfolk has invited me. I—I know that s-some of it is because I am a new witch in the village, but . . . but I think they also like me, Kitten. I really do." She rubbed her cheek against Kitten's fur, her voice lowering to a whisper. "I love you, Kitten."

Kitten stiffened and his nails dug into her shoulder once more. Alwayna felt oddly embarrassed of a sudden, as if she had said more then she ought. Forcing a laugh, she lifted Kitten from his perch and set him to the ground. "I'll race you through the woods."

Alwayna picked up her skirts and ran through the woods, elation shooting through her. She finally slowed. Gasping for breath, she turned. Of course, Kitten with his four short legs, was nowhere behind her. She waited. He always found her.

After a long moment she called out, "Kitten, I'm over here."

Her eyes widened as she heard steps within the woods. The branches parted and a man stepped into sight. Alwayna drew in her breath as her heart actually sighed with pleasure. "It's you!"

"Yes, it is me," Blake said.

He wore a simple peasant shirt and breeches. Gone was the magnificent apparel, Alwayna could not help but notice. She laughed. "Are you not a duke today?"

"No," he said, strolling up to her. His dark eyes were warm, different from the way she remembered them, and she had dreamed of them every night despite her best efforts. "Today I am just a man."

"Just a man?" Alwayna asked in a teasing tone.

"It is far more difficult then you would think," Blake said, his tone wry.

"What?" Alwayna asked, blinking, for he stood very close.

"To be just a man," Blake said. "Yet that is what I want to be. Just a man who wants to know you, Alwayna. To understand you. May we walk?"

"Yes," Alwayna said. She flushed. "I would like that."

They turned and for a few moments merely walked together. Alwayna was surprised that she was not uncomfortable. She was not even frightened of him as before. Perhaps because today he had taken the pains to come to her simply as a man and she could be just a woman. Perhaps because the thought of him had been present with her every day and night and his actual presence here now only fulfilled that thought.

"The other day you said you had lived with many people," Blake said. "Why?"

"I am an orphan," Alwayna said simply. She peeked at him. "I do not know either my father or my mother, nor does anyone else."

"How did that come to be?" Blake asked.

"The Parker family said they found me upon their doorstep one morning," Alwayna said. She smiled. "Mama—I mean Mother Parker—said I was a gift from the fairies."

"Yes," Blake nodded solemnly.

Alwayna started, peering at him. "Y-you are not surprised?"

He remained silent for a moment. "I know of magic."

"And I am learning," Alwayna said, an eagerness and pride filling her.

"Yes, you are," Blake said. A smile flashed across his face. It was neither arrogant nor seductive. It was warm and real. Alwayna started again, but he said quickly, "Why did Mother Parker say you were a gift from the fairies?"

Alwayna gazed at him and then looked away. "B-because she—she said she was a friend of the fairies. She always left them milk and gifts and . . . and that is why they left me on her doorstep one Halloween night."

"Is that the only reason?" Blake asked.

"Yes," Alwayna said, unable to meet his gaze.

"It wasn't because you bear the mark of the snowflake?" Blake asked gently.

"You know?" Alwayna gasped. Her gaze flew to his in astonishment and fear. "Who are you?"

"I am just a man," Blake said again.

"No, you are not," Alwayna said, shaking her head. "You . . . know things about me you shouldn't. You appear and disappear at will—"

"Perhaps not at will," Blake said softly. "I told you, Alwayna. I am no stranger to magic. And I think you can understand if I say that . . . I am different from other people. But I do not mean you harm, Alwayna. And, yes, I know things about you I shouldn't. I know things about the future; I know things about the past. But to know about them will not matter if I do not know you. You will not frighten me, Alwayna. Faith, you are uncommon. You are special, not strange."

Alwayna flushed. He spoke words that were a dream to her. "Thank you."

"Why would you not tell me about the mark?" Blake asked.

Alwayna grimaced. "Mother Parker thought . . . well, like you, she thought the mark special and . . . and when I lived with her I thought it was special. Only when she passed away and . . . and we moved from Chancellorville did I—I learn that others did not . . . not think it special. They thought it strange and . . ."

"Frightening," Blake said. "When did she pass on?"

"When I was five," Alwayna said. "She died of a fever one winter. Father Parker was never the same after that. He said he could not take care of all of us children and he . . . he sent me to relatives in Devonshire." She lifted her chin. "They thought me a child of the devil and took me to the parish father. He was a kind man who took me in, though he said the mark warned me that I was burdened with an unruly spirit and must strive against it."

"And have you striven against it?"

"Yes," Alwayna said, nodding. Then she sighed. "But perhaps never to the proper degree. He was happy to give me to a family that wanted a child so dearly that they overlooked my unruliness." Her spirit was lightening even more. "Mrs. Chalmers called me fey. I always like that word much better."

"Why were you fey?"

"I cannot remain indoors for too long," Alwayna said. "I must be outside. I must be in the woods. And sometimes at night, especially as a child, I would go out and merely dance and sing in the moonlight."

Blake chuckled. "There is nothing wrong with that."

"But sometimes I would forget my clothes," Alwayna confessed.

"Even better," Blake said, a fine brow lifting.

Alwayna stared. Then she giggled. "I also have a dreadful singing voice."

"Now that is a sin to be sure. What else?"

"I—I have never been able to pay attention for too long. When at lessons I would always become distracted." She flushed. "Usually thinking of pranks to play. I remember Miss Martha, an instructor of mine. She was very proud of her appearance. I—I would think of ways to ruin her appearance. Red paint upon the chair that she would sit in. Things like that."

"Indeed?"

"And I—I had a terrible habit of trying to lead people astray. It was like hide-and-seek to me." She flushed. "One evening I mislead the minister through the woods for hours by calling out to him and then running before he could catch me."

"He actually followed?" Blake asked.

"I—I pretended to be his dead wife," Alwayna said. "I know I shouldn't have. But he was going to Lucy Rothford's house to take her to task for being unwed and . . . and with child. I—I thought that was mean-spirited, so I mislead him. And in the end I told him if he said aught to Lucy Rothford I would haunt him every night. He did not like his dead wife much."

"I see," Blake said, chuckling.

"I—I don't do those things anymore," Alwayna said quickly.

"A pity," Blake murmured. Alwayna gasped. "Why have you never married?"

"Because I am fey, and the men seem to know it," Alwayna said, laughing. Her eyes twinkled. "And that without even knowing about my mark. I am sure that would totally frighten them."

Blake laughed. He stopped and grabbed her hand, startling her. "Then I am glad for that mark. I am glad it has kept other men—men who are fools—from you . . . and you from them." Almost gently he placed his hand to her shoulder, then slid it gently down her shoulder blade until it rested unerringly over the mark. "I told you that you were destined to love me. I had not realized that it would mean I am destined to love you as well."

Alwayna gazed up at him, her heart catching. "Y-you cannot love me."

"Yes, I can," Blake said. "I was surprised myself that it was that simple."

"I—I don't know what to say," Alwayna said.

"Why, that you love me," Blake said. He laughed. "Me, the man. That is what I want to hear you say when you are ready to say it."

"I—I see."

"I know of magic, Alwayna. You are learning of it," Blake said. "I have not known of love, but I am learning. We could learn that together."

"Yes," Alwayna whispered.

Blake sucked in his breath. That odd pain she had seen before crossed his face.

"What is it?" Alwayna asked.

"I—I am merely dizzy with the thought of it," Blake said, smiling.

"No, it is not that," Alwayna said softly. "You are going to leave me now, aren't you?"

"Yes," Blake said, nodding slowly. He lifted his hand and touched her cheek. "I am glad you understand. I am glad that you are fey, Alwayna." He turned to leave. Only then he halted, gazing back at her. "I used to pass time with women I never cared to know, never cared to love. Now, when I would gladly pass ages with you, I cannot. Forgive me."

He moved swiftly then, disappearing into the woods. Alwayna felt disappointment, but not lonely or lost. He would appear again. She knew that in the very depths of her heart and it filled her with joy.

FOUR

Alwayna woke slowly. She blinked and stretched beneath the covers, the chill of October waiting beyond their confines. She lay a moment, frowning. She had been dreaming deeply, she knew. She also knew the dream had felt terribly real to her. Only now she couldn't recall it. It had been odd, fantastical. That much she remembered. Something about beautiful fairy creatures, but she could not bring it back into focus. Her bemused, hazy fears evaporated as a far more real and vivid thought chased through her mind. Blake. Perhaps she would see him today. The past two weeks had been the most exciting and unusual she had ever experienced.

She and Kitten would study witchery. She would go about her daily life with Bathsheba and Dorinda. Then she would slip into the woods when she could. She never again spoke to the sisters about Blake. They would consider her crazy. They would ask questions. They would wish to meet Blake.

She and Blake had no time for that. Their moments together were too precious. These moments were their very own. Often they would sing and dance with no music but that of their own. Many times Blake would laugh and beg her to dance as she had done as a child. She would talk to him of her secret thoughts. He would tell her of exotic places, of different woods and skies that he would have her dance under someday.

Then, within an hour or two, that look would cross his face and he would say he must leave. Always when he departed he would touch her face and say he was waiting for the day she could say . . .

"I love you," Alwayna whispered tentatively. She waited to see what emotions came. There was no fear anymore. Indeed, now the words felt so perfectly and marvelously right. "I love you, Blake!" she shouted out in joy. She threw the covers back, peering around as if her room was strange and new. Just saying those words and knowing they were true had changed everything. She glanced at the foot of the bed, where a small black ball of fur rested. "Kitten, I can say it! I love Blake!"

The ball of fur slumbered on.

"Kitten, did you hear me?" Alwayna asked. She shifted the blankets and prodded him with her toe.

The small ball jumped. Kitten lifted a groggy head and meowed in a dazed tone. Alwayna giggled. "Wake up sleepyhead! What is the matter with you? You are always awake before me. Oh, never mind!" Alwayna bounced across the bed. "Do let us hurry. It is going to be a special day. For today, Dorinda and Bathsheba are going to teach me their wine spell." She teased him awake, playfully brushing a finger lightly across the pointed tip of an ear, chuckling as it twitched in agitation.

Blake woke slowly. Alwayna had called him—that he knew. He shook his head. Through his sleepy haze, he saw Alwayna's pixie face as she peered down at him. Her hair was tousled from sleep and her green eyes sparkled. She was the most beautiful vision. He meowed.

Alwayna giggled and sprang from the bed. "Slugabed! Hurry. Today is going to be a wonderful, fantastic day and I do not want to tarry."

Blake stifled a groan. He was exhausted. The offering of his powers to Alwayna required effort. He enjoyed it, for each time they practiced magic together, he could feel their bonding. Yet it taxed him. As did drawing enough magic together to then turn himself into a human. Each time it became more and more of a struggle to fight Trillion's spell. Each time the cost was higher, the consequences more painful.

Such must be the torments of hell. The hours he could spend with Alwayna meant everything to him. Blake desperately wanted to hold her and swear to her his love. Still, he waited. He did not want to seduce her. He did not want to fool her either. He wanted her love as she could only give. Without her love he was doomed. Even if there was no curse to fight, even if Trillion did not come to claim him, Blake knew that, without Alwayna's love, he was doomed.

Alwayna came to kneel beside the bed and rest her head next to him. Her eyes were bright and filled with something he hadn't seen before. "Then, Kitten, my dearest familiar. Then I will see Blake. I know I will." Her laugh was music to him. "Because I have something I must tell him."

Blake meowed, shaking off his exhaustion as hope flared. Yes, she would see him today. He would move heaven and earth to hear her say she loved him.

Alwayna attempted to train her thoughts on her studies with Bathsheba and Dorinda. It was the sisters' habit to make their own elderberry wine, of which they would partake one glass every day at eventide. Upon each cherished bottle they would cast a chant to make the wine's spirit strong and sweet. Today was their day to perform the chant. Both very proud of Alwayna's stunning progress in the arts. They had decided it was time for her to learn the very special secret to fine elderberry wine.

"Do you think you have the words correct now?" Bathsheba asked, her blue eyes solemn.

"I think I do," Alwayna said, nodding. She peered at the bottle. Her mind was focused upon the chant and its particular phrasing, while her heart pounded with the desire to see Blake today.

"Then try it," Dorinda said. "It's the only way to find out."

Alwayna petted Kitten, whom she held in her arms. "Are you ready, Kitten?"

"Meow," Kitten consented.

"Very well." Alwayna smiled. She began the chant, eager to perform her best. She experienced the welling of power, which always felt more like an outside force than her own. Only this time it felt as if it were hers—all hers.

Kitten actually mewed and squirmed in her hold. Alwayna shivered and glanced down at kitten. "What—what is the matter?"

"Humph," Dorinda said, looking at the bottle. "Wonder if it took."

"We will have to test it," Bathsheba said, her tone eager.

"That we will," Dorinda said, grinning.

She speedily uncorked the bottle. Bathsheba lifted a dainty teacup the sisters used especially for their elderberry wine. Dorinda poured a little into each cup. Alwayna waited anxiously while the two sisters sipped the wine.

"My stars!" Bathsheba gasped, sputtering.

"Gracious," Dorinda gurgled, straightening.

"What?" Alwayna asked. Her heart sank. "How bad is it?"

"No-o-o," Bathsheba said, her eyes wide as she took another sip. "It is not bad."

"Only p-potent," Dorinda said, her words muffled behind her raised teacup.

"Then . . . then I did good?" Alwayna asked, relieved.

"Oh, yes, indeed," Bathsheba said. "You have given it a fine spirit. Why it positively makes one tingle. It . . . it makes one think of—"

"L-o-v-e," Dorinda breathed. Then she stiffened and glared at them, her face flushing deep red.

"It does, doesn't it?" Bathsheba said, sighing. She offered Alwayna the cup. "Here, dear. See for yourself."

"No," Alwayna said, her heart soaring. "I don't need to. I already—" She halted and bit her tongue. She had almost said she knew what love tasted like, for it seemed to fill her this day. "I am not accustomed to wine. I wouldn't know if it was good or not."

"Oh, this one you would," Bathsheba said, giggling.

"Don't press her, sister," Dorinda said sternly as she swiftly reached to refill her teacup. " 'Tis very potent."

"But I only wish for her to see how ver-ry well she did upon her spell," Bathsheba exclaimed.

"I shall take your word for it," Alwayna said. She laughed. "Now if you would permit it, I would like to go to the woods . . . to hunt out more herbs."

"Hmm, yes. If you wish. That's a good girl," Dorinda said, sipping from her teacup.

"Yes," Bathsheba said, reaching for the bottle. "Such a good girl."

Alwayna bit back a grin, and calling Kitten to come with her, she left the kitchen, her heart eager. She headed toward the woods. She glanced back to see Kitten slipping away in the other direction. She shook her head, smiling. He was developing a greater and greater sense of adventure since that first day she had found him. She never doubted it was natural as a kitten matured into a full-grown cat. Since he always reappeared in due course, Alwayna did not concern herself. At least she tried not to concern herself.

She walked deeper into the woods. It was a gloriously cool day and she breathed in deeply.

"Alwayna," Blake's deep voice called out from ahead of her.

"Blake," Alwayna cried. She picked up her skirts and dashed toward his voice. Breaking through a grove of trees, she saw him.

"Blake!" She ran toward him, wishing to throw herself in his arms. Realizing her overzealous behavior, she slowed. Sudden embarrassment overtook her. "Hello."

"No," Blake said, his eyes dark and wild. "Do not stop, Alwayna. Come to me."

Alwayna started in astonishment. It was as if he knew. Then she laughed. Of course he knew.

"Blake!" She charged at him and did indeed throw herself into his arms.

"Alwayna," Blake murmured as he held her tight and swung her around. He finally set her down, his dark eyes jubilant. "I was right! Say it, Alwayna. Say it."

"I . . ." Alwayna blushed, though her smile was teasing. "Say what?"

"Say it, vixen," he ordered with a laugh, all but squeezing the air from her lungs. "Say what I've been waiting to hear you say."

"I . . ." Alwayna gasped. "I love you!"

"Say it again," Blake said, grinning.

Alwayna laughed. "I love you!"

"Again," Blake said, only this time more softly, his head lowering toward hers.

"I love . . ." Alwayna didn't finish. Blake covered her lips with his, warmly, firmly, possessively. A whirling sensation filled Alwayna. She'd always spurned men's kisses before, because she had never felt anything with those who attempted to steal them from her. Now she felt everything. It was like performing her first spell. It was like dancing under the stars. Only it was all consuming and encompassing.

Alwayna moaned and she returned Blake's kiss with an unleashed fervor, pressing herself against him. She gloried in the sensations, with no thought of hiding her newborn desire. An odd growl came from Blake. He deepened the kiss, revealing to Alwayna the sweet power of lips and tongues mating. His hands moved surely over her body, creating a wild heat wherever they roamed. Shivering in delight, Alwayna's hands roamed across Blake's broad shoulders and down his back. He groaned.

"Enough!" Blake said. He tore himself away from her.

"Enough?" Alwayna blinked, feeling both dazed and abandoned.

"You are making me lose my senses," Blake said. He laughed hoarsely.

"You feel that way, too?" Alwayna exclaimed. Her pleasure returned and she moved toward him eagerly. "For I am losing mine."

"No, remain where you are," Blake ordered, holding out a staying hand.

Alwayna halted. His look was one of grim determination and almost of fright. A laugh escaped her. For Blake to show such fear was amusing. Suddenly she felt strong and brave and free. "First you tell me to come to you, and now you order me to stay where I am. Do make up your mind, Duke."

"Do not tease me, lady," Blake said, a glimmer of humor answering hers. "You do not know what powers you play with."

"Yes, I do," Alwayna said, grinning "It is magic, sheer magic."

Something odd passed through Blake's eyes. "Alwayna . . ."

"The minute you kissed me, I knew," Alwayna breathed, stepping toward him. "Kiss me again, Blake."

"No. There will be plenty enough times for that after we are married," Blake said, his tone firm. He winked wickedly at her. "For even more than just kisses, I promise you."

"Married?" Alwayna asked. She halted.

"Yes," Blake said, frowning. "Married. And I would that we could do it within the next few days."

"S-s-o soon?" Alwayna asked, swallowing. She did not feel as strong and brave and free as before.

Blake's gaze grew solemn. "You said you loved me, Alwayna."

"I do," Alwayna said quickly. "I—I do. But . . . but t-to marry so swiftly?"

"I would give you all the time in the world, Alwayna,"

Blake said. Regret and a naked torment filled his gaze. He walked slowly up to her. "But . . . but that is something I cannot give you. That is something we do not have."

"Why?" Alwayna asked. A shiver coursed through her. "Why not?"

"If you will not marry me now because you love me and I love you," Blake said, softly, "then anything else I tell you will not matter. It will not change things."

"Change things?" she whispered.

"I need you to love me, Alwayna," Blake said. "I never thought I would need anyone, let alone need her love. But I do, Alwayna. I need yours. I will confess that, when I first came here, I thought only of you loving me and you marrying me. I had not realized that such could never be enough. That it would be a curse in itself, because love must be shared for it to be true."

"I do love you," Alwayna said. Feelings of love rose within her to testify to that truth. Yet a feeling of fear rose to war with it, to warn her not to trust it so readily.

"But . . . but . . ."

Blake bent down and kissed her. He neither touched her nor held her, but merely kissed her gently, tenderly. Then he drew back. "This is the magic, Alwayna. This is love. I have been powerless to show you anything to make you believe in me or the future. I can only ask you to believe in this right now. In our love. Marry me, Alwayna. Marry me!"

"I . . ." Alwayna trembled. Her fears grew. They clamored loudly, drowning out any sound of love. She was different. Love and belonging were meant for other people. People could not depend on her or she on them. Instinctively, as a frightened animal, Alwayna picked up her skirts and, turning, ran from Blake and her emotions.

"Alwayna . . ." Blake's voice called. "Come back!"

Marry me, Alwayna. Marry me . . ." The words whirled in her head as she darted through the woods. Love and fear tumbled and roiled with it. Gasping for breath, tears streaming down her face, Alwayna finally halted. It took every particle of strength to do so, but she stopped.

As Alwayna stood and quivered, her mind cleared. Her heart lurched. She was running from the very thing she desired. Love. All the precious moments. Time.

"Blake!" she cried. "Blake, I'm sorry."

Spinning, she ran once more through the woods. This time toward love and away from fear. She shouted Blake's name and it rang through the woods. She swore she heard the shimmer of laughter just as she returned to where she had left Blake, but she ignored it.

"Blake . . . I will . . ." Alwayna's voice faded away. He was nowhere to be seen. Kitten, however, sat upon the ground. "Kitten, where did Blake go?"

"Meow," Kitten said. His gaze seemed as lost as she felt. She lifted him up and hugged his tiny body close for comfort.

"Blake! Blake! Please come back," Alwayna cried. Holding Kitten against her heart, Alwayna chased throughout the woods, searching for Blake.

Numb with exhaustion, Alwayna walked slowly toward the cottage, still clutching Kitten to her. The afternoon sun had melted into fall's early darkness. She'd searched for Blake throughout the woods. She knew intuitively that she would not find him, but still she had searched.

She cringed. It had seemed as if the very woods whispered about her. She would wait and look around. Kitten would hiss and growl low in his throat. She had always considered nature to be her friend when mankind was not. Now it suddenly felt as if nature had turned on her.

Shaking off her strange imaginings, she opened the cottage door and entered into the kitchen. Kitten yowled. Alwayna shook her head, thinking it another phantasm of hers. The kitchen was awash with red, white and gold. Grandiose Valentine hearts, deep red and laced in white, wafted about the room wherever a breeze took them. Statues of cherubs populated the room: sitting cherubs, flying cherubs, laughing cherubs. The greatest statue of them all towered to the ceiling. Venus!

Two off-key voices raised in a ballad drifted to Alwayna. She attempted to define the words, recognizing it as a medieval ballad of love lost. Skirting cherubs and hearts, Alwayna navigated through the kitchen toward the mournful singers in the small parlor.

The parlor was another shrine to love. Green vines swung from the ceiling, dripping red roses. Bathsheba lay sprawled upon the settee, teacup in hand, waving it and singing lustily. Intermittently she would intersperse her song with gusty sighs. Dorinda sat stiffly in her chair, holding upon her hand a white turtledove. She sang just as loudly. Tomolina sat perched upon the mantel shelf, her hair raised, her yellow eyes slit in distaste. She yowled and hissed as Alwayna entered. Kitten hissed in return. Alwayna only gurgled in shock.

"Oh-h-h, hello, dear," Bathsheba said with a wide smile.

"H-hello," Alwayna stammered. "Are—are you all right?"

"Oh, y-yes," Bathsheba said. "We were just s-s-singing of lost l-o-v-e."

"Sad, very sad," Dorinda said with an unladylike belch.

Alwayna's heart wrenched. Had she lost Blake?

"Y-your wine is specta-wonder-er-er-ful," Bathsheba said. "Y-you must taste it."

"Yes," Dorinda said. She leaned forward, the dove flapping away as she reached for the bottle set upon the carpet beside her. She lifted it and then set it down once more. "S-sorry. It is all gone."

"Oh, dear," Bathsheba said. "It was lovely. So—so lovely. Now it is all gone. G-gone."

"Y-yes," Alwayna said, refusing the pain in her heart. She stared at the two sisters, frowning. What did one do with two sentimental witches drunk on love-enchanted elderberry wine?

Her mind too numb to think of an answer, Alwayna

moved silently to sit in a chair. She listened to the songs
until Bathsheba's head drooped and Dorinda nodded off.
She roused them, helping them to their respective rooms.
Only then was she able to stumble to her own room. She
changed quickly into her nightclothes and fell into bed.

Bathsheba's voice drifted in her mind. *So lovely. Now it
is all gone. G-gone.* Had her love been the same? This morning she had been drunk with it. She had tasted deeply of
it. Now, tonight, because of her own doings, it was gone.
Perhaps all gone.

One lone tear slipped down her cheek.

"Alwayna, come to me!"

Alwayna's eyes snapped open. She stared into the darkness. Had she dreamed a voice calling to her.

"Alwayna, come! I need you!"

Alwayna blinked. Sleep clouded her mind. She could
not determine if the voice was male or female.

Sitting up, she gazed about the room. Moonlight dusted
it to silver. Someone was calling her. Someone needed her.
She sprang from the bed. Kitten meowed slightly. She
peered at the small ball of fur at the foot of her bed. It
did not stir.

Alwayna's thoughts immediately turned to the sisters.
She hastened from her room and went first to Bathsheba's
room.

"Bathsheba?" Alwayna called softly. A high, petering
snore greeted her.

"Alwayna, come!"

Alwayna gasped, spinning. The voice called her, yet she
and the sleeping Bathsheba were the only ones present
within the chamber. It must be Dorinda in trouble. She
hurried from the room and stumbled to Dorinda's, opening the door and entering. "Dorinda?" Alwayna whispered, walking to the bed.

A deep, staccato snore arose in answer.

"Alwayna, come to me!"

Alwayna stilled. "Where are you?"

"Come into the night." The voice finally took shape and form. Blake! Alwayna ran from Dorinda's room. She chased through the cottage and tore out of the kitchen door, leaving it swinging on its hinges. "Blake! Where are you?"

"Come to me!" his voice called.

"Yes!" Alwayna sprinted toward the woods. "Blake! Where are you?"

She halted of a sudden. She did not gasp. Her heart did not even pound. Perhaps it merely stopped as she stared in awe. Wonderment, both warm and pervasive, filled her.

The most beautiful woman stood before her. Moonlight glistened on her and through her, as if she were its embodiment. Her blue eyes glowed with a supernatural power. Translucent wings whispered.

"Hello, Alwayna," the woman said, her voice silver music to the ear. "I have been waiting a long time for you."

"Who are you?" Alwayna whispered.

"You may call me Trillion," she said, smiling. "I am a princess of the fairies."

Alwayna could not doubt it. The woman was too beautiful to be anything else. "Y-you've been w-waiting for me?"

"Yes, dear one," Trillion said. Her voice sounded so loving. "It is time you join your own."

"M-my own?" Alwayna whispered.

"Yes," Trillion said. She drifted close. "You know you are part fairy."

"I—I am?" Alwayna asked.

"You bear the mark of the snowflake," Trillion said, nodding. "You are both human and fairy. Very special. You belong with us."

"I—I do?" Alwayna asked. Happiness welled within her. She belonged with this beautiful woman. Her loneliness and hurt disappeared. It all made sense. That was why she had always felt lost before.

Yet the smallest question teased at her. "Wh-why have you c-come now?"

"I could not come before," Trillion said, her tone sad. "But I have found you now. And just in time. A mortal seeks to break your heart, does he not? He seeks to capture you and hold you tied to him."

Alwayna started back. "H-how do you know?"

"I care about you," Trillion said in response. "Come away. Mortals will only cause you pain. Especially the men."

"Th-they will?" Alwayna stammered.

"They say they love you," Trillion laughed lightly. "And when you offer your love, they leave you."

Burning blood rushed to Alwayna's cheeks. "Is . . . is that what Blake did?"

"They cannot be faithful," Trillion said, shaking her head. "Only look at them. They live such a short time. I suppose it only makes sense that they cannot be faithful."

"But . . . but I am mortal, too," Alwayna said.

"You need not be," Trillion said, the oddest smile upon her lips.

The dark, dark woods behind her disappeared and the most fantastic vision replaced them. It was of a beautiful plain and a glass smooth pond. Mountains soared—purple, blue, and green, high in the distant background. The landscape glowed, as with moonlight. Yet the colors were kaleidoscopic—clear and vibrant at the same time. Where most colors blend, reflecting from one object onto the next, here the hues cut sharply, each to its own. The pond was sapphire blue, with silver tracing through it, like the veins on a leaf. The grass of the plain was deep, verdant green, each blade tipped with brilliant light as if a diamond of the highest quality was set upon it.

"Come into our land," Trillion said softly.

"It is real?" Alwayna breathed. It called. Enchanted. And filled Alwayna with dreams promised.

Yes," Trillion said. "It can be your home. Forever. It is eternal. You belong, Alwayna. You belong with us."

Dazed and breathless, Alwayna took a step forward.

* * *

Blake woke. In a moment he knew Alwayna was gone. In the next he knew that she was in danger. He could feel the different powers in the air. He could feel it to the core. He looked about the moonlit room, detesting the shimmer of it.

Meowing his fear and rage, he jumped from the bed and ran through the cottage. His hair stood on end and he yowled as he saw the open kitchen door. He darted through it, out into the cold, bright night. He did not need to search, for the magic was so strong it scorched his nostrils.

Blake suddenly halted, his nails digging deep into the earth. Trillion stood, glittering with power, her eyes filled with malicious glee. Alwayna, bathed in that power, stood next to her. Blake stared, unable to believe what he saw. Trillion's land was exposed to them.

Dear God! Trillion was showing Alwayna their land. It lay before them, speckled with varying brilliants of silver. Fairies of every type stood, watching from the plain. Their eyes glowed as maliciously as Trillion's.

Stories and legends abounded, but rarely did the fairies show mortals their land, for if a mortal possessed the strength to turn away from it, that mortal could not help but be touched by the power and would carry it with him.

Blake growled deep in his throat. How confident Trillion must be to dare show Alwayna their land. If Alwayna entered it willingly, she would be Trillion's forever.

Trillion could not do that! Blake had until Halloween night to wed Alwayna. That was the agreement. He growled in his throat. His father had warned him that a fairy's sense of honor was skewed.

Alwayna took another step closer to the land.

"Come, you belong with us," Trillion said.

"Yowl!" Blake howled. He sent the force of his thoughts to Alwayna with the urgency of his cry.

Alwayna stopped and turned. She was beautiful, her red hair and green eyes traced with the fairy's glow. "Kitten, look! Isn't it beautiful?"

Blake yowled again.

Trillion did not flinch. She smiled wickedly as she looked at Blake. "Forget the creature, dear."

"What?" Alwayna gasped.

Blake saw Alwayna's surprise and how her face worked in confusion. Hope flared within him. He lifted his paw as if injured. Rather than yowling his anger and hate, he meowed as pitifully as he could. All his love and all his need went into that meow.

"What is the matter, Kitten?" Alwayna asked, staring at her small familiar, feeling confused and disorientated.

"Meow," Kitten burred, lifting his paw again.

"Leave him," Trillion said. She waved her hand. "Look, Alwayna. How can you turn from our land. Your land. It is eternal. You will never die."

Alwayna looked. The land drew her again. Visions and dreams filled her, promising marvelous things. She would belong. She would be great. This was her destiny.

"Just one more step, and it is all yours, Alwayna," Trillion whispered.

"Meow," Kitten said, his cry pitiful and pleading.

Alwayna halted and looked at Kitten. He had never acted like this. He was always feisty and independent. But he was hurt now. She could hear it in his voice. He was in need. She could feel it.

"Alwayna," Trillion said again. "Come now!"

Alwayna looked to Kitten. He was her familiar. In the few short weeks since he had entered her life, he had changed it. He had been her constant companion. They had worked spells together. She had felt closer to him than to any other creature. Then her thoughts, unaccountably, flitted to Blake. She had also fallen in love. It stunned her of a sudden. Her feelings for the two were different of course. Kitten was a small animal and Blake was a man. Yet she realized, in an odd manner, her feelings were equally strong for them both.

"He's nothing," Trillion said. "He's just a cat."

"No, just a kitten," Alwayna whispered. "Can he come with me?"

"He won't come with you," Trillion said, snorting.

"Why not?" Alwayna asked, frowning. She turned to Kitten. "Come with me, Kitten."

Kitten, injured paw and everything, scurried back so quickly that he toppled and rolled tail over paws. Alwayna could not help but giggle.

"I told you he would not come. Leave the creature for now," Trillion said. She gazed at Kitten, a challenging smile upon her lips. "If he has the strength he might follow."

Kitten hissed and growled.

"I did not think so," Trillion said, laughing. "But that could have been a choice. An amusing one, of course, but still a choice. It can never be said that we fairies are not fair." Kitten hissed low and deep. She looked to Alwayna. "Leave him. He is nothing."

"I cannot," Alwayna said. "He is hurt and needs me."

"Do not be so mortal," Trillion said, her voice cutting. Alwayna started back. She stared at Trillion. In that moment she did not appear so very beautiful, for the glitter in her eyes was hard and razor sharp. "But . . . but I *am* mortal."

"Only part of you," Trillion said, sniffing. "You have fairy blood as well. You can be one of us. We are eternal."

"And mortals are not?" Alwayna asked.

Trillion paused and then she waved a hand. "You mortals pass from this land of yours in an instant of our time. Our land never disappears, nor must we leave it for another."

Alwayna nodded slowly.

Kitten meowed.

Alwayna looked to Kitten and suddenly knew why her feelings were as strong for a kitten, a mere animal, as for Blake, a man. She loved. It was that simple. It did not matter that one was a lesser creature of the earth, or so she had been taught, or that one was a human who she might never see or love again. It only mattered that she loved and believed she received it in return. It was life and breath to her. And it was mortal.

Alwayna gazed solemnly at Trillion. "Forgive me. I cannot go with you."

"Mortal fool!" Trillion cried. Her beautiful, glowing hands seemed to turn to talons as she clenched them. "You dare turn from all I offer? You dare turn from eternity?"

"I—I do not think I turn from eternity, only from eternity as you know it in your land. And, yes, I dare. I fear I am too mortal," Alwayna said. She actually found herself smiling. "I will not leave the ones I love."

She turned then and walked over to Kitten. Bending down, she lifted him into her arms. She could feel his small heart pounding as he dug tiny claws into her. She felt the small stings of his fear and his need. She felt her own heart beating in return. She looked at Trillion. "Far too mortal!"

"Fool! Idiot!" Trillion screeched. Her hands indeed turned to talons and her wings flared high, whirling shooting bolts of lightning.

Alwayna gasped. The enchanted land behind changed. The vibrant colors faded, leaving only icy-cold shades of silver. She could see other fairies now. They populated the plain she had thought empty and tranquil. Their eyes were cold and malicious.

"It matters not," Trillion said. "You will be ours, Alwayna. I only thought to make it easy for you, but we will proceed to the end. All Hallow's Eve is not long away. You do not have the strength to fight our powers. Indeed, this will be far more entertaining for us, if not for you."

Trillion and the land and the other fairies disappeared.

Alwayna blinked. She held Kitten close, his purring a comfort. She turned and walked back to the cottage. As she walked, the scene and images were already disappearing from her mind.

She entered the cottage and went to her room. Sighing,

she lay down upon her bed, Kitten curled up in the curve
of her arm. Her last thought as she drifted off into a deep,
deep sleep was that she was glad she was too mortal.

FIVE

Dorinda and Bathsheba drove their cart into Chancellorville late the next morning. Every time the cart jiggled, Bathsheba moaned.

"Do be quiet, Bathsheba," Dorinda said, her own voice tight as she winced.

"But my head hurts so frightfully," Bathsheba said.

"So does mine, but you do not hear me crying," Dorinda said, tartly. They jolted again. Dorinda sucked in her breath.

Bathsheba moaned. "Why did our spell for the overimbibing of elderberry wine not work?"

Dorinda snorted. "Most likely because our heads hurt so much that we could not concentrate."

"Perhaps we should have awakened Alwayna. She could have helped us."

"You saw how she was sleeping as if dead," Dorinda said. "It would have been far too unkind to have awakened her."

"Yes," Bathsheba said. "I know. But since it was her spell on the elderberry wine . . ." She halted and blinked.

At the same time Dorinda sawed on the reigns of the horse, who neighed in fright.

"Dorinda?" Bathsheba asked. "D-do you see a . . . a little man doing a handstand in the middle of the road?"

"Yes," Dorinda said. "I do. Looks like a fairy to me."

"Good. I thought only I saw him."

"It's not good, Bathsheba," Dorinda said tartly. "We

must still be suffering from the w-wine. We must keep our meeting with Great Granny."

"Y-yes, I—I am sure you are correct," Bathsheba moaned, closing her eyes tightly. "But—but could we please stop for some powders at Mr. Talboth's? It—it is clear our spell for drinking too much elderberry wine must have . . ."

"Backfired." Dorinda nodded and slapped the horses reigns, driving directly at the little man, who swiftly disappeared.

The sisters remained silent as they drove into town, both stoically ignoring the sound of laughter that followed them. They could not be so stoic, however, as they drove down the single street running through Chancellorville. Thomas Fareweather, the bruising smithy, stood in the middle of street. He grunted and boxed at thin air, cursing all the while. On the sidewalk, Mildred Templeton, a distant cousin of the sisters, was shrieking and slapping at her skirts, which seemed to fly up on their very own.

"Oh, dear," Bathsheba moaned. "I must have a powder quickly."

"We must have done something frightfully wrong," Dorinda said, drawing the cart up before Mr. Talboth's. "We must make a rule. We never attempt to do a spell when under the, er, the weather."

"Indeed," Bathsheba groaned as little Tommy Fareweather leapfrogged with an imaginary playmate. Only when she blinked, she thought she could see the imaginary playmate. It was a dainty blond fairy creature. "Do let us hurry!"

The two sisters clamored down from the cart and all but loped into Mr. Talboth's store.

Mr. Talboth looked up as they entered. He grinned. "Hello, Bathsheba and Dorinda. What can I do for you?"

"We are here to buy headache powders," Bathsheba gasped.

"Yes," Dorinda said, panting. "What kinds do you have? I'll try one of each."

"Ha! Powders?" Mr. Talboth asked, laughing. "That I have. Thought you might be wanting to buy a talisman and I'm fresh out. Sold the last one a minute ago. And don't ask if I have any rowan wood, Saint-John's-wort, or red verbena. Am out of that, too. If I had known there was going to be such a demand, I would have set in a supply."

"Wh-why w-would we want any of that?" Bathsheba asked, her voice hollow.

"You didn't see anything queer coming here?" Mr. Talboth asked, his brows raising.

"Well . . ." Bathsheba said, appearing shamefaced. "Perhaps."

"You are like me then," Mr. Talboth nodded. "I ain't seen a one of *them*. But there are a lot of folks who *are* seeing them."

"You—you couldn't mean . . . fairies, could you?" Dorinda asked.

"That's what I mean," Mr. Talboth nodded.

"Gracious. Then it wasn't because we were—" Bathsheba halted and flushed. "Then they are real?"

" 'Fraid so," Mr. Talboth said. "I don't see them. They ain't bothering me, but it seems since last night they've been frolicking something fearful."

"Goodness me," Bathsheba murmured.

"There won't be a cow who's not drained dry by tonight," Mr. Talboth said, grinning. "Though the way it appears, a pool of milk set out might not be enough for the little folks." He shook his head. "And All Hallow's Eve just a few days away."

"We must go," Dorinda barked, her face alarmed.

"But . . . I want my powders," Bathsheba said.

"Forget your powders," Dorinda snapped. "They evidently won't help."

"You might go to Father MacKenzie," Mr. Talboth suggested. "He should have holy water for you. Or some churchyard mold perhaps. That might do the trick. Though he might have gone out hunting for the church bell. He meant to start ringing it this morn . . . only some fairy took off with it last night. Left a child's rattle hanging in its place."

Dorinda quivered. "We must see Great Granny."

"Oh, yes," Bathsheba said, her tone relieved. "She will know what to do."

The two sisters hastened from the store. After springing into the cart with stunning speed for two suffering such headaches, they made their way to Great Granny's cottage. Upon drawing the horses to a stop, however, they did not alight.

They watched silently as puffs of smoke rolled out from the cottage windows. A bright fuchsia cloud billowed from the right window first. Then a blue cloud mushroomed from the left. Finally one of green spouted from the chimney. Great Granny's querulous cries and shouts could be heard even from the cart.

The cottage door suddenly swung open. Smoke did not spew out. Rather, a fairy darted into the yard, laughing gleefully and waving what appeared a banner of red. Great Granny hobbled after him in shrieking pursuit. "Come back with those, you little blighter. Them's my favorite drawers!"

Dazed and tired, Alwayna moved quietly about the kitchen. She ignored the cherubs and hearts while waiting for the kettle to boil. She desperately needed a cup of tea. Perhaps it could help clear her befogged head. Kitten sat watching. His eyes drooped in patent exhaustion.

"Did you have strange dreams as well?" Alwayna murmured. She pushed the unsettling memory of the dreams she had had from her conscience. Faith, how had her imagination gone so very far afield as to make her believe that a princess fairy would ever come to her and invite her to enter the land of the fairies? It had seemed so terribly real at the time. Yet dreams could be that way.

Her heart wrenched. If only yesterday afternoon could

have been a dream as well. Unfortunately, she knew it was not. The pain slicing at her told her it was real. Would she ever see Blake again? Aching regret filled her. If only she had not run. If only she had not rejected him. She loved him. If she could only see him again, she'd not let fear destroy it.

The teakettle steamed and Alwayna moved to take it from the fire just as she heard noises from outside. The kitchen door opened and Bathsheba and Dorinda entered.

"Hello," Alwayna said. She forced a smile as she crossed to pour the steaming water into her cup. "I wondered where you two were."

"Tea! Thank heavens," Bathsheba exclaimed. "How I need some."

"Do you?" Alwayna asked. A true smile escaped her. After last night's foray, she never doubted Bathsheba required tea.

"Tea?" Dorinda snorted. "You want a cup of tea, sister, when the entire village is overrun with fairies?"

"What?" Alwayna gasped, freezing in shock.

"I cannot help myself," Bathsheba said, her tone reproachful. "I need a soothing cup."

"Did you say f-fairies?" A chill ran through Alwayna.

"Well, tea ain't going to help us much," Dorinda said, her tone exasperated.

"I know that, but—" Bathsheba stopped. Her eyes widened in alarm. "Alwayna dear, take care. You are pouring out all the water!"

"What?" Alwayna asked. Starting, she looked down. She still held the teapot over the cup. It was full and the water was splashing onto the table. She jerked the kettle up, and shaking, she set it upon the table. Her legs gave out and she stumbled to the nearest chair, falling into it. "I'm sorry."

"Are you all right, dear?" Bathsheba asked in concern.

"I—I don't know," Alwayna murmured. "What—what is this about fairies?"

"Humph. The creatures are everywhere this morning,"

Dorinda said. "Full of juice and bedeviling the entire village of Chancellorville."

"Indeed," Bathsheba said, nodding wide eyed. "Dorinda and I saw one little fellow. Only we thought it our imaginations, because we were—"

"Bathsheba!" Dorinda said sternly. "Do not rattle on so."

"Oh, yes," Bathsheba said. She turned red. "Well, anyway. We thought it our imagination."

"And I thought it a dream," Alwayna said, paling.

"Thought what was a dream?" Dorinda asked.

Alwayna turned a frightened look to Dorinda. "I dreamed a fairy princess called to me. She said I could call her Trillion."

"Yes, yes." Dorinda nodded. "Means she didn't give you her real name. Go on."

"Sh-she told me I was part fairy and belonged with them. She invited me to enter their land. It was so very beautiful."

"You saw their land?" Dorinda asked. Her tall sparse body twitched.

"I thought it was a dream," Alwayna murmured.

"Merciful heavens!" Bathsheba exclaimed. She tottered to the table and crumpled into another chair.

"What?" Alwayna asked. "What is the matter?"

"Few humans ever see their land," Dorinda said. "Or at least that is what we think. Truth is, we can't be certain, because once a human sees their land he doesn't commonly walk away."

"I—I did," Alwayna said. She frowned. "I remember it now. She was angry when I would not enter. Then . . . then . . ." Alwayna halted, unwilling to continue.

"Then what?" Dorinda barked.

"Yes, dear," Bathsheba asked, leaning over. "Then what?"

"She—she said it would not matter. That I would be theirs and that she had only thought to make it easy for me, but" —Alwayna flushed— "she would proceed to the end. And that it would be more amusing for them . . . if not for us."

"Amusing!" Bathsheba exclaimed, her voice indignant. "They are not amusing, not one whit!"

"What—what did I do?" Alwayna asked.

"I don't know," Dorinda said. "But I don't like it. We need Damian."

"But, dearest," Bathsheba exclaimed, "you know Sarabeth and Damian are in London. They do not want little Andrew to experience All Hallow's Eve here in Chancellorville. There is always too much magic flowing about on such a night. It is a very dangerous thing for a baby warlock."

Alwayna gasped. "All Hallow's Eve! She mentioned that, too!"

"We must call Damian back," Dorinda said. "I don't think it's little Andrew who's in danger right now."

"No," Bathsheba said, her blue eyes widening. "It's us, isn't it?"

Dorinda nodded. "Great Granny wasn't chasing a fairy for her red drawers for nothing."

Blake prowled about the parlor. Alwayna and the two sisters sat quietly upon the sofa and chairs. All of them were waiting.

"Come here, Kitten," Alwayna said. "There is nothing to be nervous about. Damian will be here soon."

That was exactly what Blake was nervous about. There wasn't one warlock who trusted another warlock. It was never safe to do so. Also, he knew full well this Damian would not be of any help. If Blake's own father could not help, this Damian wouldn't be able to either. In truth, this warlock could only muck things up all the more.

Blake groaned. He should have told Alwayna everything when he proposed. Yet he had feared her reaction. Now it could very well be too late. Blast his lack of powers! Blast Trillion!

A knock sounded at the door. Bathsheba and Dorinda both squealed in excitement and jumped up.

"And blast son-in-law warlocks!" Blake stormed to himself.

He noticed as the sisters rushed out of the room to the door that Alwayna remained behind. She appeared nervous. He meowed. She smiled back. "He . . . he always frightens me a little." Blake padded over and jumped into her lap. She petted him. "You are right. There is nothing to be concerned about. He is here to help us."

Bathsheba and Dorinda entered the room, accompanied by a tall, dark-haired man and a beautiful blond woman. Blake's eyes narrowed. Damian was indeed a warlock to be respected. He could read the power emanating from the man instantly. It was not only strong, but clearly inbred from a long line of warlocks, as was Blake's power—or the power he once had, he amended. Blake tensed as the man smiled and looked at Alwayna. "Hello, Alwayna. We came as fast as we could."

"Thank you," Alwayna said, lowering her gaze.

"We stopped merely to settle Andrew and Nurse at the castle," the blond woman named Sarabeth said. Blake studied her. She held no magical powers, but the warmth of her personality and her beauty certainly could cast its own charm. "We rode through Chancellorville. It seemed quiet."

"Perhaps the fairies went away," Alwayna said.

"No," Dorinda said. "Fairies have short attention spans. Long memories, unfortunately. If they want something that is."

"Oh," Alwayna said, sighing.

"And what they want is what we must determine," Damian said, as the ladies sat and he settled himself next to his wife. He gazed solemnly at Alwayna. "I would imagine that it is you, my dear."

Blake meowed in agreement. Damian glanced at Blake. He frowned. Blake stared back, tense and waiting.

"This is Kitten," Alwayna said quickly. "He is my familiar."

"Is he?" Damian asked.

"Oh, yes," Bathsheba said. "Alwayna has finally found her powers as a witch, Damian. And this darling little kitten is her familiar."

"I see," Damian said, his frown lessening somewhat.

"She just found her powers, dear," Sarabeth said, putting a hand upon him. "Could that be what has drawn the fairies to her?"

"Perhaps," Damian said, finally turning his gaze to his wife. "I doubt it is a coincidence."

Blake smirked. Damian could not be such a great warlock or he would have recognized that Blake was one. Else, Blake thought in sudden fear, Damian could not see his power because Trillion had truly taken it away from him this time.

Damian's focus was upon Alwayna. "Please tell us everything you can remember. Everything that has been strange and out of the ordinary."

"I—I do not know where to start," Alwayna said. "There are so many things that have happened. I found Kitten. I came into my powers. And I—" She halted.

"Yes?" Damian asked gently.

"And I" —Alwayna lifted her chin— "fell in love."

"What?" Dorinda exclaimed.

"Dearest, how could this be?" Bathsheba cried. "And why didn't you tell us? How marvelous. Who is he?"

"He—he says he is a duke," Alwayna said. She studied Damian. "Which I think he must be. He—he acts very much like you. I mean . . . he has an air and . . . and a certain . . . er . . ."

"Arrogance?" Sarabeth asked, chuckling softly and gazing at her husband with open love in her eyes.

"Yes," Alwayna nodded. "Exactly!"

Damian stiffened at the very moment Blake's hair rose in indignation. "I see."

"A duke? My stars," Bathsheba gasped. "Never say you

mean the crazy one you said you saw that day. The one who was wearing my petticoat."

"Er, yes," Alwayna said, a flush rising to her cheeks. Blake himself had a sudden desire to hide his head in his paws. "I've—I've seen him since then. But he was fully dressed on those occasions, I assure you."

"Why didn't you tell us?" Dorinda said, her voice stern.

"I—I don't know," Alwayna said. She shrugged her shoulders. "I am sorry."

"He claims to be a duke?" Sarabeth asked, frowning.

"Yes," Alwayna said. "The Duke of Trenton."

"Trenton!" Damian exclaimed.

"You know him?" Alwayna asked, leaning forward.

"I know *of* him," Damian said, his tone severe. "We do not move in the same circles."

"Y-you do not approve of him?" she asked, her voice disheartened.

Damian paused a moment. "I will not lie to you. He has the reputation of a rake and reprobate."

Blake growled. One warlock could never trust another.

"I see," Alwayna said, her voice low and weak.

"What I fear even more is his appearance at this time," Damian muttered. His gaze grew piercing. "Tell me more of him."

"He—he knows magic," Alwayna said. "He said so."

"The devil," Damian said. He looked sincerely at Alwayna. "Beware of him in the future. If he is a warlock he cannot be trusted."

"Dearest," Sarabeth said gently, "you are a warlock and I trust you."

"I know, but I am different," Damian said, his tone terse. "Other warlocks cannot be trusted."

Blake blinked. His own thoughts exactly, only turned against him.

The ladies stared at Damian in confusion, the kind which any wise man knew portended a plethora of questions. Clearing his throat, he rose swiftly. "There is much to discuss to be sure. However, the most important matter at hand I believe is for you ladies to remove to the castle Tor directly. It possesses its own wardings and I will feel better once you are under its protection . . . and my protection. I fear I know very little of fairies. Chancellorville has not seen this sort of activity from them in ages. Our only hope is that the castle library might tell us more and show us what we can do to combat them."

Blake rested upon the large four-poster bed, watching Alwayna as she unpacked her clothes from a satchel. Worry lined her eyes and mouth. Her tension was palpable.

"Meow?" he said, tormented. How he wished she could comfort her, hold her, tell her everything would be all right. "Meow?"

Alwayna glanced up. She smiled weakly. "I'm all right. Truly I am."

"Meow."

"Very well," she sighed, moving to sit upon the bed. Blake jumped to her lap and she immediately smoothed her fingers across his fur. "I—this castle is so grand. Everything is so grand. It frightens me."

"Meow, puuurrr," Blake said, attempting to send her a feeling of confidence.

The castle Tor indeed was grand and impressive. It was not its size in itself. Blake's family seat was built on a grander scale with greater conveniences. What was impressive, invasive, and so deeply imbedded into the very stone walls of the castle was its magic. Damian had said it possessed its own wardings. Indeed, Blake could see it upon their approach. The castle itself, hewn of rough stone, struck one as ominous. Yet to those who could see the magic, it glowed with a blue light, strong and impenetrable.

A knock sounded at the door. Alwayna started. "Yes?"

"It is Sarabeth," she called. "May I come in?"

"Certainly," Alwayna said. She tumbled an astonished Blake from her lap and stood promptly as Sarabeth entered. Blake growled. Alwayna's attitude was that of a peasant before royalty. She should not belittle herself so.

Sarabeth, beautiful in a green figured silk dress, halted. She studied Alwayna solemnly. "There is no reason to stand for me, Alwayna," she said in a gentle voice as she walked across the room and sat down upon the bed.

"Y-you are—are a Duchess," Alwayna stammered.

"I am a Duchess now because the man I love is a duke, but I grew up in Bathsheba and Dorinda's cottage. I am of no greater rank than you." Sarabeth laughed. "We are both peasants. Now please come and sit beside me."

"Yes, er—" Alwayna gurgled into silence.

"Sarabeth," Sarabeth said.

"Yes, Sarabeth," Alwayna said, moving to sit upon the bed. She shifted in discomfort.

"I have been forced to give up much to become a duchess," Sarabeth said, her tone teasing. "But I refuse to give up having those I wish to have as friends call me anything but Sarabeth."

Blake sprang up to the bed and settled back on Alwayna's lap, purring his approval. He did not care for Damian, but he liked Sarabeth very much.

"You gave up much to become a duchess?" Alwayna asked shyly.

"It can be very daunting at times," Sarabeth said wryly. "When one is not accustomed to it, as I am not. The secret is not to take it too seriously. I remind myself when I make a social error or disgrace myself in some fashion, which I do often, that what other people think of me does not matter. What Damian thinks does. He loves me regardless and that is enough. More than enough in fact."

"Th-that must be wonderful," Alwayna said softly.

"It is," Sarabeth said. She looked down a moment and then lifted a very concern gaze to Alwayna. "Love is one of the most powerful forces. It is magic itself and as such can be coveted and used by evil as well as good."

"Y-yes?" Alwayna whispered.

"Damian means well when he warns you against the Duke of Trenton."

"I—I understand," Alwayna stammered.

"However," Sarabeth said, smiling a small smile. "From what I understand from others, Damian was quite a rake himself before I met him. He did not believe in love. He also did not come into his powers until we met. He fought them until then."

"Why?" Alwayna asked. Blake was glad she had asked the question, for he could not fathom any warlock not wanting his powers.

"He grew up believing he was only mortal and he was taught not to believe in magic. But I think the truth is that he was frightened of his power. He could not be sure it was good. He also feared he could not control it." She tilted her head. "It is very much like love in that respect."

Blake stared. He had never worried whether his powers were good or bad—he had merely used them for his own purposes and pleasures. He, of course, had never dabbled in the dark arts. He had never needed to do so. He had never desired to side with evil. Yet he had never desired to side with good either.

"I believe you have many things to face as well, Alwayna," Sarabeth said softly. "I do not know what powers you must come into or what you must fight, but I believe the strongest power lies already within your heart, if only you will listen to it and not turn back from it."

"I will try," Alwayna said, nodding sincerely.

"I know you will," Sarabeth said, smiling. She rose, drawing in a deep breath. "Damian would like you to come down to the library."

"Yes, of course," Alwayna said. Blake obligingly jumped down and permitted her to stand.

The three silently passed through the castle and down to the large hall, where the library connected. Blake narrowed his eyes as he observed the entourage awaiting them. Bathsheba, Dorinda, and Damian all stood at the library door. Apparently it was going to be quite a group search.

"Hello, Alwayna," Damian said, smiling. "Are you ready?"

"Yes. Yes, I am," Alwayna said, her smile a tremble.

"Excellent," Damian said. His smile was all encouragement. "Let us see what the library can reveal."

Bathsheba bustled forward and enveloped Alwayna in a hug. "Good luck, dearest."

"Yes," Dorinda nodded. "You have us all cheering for you."

Blake stared at them. His tail twitched in an odd presentiment.

"Y-you are not coming with me?" Alwayna asked.

"Good gracious no!" Bathsheba gasped, all but jumping back from Alwayna.

Dorinda flushed and cleared her throat gruffly. "We—we don't do well in the library."

"The library is very old and possesses every kind of book on magic," Damian said quietly. "Each one exudes traces of the magic it holds within. I believe it is best if only you and I enter. If and when you become accustomed to the library, I will then leave you to your own private study."

"My own study?" Alwayna stammered.

"It is clear you are integral to what is happening in Chancellorville," Damian said. "The princess wants you, Alwayna."

"But why?" Alwayna cried.

"That we do not know," Damian said. "Perhaps the library will have an answer. If it does not, it will at least offer you an understanding of the fairies. It might show you what you must do to fight them."

Blake meowed in eagerness. Damian might be correct for once. The library might tell of the legend. If it was as great as Damian purported, it might offer new powers.

Damian glanced down to him. "Your familiar, of course, must never enter the library. It could be dangerous for him."

Blake arched his back and howled.

Alwayna looked at him with frightened eyes. "You must stay out here, Kitten. I—I will be all right, I promise you."

Alwayna laid her head down upon the large oaken table centered in the library. Around it, wall after wall of dark-hued volumes were packed tight on shelves reaching from floor to ceiling. The solemn, deep tones of the great clock in the hall drifted to her as it rang the half hour. It had become her one tie to the outside and reality. She had not left the library since she had entered it the night before. Damian had remained with her until four hours before. Only then had he felt secure in leaving her alone.

The large windows at the end of the oblong room were the only things to break the continuous line of shelves. They were hung with thick heavy curtains, drawn tightly against the night and the silver of moonlight and fairies. One meager candle glowed in its stand on the table. Alwayna, knowing her powers to be negligent, could still hear whispers from the books themselves.

She had studied many of them. Fairies must be warded against, for they stole human babies and left changelings in their place. Tales of the fairies enchanting and capturing humans to make them their servants abounded. Trillion had told Alwayna she would belong in their land. Now Alwayna realized that she would have belonged in their land as a servant.

Chants against the fairies and their powers whirled within Alwayna's mind. Ancient potions of ridiculous ingredients that came from books reeking of magic teased her. Damian explained that the properties of the potions held no power, yet the belief of the witches and warlocks who scribed them was still strong magic. Jumbled within it all, or perhaps actually an untouched stream running beneath, was Alwayna's yearning for Blake Farewell. Be he a reprobate duke, be he a dangerous warlock, or be he in league with the fairies themselves, her love for him burned deeply in her heart. It glowed brighter with the missing of him each day.

The strongest power lies already within your heart, if only you will listen to it and not turn back from it.

Alwayna heard the words as clearly as if Sarabeth stood within the room and spoke them once more. Yet that was not unusual in this library. Thoughts actually took up their own reality here.

A tear slipped down Alwayna's cheek. No power lay within her heart. Only this love did. Only this overpowering, longing need. She had learned of love in such a short time. Brief, unusual moments. Precious moments. She had turned back from Trillion and the promise of eternity in a glittering land because she was too mortal, and because she loved. It had offered her strength.

A second tear slipped down her cheek. Now that love was her weakness. She needed to study and find the magic with which to fight Trillion. Exhausted, frightened, and confused, she could only think of Blake. She could only remember him vowing he loved her. She could only remember his kiss. She could only remember returning to promise she would marry him and discovering him gone.

The third tear fell. She did not think of magic. She did not think of anything. She only whispered one plea as she watched the candle flicker out in its wax and she let her spirit sink into the oblivion of rest. "Please let me see Blake again. I love him."

Blake scratched once at the library door and meowed. He then paced almost drunkenly back and forth outside the library door. Alwayna had been closeted within the library since the evening before. An entire evening and day. He had waited and waited. She never came out. They sent food into her, shooing him away or picking him up when he fought, always entering and exiting while holding him helpless.

He scratched the second time. He needed to see Alwayna. If it must be as a kitten he did not care. He simply needed to see her. He must know that she was safe and well. He could not control the driving force within him, nor did he care to control it. He loved her. He must be able to see her.

He scratched the third time. Numb and exhausted he fell to the ground with a meow. He had never sided with good or evil. He had never needed to do so. Now he did not think of magic. He did not try to draw it to him or use it. He finally sought good, for he sought love.

"Let me see her. Please let me see her," he asked as sleep claimed him.

The chimes of the great clock rang out the twelfth hour into the silence of the castle.

A blue-white light grew, a small nimbus in the darkened library, where the candle had flickered out. It glowed brighter, spilling its light over the table and the sleeping form of Alwayna. Silence reigned. No whispers from the books of magic sounded; nothing stopped its glow.

It spilled over the table, streamed along the floor, and flowed beneath the library door. The blue-white light engulfed the figure of a sleeping kitten on the other side, wrapping about it like a gentle cocoon. The light glowed deeper and brighter as the shape of the kitten changed and evolved into the long length of a man. The man's arm was stretched toward the door.

The light crackled along that man's reaching arm and leapt to the door. The door flared with light and swung wide open as the man's eyes slowly opened.

Alwayna's lashes fluttered. Almost against her will, she opened her eyes. A sweet glow of blue-white light comforted her. Confused, she glanced to the candle. No flame flickered there. It mattered not, for her gaze turned as if by demand to the library entrance. A man stood within a blue-white light. It seemed as if it was the most natural of lights, neither sunlight nor moonlight or the yellow of a fire's flame.

"Blake?" Alwayna whispered, her heart warming to the glow of that light. "Is it you?"

"Yes," Blake said, his voice soft and confused.

"Blake!" she cried. Alwayna sprang up and stumbled toward him. "You've come back to me."

"I never truly left you," Blake said hoarsely, catching her into his arms. He kissed her roughly with a need that communed with hers. "My God, I never thought to hold you again."

"I feared the same," Alwayna whispered, clinging to him tightly. The light shimmered around them. She gasped in fear, drawing back. "I am not dreaming, am I?"

"No, unless we are both in the same dream," Blake whispered. "It's magic."

Alwayna gazed around the library. She shivered. "Magic, yes. But will it be enough?"

"It must be," Blake said softly. "It simply must be."

Alwayna gazed up at him, a deep knowledge filling her. "You know, don't you? You know wh-what is happening?"

"Yes, I do," Blake said solemnly. "But they are wrong. I am not dangerous, Alwayna, not to you. Never to you."

"What—what is happening?" Alwayna asked. She swayed. Whether from exhaustion or dread of what he might say, she did not know.

"Blast!" Blake swiftly lifted her into his arms. "This is enough. Come."

"Where?" Alwayna sighed, laying her head upon his shoulder.

"You are going to get some sleep," Blake said, his voice stern as he carried her from the library.

"That would be nice," Alwayna sighed, closing her eyes. Then she snapped them open. "No, I do not want to sleep. I do not want you to leave me."

"Hush, sweetheart," Blake said, carrying her through the castle and up the stairs.

"You will disappear," Alwayna said. "I know it."

"I won't disappear," Blake said as he entered the bedroom. "Not really."

Alwayna frowned in bemusement. "H-how did you know this was my room?"

Blake settled her upon the bed. He lifted her hand and held it tightly. His gaze was solemn. "Alwayna, will you marry me?"

"Yes," Alwayna said, smiling. "Yes, I will."

"Do you love me enough to marry me before midnight tomorrow night?"

Tears stung Alwayna's eyes. She felt no hesitation, only a humble gratefulness that she could answer him. "Yes. I love you enough to marry you before midnight tomorrow night."

"It must be before midnight tomorrow night," Blake said, his voice urgent. "Or we will all become the servants of the fairies."

"What?" Alwayna asked. "What do you mean?"

He groaned, his face twisting with regret. "Alwayna, I cannot remain like this."

"You are leaving?" Fear filled Alwayna.

"No," Blake said. "Alwayna, I am Kitten."

"Kitten?" she asked, laughing. "What do you mean?"

"I should have told you all these past times," Blake said roughly. "But I wanted and needed your love for me, Blake Farewell, the man. Now I must ask you simply to love me whether I am a man . . . or the kitten Trillion has turned me into."

"Trillion turned you into a kitten?" Alwayna gasped.

"Yes," Blake said. "It is a long story that started with my forefather and Trillion. I do not know if I will have the time to tell it to you. Right now I must beg you to please marry me tomorrow. If we are wed before tomorrow night midnight, the fairies cannot hurt us. They cannot take the descendants of the Farewells into their land."

"I will," Alwayna vowed. "I do not ever want you to leave me."

"I won't," Blake said. He smiled warmly. "You do not know the attention I will shower upon you when we are husband and wife. We shall have a splendid life together."

"Yes, we shall," Alwayna murmured, exhaustion claiming her. She fought it. "I never asked. Do—do you like children?"

"We will have as many as you like," Blake said, chuckling.

"Father Parker had ten," she said.

"Then we have an even dozen," Blake returned.

Alwayna chuckled. "Six of each . . ."

"It will be a powerful family," Blake said.

"What is your favorite color?" Alwayna murmured.

"Red," Blake said. "Like your hair."

"Flatterer," Alwayna murmured.

"Hmm . . . green like your eyes?"

"No, what color do you truly like?" Alwayna asked.

"Blue," Blake answered "For the skies I'll watch you dance beneath."

"I like that," Alwayna said, with a smile. Her eyes closed.

She fell asleep before she could ask another question. She fell asleep before the hand she held so tightly turned into a tiny furred paw.

SIX

Alwayna awoke the next morning. She started up, memories flooding back. Or were they dreams? Her gaze turned in question to Kitten, who slept beside her. "Kitten . . . Blake?"

Kitten woke. His cat eyes widened and then he meowed. He swiftly stood and crossed to run a kitten tongue on her hand as a kitten kiss.

"Did I dream it?" Alwayna asked, her heart beating wildly. "Or did it truly happen?"

"Meow," Kitten said. He stared at her intently.

She felt a sudden warmth, comfort, and support, the same feeling she had always gained from Kitten when she performed spells. She had always thought that that was natural between a witch and a familiar. Perhaps. Or perhaps it was natural between two souls who loved and belonged together. She drew in a deep breath, grinning in exuberance. "We are going to be married today!"

She sprang from her bed and dashed toward her wardrobe, drawing out a dress. She gasped and spun. "Kitten . . . Blake . . . you must leave. I'm dressing." She flushed. "But you've . . . ." It was too confusing to think about at the moment. "Oh, never mind. Only do leave."

"Meow!" Kitten said. He jumped down from the bed and stalked to the door. His tail was raised at a cocky angle. Now that Alwayna knew, she could almost see the similarity in walks between Kitten and Blake.

Laughing she went and opened the door to let him out. She then dressed quickly. Her thoughts were in a whirl. Was she crazy? No. Sarabeth had said that the power would lie within her heart. Blake had returned to her. It could not have been a dream.

When she opened the door, Kitten was patiently waiting. "Very well. Let us go."

They hastened down the stairs. When they entered the great hall, Alwayna halted. It was populated with people. Sarabeth stood amongst them, her servants passing out refreshments.

"Sarabeth," Alwayna said, hastening to her. "What is happening?"

"The villagers are seeking refuge," Sarabeth said in a calm voice, though her gaze skittered about in a harried manner.

"Refuge?" Alwayna asked.

"Yes, the fairies are bedeviling these poor souls," Sarabeth said. "Since All Hallow's Eve is tonight they hope that Damian and the castle's warding might offer protection."

"Do—do you think that it can?" Alwayna asked.

"It seems to do so," Sarabeth said. "The fairies have not attempted to tease us here. Though tonight we cannot say. All Hallow's Eve looses greater powers for all."

"Are they descendants of the Farewells?" Alwayna asked, gazing at the villagers.

"What?" Sarabeth asked, frowning.

"Are they descendants of the Farewells?" Alwayna repeated.

"Farewells?" Sarabeth repeated. "Yes, I suppose they might be. It is a very common name in Chancellorville. It has always been a small village. I fear many of us are cousins and would not even know it."

"I must talk to you and Damian immediately," Alwayna said. Kitten meowed.

Sarabeth looked at her intently. "Certainly. I—I believe

the parlor to be vacant. I will get Damian. He is in the library."

"Thank you," Alwayna said.

Skirting the small crowd, Alwayna went into the parlor, grateful that one room was empty. She paced back and forth, her thoughts turning to how to present the subject. She looked to Kitten—or Blake. "I am right, aren't I? It wasn't a dream? You know I love you, and I promised . . . but . . . but how am I to tell them?"

"Meow," Kitten said. He rubbed up against her skirts.

"Yes, but . . ." Alwayna began.

At that moment Sarabeth and Damian entered the parlor.

"Sarabeth said you wished to talk to me?" Damian said. "Did you discover anything to help us last night?"

"Yes, I did," Alwayna said. Kitten stiffened and meowed. She clasped her hands together. "I saw—saw Blake last night."

"What!" Damian exclaimed, his brows snapping down.

"You did?" Sarabeth asked, her eyes widening.

"Y-yes I did," Alwayna said.

"How? How were you able to see him," Damian persisted. "You left the castle?"

"That was not wise," Sarabeth said.

"I did not leave the castle," Alwayna said. "I—I saw him in the library."

"Explain!" Damian barked. Kitten growled and hissed.

"It is all right," Alwayna said. She looked at the thunderous Damian. She lost her courage and took the tiger— or the kitten—by the other tail. "I—I want to marry him."

"Alwayna," Sarabeth gasped. "Are you sure?"

"Yes," Alwayna said. "I want to marry him and I must marry him. He did not have enough time to tell me it all, but if we are not wed by midnight, we and all the descendants of the Farewells will become servants to the fairies."

"Good Gracious," Sarabeth said. "That is why you asked about them."

"Wh-what . . . rot!" Damian exclaimed. "Surely you did

not believe his story. He is a warlock. You cannot trust him."

"I do trust him," Alwayna said. She lifted her chin. "And I believe him."

"It is ridiculous," Damian said. "Just why would such a thing happen?"

"He didn't have time to tell me that," Alwayna said, flushing.

"And why not?" Damian demanded.

"Because . . . because h-he turned back into . . . Kitten," Alwayna said.

"What?" Damian roared.

"That is Blake Farewell?" Sarabeth asked, peering at Kitten.

"Trillion turned him into a kitten," Alwayna said.

"Impossible," Damian snorted.

"It is not impossible, dear," Sarabeth said, her tone calming. "You know that it is not."

"I know nothing of the sort," Damian said curtly. "Just because it happened to you does not mean it can happen to other people."

"It happened to you?" Alwayna gasped. A surprised meow came from Kitten.

"A witch made me invisible to Damian," Sarabeth said. "And it was Bathsheba and Dorinda who turned me into a kitten by mistake when they were trying to make me visible again." Damian muttered a curse. Sarabeth's green eyes twinkled a moment. "But we need not discuss the past. What is important is *now.*"

"Yes, what is important is now," Damian said. He drew in a deep breath. "Let us all sit down and discuss this more calmly."

"An excellent notion," Sarabeth said. She quickly took up a seat, just as a knock sounded at the door.

"Who is it?" Damian called, his voice exasperated.

"It is Bathsheba and Dorinda," Bathsheba's voice called through the door softly. "We heard, ah, voices. Is everything all right?"

"It damn well isn't," Damian muttered.

Alwayna, trembling at his anger, realized that the two sisters would need to know sooner or later. "Yes, please come in."

The door opened and Dorinda and Bathsheba entered.

"Is aught wrong?" Bathsheba asked, bustling over.

"Yes," Damian said. "Alwayna claims she is going to marry Blake Farewell . . . and he is that blasted cat there!"

Both Bathsheba and Dorinda exclaimed.

"Dearest," Sarabeth said. "You said we were going to sit and discuss this calmly. Now sit!"

"You are going to be married?" Bathsheba exclaimed.

"To Kitten?" Dorinda asked.

"Everyone sit!" Sarabeth said in an imperious tone.

Amazingly, everyone sat.

"That is better," Sarabeth said, nodding.

Immediately the room broke into babble. Sarabeth's groan of exasperation was drowned out. Dorinda and Bathsheba fired questions at Alwayna.

"I thought you said Blake Farewell was a duke," Bathsheba said.

"He is," Alwayna said.

"He *says* he is," Damian corrected.

"Then why is he Kitten?" Dorinda asked.

"Trillion, the princess of the fairies turned him into Kitten," Alwayna said. "He told me so last night in the library."

"You *thought* he told you," Damian said. "You were tired. The magic from the books created your wish."

"Who would wish to marry a kitten?" Dorinda asked.

"That is a good question," Sarabeth said.

"No, that is a good *point,*" Damian said. "Alwayna cannot marry a kitten because she has been deluded. The fairies must have entered the library after all. I didn't think it possible, but that is what must have happened."

"That is not what happened," Alwayna said, a headache beginning to pound behind her eyes. "Blake was there. He was real. He is real."

"Where *is* he?" Sarabeth suddenly asked.

"Blake?" Alwayna looked about. He had disappeared. Her heart sank. Where had he gone? Her very strength felt as if it was ebbing. So did her faith. How could he have left her at this moment?

"What does it matter where he is?" Damian asked. "It is not as if he is going to be able to join the discussion—unless someone can speak fluent kitten."

"Damian," Sarabeth said, her tone reproving.

"Well, can you?" Damian retorted. "Please, Alwayna, there are far too many forces here at work. You cannot marry a kitten! What if I am right and it truly is just a kitten. What then?"

"I—I don't know," Alwayna said. "I—"

"Gracious," Bathsheba exclaimed.

"My stars," Dorinda said.

Alwayna swallowed any confession of doubt she was about to speak as Kitten entered the room, dragging after him a blue negligee.

"What the devil!" Damian cried as Kitten came to a halt in the very center of them all.

"I believe," Sarabeth said, laughing, "he has just joined the discussion, my love."

Alwayna, her heart pounding, stood quickly and moved to bend down next to him. He had in his teeth the negligee's ribbon, which laced its neck. Sparkling and twirling upon that ribbon was a diamond ring.

"Where ever did he get that?" Bathsheba breathed. "Magic?"

"It's not magic," Damian said. "Those are Sarabeth's."

"Yes," Sarabeth nodded. "Your fiancé is a thief, Alwayna."

"That he was from the very beginning," Dorinda said, frowning.

"First my petticoat and now Sarabeth's nightgown," Bathsheba said. She giggled. "He *is* a wicked one."

Alwayna's fears drained away. She laughed in sheer delight. "He brought it to me because he likes blue. Blue like the skies I have danced beneath."

"Ah, that explains it," Sarabeth said, chuckling. "He must have had to search for it. I possess very little blue in my wardrobe. Damian bought that gown for me."

"Well, I like blue," Damian objected. A wry grimace crossed his face. "Too."

Sarabeth laughed. "It seems the groom has at least two of the items necessary for the wedding. Something borrowed . . . and something blue. We best hurry if we are to provide the rest."

It was an odd collection of wedding guests who sat waiting in the great hall of the castle Tor. Indeed, almost all of Chancellorville was present. Those who had arrived that morning were dressed in the manner in which they had come. Those who had received news of the event prior to arrival had come more properly attired. The greatest portion, whether fine suit or not, had their coats turned inside out, a well-known precaution against the fairies. They were adorned in amulets of rowan wood and ash wood. Many appeared very devout with their crosses and vials of holy water. Bells tinkled and rang amongst the crowd, another well-known warding.

"Ish—ish sh-she r-really going to mar-ry that cat?" Jacob Renson asked, hiccuping. Every village had one member who receives the honorary title of the village drunk. Jacob had held that title, uncontested, for fifty years. He alone was suspiciously free of any amulets or protection from the fairies. He had often boasted he had never been pixie led in his life. No doubt because he had always been so gin logged that even a fairy calling to him could not have distracted him from his purpose. That or he went wondering lost upon his own volition so often the fairies considered him poor sport. "We-ell, I've seen many of str-ange thingsh in my life, but never a gel marrying a cat afore."

No one questioned that he had seen strange things before. Not of a man who had sworn to having seen purple elephants dancing in the streets last May Day.

"He ain't a cat," Great Granny did say in a querulous tone. "He's a duke."

Jacob leaned forward, almost falling from his chair as he peered blurry eyed to the front of hall, where the wedding party was assembled. "Is-s he? Strangest d-duke I've ever seen."

"Be quiet," Great Granny said. "Or I'll turn you into— Oh, never mind. It would be useless." She sighed, even as she received sympathetic glances from the rest of the crowd.

"When do you think they will start the wedding?" Martha Fareweather asked in a nervous tone.

"When the duke finds Father MacKenzie, of course," Great Granny snapped.

"Thought you said that cat was the duke," Jacob said, burping.

"I mean the other duke, you soused want wit," Great Granny said.

"Do you think he can find him?" Martha asked. "I mean, the fairies levitated the church into old Samuel's farm last night."

"If anyone can find Father MacKenzie, it will be Damian," Great Granny said in a sage tone.

"I do hope so," Martha said. She paled. "It is already dark. We have but five more hours before midnight."

"Oh, Mother, do not be so scared," Betsy said in an exasperated voice. She leaned back in her chair and crossed her arms. "Alwayna is just doing this for attention and nothing more. You will find this is all a sick Halloween joke of hers and nothing more. You know she is fey."

Great Granny peered at Betsy, who wore a thick coat of white powder upon her face. A blue hue still showed through. Great Granny broke out into a cackle of laughter.

"You look lovely, dearest," Bathsheba said, fluttering about Alwayna, straightening a curl here and a ruffle there. Alwayna, wearing a white brocade gown that Sarabeth had supplied, sat still and tense. Her hands gripped a bouquet of red berries. She gazed at the bridal arch they had constructed of rowan wood, brilliant fall leaves entwined within it. She looked to Blake, who prowled back and forth, his tail whipping with impatience.

"When will they come?" Alwayna asked.

"Damian will find Father MacKenzie," Sarabeth said with confidence. "Do not worry."

"No, of course not," Alwayna said. She did worry. Every minute ticking by frightened her. She never wanted anything more then to be married to Blake Farewell, even if at the moment he was a cat. When she had imagined her wedding day, it had never been anything like what was transpiring now. She did not care as long as she could marry Blake.

The large doors to the castle burst open. Alwayna sprang up in hope.

Damian entered. He all but carried a thin man who wore the collar of the church. The wedding guests applauded and rang their bells. Alwayna broke into a relieved smile.

Damian slammed the door shut, speaking a brisk chant of warding. He then assisted Father MacKenzie over to the waiting bridal party.

"It's good to see you, sweetheart," Sarabeth said, her eyes filling with delight.

"So it is," Bathsheba said. "We were worried."

"Where did you find Father MacKenzie?" Dorinda asked, driving directly to the point.

"Four counties from here. He is slightly dazed," Damian said lowly.

"When he meows, that means yes," Father MacKenzie said in an odd voice, nodding his head.

"It took me an hour in itself," Damian said, "to convince him to wed Alwayna to a cat. I told him the bishop need never know."

"He's not a cat . . ." Sarabeth began.

"I know, I know," Damian said, smiling. "Now do let us proceed before good Father MacKenzie faints on us. I believe the fairies overexerted him this day."

"I am ready!" Alwayna exclaimed, her heart pounding. She heard a meow and looked down. Blake stood close to her, gazing up at her, his eyes snapping in anticipation. She smiled. "Do let us hurry."

Everyone moved into position. Father MacKenzie meandered to behind the rowan wood arch, taking a swaying stance. Alwayna stood beneath it and Blake jumped up to the marble pedestal awaiting him and sat squarely upon the blue velvet cushion on top of it. Damian took his place beside him as best man. Bathsheba and Dorinda stood to the other side of Alwayna. Bathsheba's eyes were already tearing and she sniffed. The sisters had been honored when Alwayna had asked them diffidently if they would please be the ones to give her away. Sarabeth stood close by as the matron of honor.

Father MacKenzie peered about a moment. Unfortunately, his expression looked as befuddled as Jacob Benson's. He cleared his throat. "Dearly departed . . . I mean beloved . . . we are gathered here . . ."

A sudden wave of dizziness overpowered Alwayna. The sound of wind whirled in her ears. She blinked. The image of Father MacKenzie shimmered and evolved into Trillion, her elfin face bright with malice.

"We are gathered here to claim these mortals as our servants," she said.

"No!" Alwayna cried. She stood upon a silver plain, beside a silver pond, with silver mountains rising in the background. Uproarious laughter surrounded her.

She spun. A multitude of fairies, surely too many past the count of hundreds, populated the land, capering and dancing. Alwayna's blood chilled. Amongst them were frozen images, real but not quite real, of Bathsheba and Dorinda and Sarabeth and a great many of the Chancellorville villagers. There were others, too, frozen in different postures as if drawn unsuspecting from their various lives.

"So many of the Farewell line," Trillion laughed. "I have waited ages for this moment. Ah, but what a marvelous harvest."

"Blake!" Alwayna gasped, spinning back. "Where is Blake?"

"I have not forgotten the best," Trillion said, grinning.

Blake suddenly appeared beside Alwayna. He stood tall and stern. He didn't appear surprised. His eyes narrowed. "Hello, Trillion."

"Hello, my sweet lover," Trillion said with a malicious look.

Blake stared steadily at her a moment. Then he turned his gaze to Alwayna. She swallowed hard. She could read everything within his eyes—dreams promised and dreams lost. "Alwayna, my love."

"Ha!" Trillion laughed, though her eyes glittered like shards of jagged glass. "Arrogant as ever, are you not, Blake dear? Did you not learn anything? Perhaps I should turn you back into a kitten for the next age."

"No!" Alwayna cried.

"Do, Trillion," Blake said quietly. "I am no longer like you, Trillion, and I thank you."

"What?" Trillion asked, her hands clenching.

"You can only want and desire," Blake said. "When you took my powers from me and turned me into a kitten I actually learned to be human. I learned to love."

"Love! Much good it will do you, fool. You are now mine." She flung out her hand. "As they all are." She pointed to a figure of an older man. "Your father there. Those silly sisters. All those Farewells. Chancellorville shall miss them." She smiled wickedly. "And Alwayna, of course. Our very own."

"No!" Blake roared. Rage flared in his eyes. Alwayna felt the powerful magic even before he spoke. It shot from him, a crackling lightning bolt at Trillion.

Alwayna, the power she had found and shared with Blake welling within her, chanted ancient words from the books of the library. They flowed from her like the magic shooting at Trillion.

Trillion was engulfed with sudden blasts of color—

vibrant reds and greens and golds. Alwayna's heart prayed.

Trillion waved her hands. The colors dispersed and all was silver moonlight about her again. She cast a derisive glance to Alwayna. Alwayna stiffened and choked, feeling as if shackles chained her, though she could not see them.

Trillion then leveled her gaze at Blake and pointed. A spasm of pain crossed Blake's face. It contorted his body. Slowly, very slowly, he fell to his knees. Trillion's eyes glowed.

"That is your proper demeanor, fool. You have nothing to stop me. You are in my land. There is not a power that can save you." She strolled up to him. "You will be my servant for eternity. Ah, if only you had chosen to be my lover. But like your ancestor, you turned away from me. And you shall pay since he did not." A slyness entered her eyes. "But I might be merciful if you ask me—no beg me—to keep you in this land as my consort."

"No," Alwayna gasped. The torment in Blake's eyes was too great. So was his will. She knew he would not beg. "But I will."

"What?" Trillion asked, frowning.

"I will beg. I will plead," Alwayna said, her heart tight. "Be merciful. Release Blake and . . . and I will do anything you wish."

"You will?" Trillion asked, grinding. "Do you beg to enter my land and be my faithful servant? Perhaps a scullery maid?"

"No," Blake choked out. "Let Alwayna go. Release her and I will d-do whatever you wish."

"Look at the two," Trillion laughed. The fairies about her giggled and whispered. "Are they not amusing? Each of them is willing to give up his love if I but send the other back to his dreary mortal sod."

"I do not give Blake up," Alwayna said. Her heart filled with a deep, burning truth. It felt as if the magic shackles fell from her, though it might have only been her soul's shackles. She looked at Blake, hoping he could see the dreams promised and the dreams lost within her eyes. "Nor do I do give up my love for him. It will be forever. I shall always love him. I shall always be his, in any world and at any time."

The fairies' laughter died. A stunned look crossed Trillion's face. "Be quiet, mortal."

"And I will be Alwayna's," Blake gasped, his eyes blazing a strong, bonding power upon her. He slowly, amazingly rose. "I shall always love her. I shall be hers, in any world and at any time."

"Do not speak!" Trillion shrilled. "Be quiet, I say!"

A sudden bong sounded. It rang clear and deep. The sound actually rolled across the silver plain like a wave, rippling and contorting it.

"What was that?" Blake asked.

"No!" Trillion cried. "Impossible!"

"It is the castle clock," Alwayna gasped. She knew the sound of it well.

"Human time cannot not enter our world," Trillion shouted, glaring about feverishly. The other fairies fell silent, cringing back.

The second bong sounded. Alwayna's heart leapt. The tolling clock had been her one grasp with reality when in the library. It was her reality once more. "It's ringing for us, Blake. I know it is!"

"Do not listen," Trillion said. "Nothing can save you now."

The third bong sounded. This time it rocked the land.

"It's ringing for us because it's not yet midnight," Blake said, "not in our world, is it?"

"Do not listen!" Trillion screeched above the fourth bong.

"Listen to your heart. That is where the power lies," Alwayna gasped.

Blake, his eyes shining with hope, stepped forward and grasped Alwayna's hand. "Alwayna, I vow before man and God and fairies that I will be your husband. I shall love, honor, and cherish you until death do us part."

Alwayna, her heart surging with joy as the clock bonged again, gripped his hand tightly. "Blake, I vow before man and God and fairies that I shall be your wife. I shall love, honor, and cherish you until death do us part."

The clock bonged. The fairies covered their ears, moaning. Blake looked to the quivering Trillion. "Would you like to pronounce us man and wife, Trillion?"

"Leave mortals!" Trillion shrieked as the clock rang out once more.

"Tsk. You are to say I may kiss the bride," Blake laughed. He drew Alwayna into his arms. Lowering his head, he kissed her deeply. Alwayna sighed and held her husband close as the castle clock rang out its twelfth and last chime for the midnight hour of All Hallow's Eve.

Silver landscape warmed into the colors of the great hall. Alwayna drew back from Blake, but only enough that she might gaze at him. She smiled tremulously. "We are safe. We are home."

"Yes," Blake said with a warm, knowing smile. "Home on this mortal sod."

Alwayna giggled. Then she gasped, peering about. She had been so focused upon Blake she had considered naught else. Fear seized her for a moment. Everyone in the great hall appeared asleep or frozen. Yet as she watched they came to life, some jerking awake, others blinking and shaking their heads as if to clear it. "Thank heaven!"

"No," Damian said as his eyes gained focus. "Thank *you.*"

"You saved us all," Sarabeth cried even as she moved into Damian's arms. She shivered. "It was frightful to watch."

"You saw?" Alwayna gasped.

"Oh, yes, dear, we were there," Bathsheba said, blinking. Then she dimpled and looked at Blake. "You are right, dear. He is very handsome."

"Bathsheba, for shame," Dorinda said, her tone severe as she regained focus. She nodded to Blake. "I am pleased to meet you, Your Grace. That is, in person. Not that you weren't a nice kitten." She halted, flushing.

Blake laughed. "I completely understand. I myself will not miss the fur and tail."

"I would miss Kitten," Alwayna objected, then grinned at Blake, "if I did not have you."

"Only wait," Blake said, a wicked glint in his eyes. "There are many benefits of me being a man rather than a kitten—all of which will be my pleasure to show you."

"Oh, my," Bathsheba said, fanning herself even as Alwayna blushed. "It is good you are getting married."

"We are already married," Blake said. He smiled. "Though we should perform the ceremony again. I think it good to have it recorded here as well. We must think of our children and grandchildren."

A sudden thunderclap sounded. An older man materialized. Everyone stared. The man arrogantly ignored them. He grinned at Blake. "Good work, son. You did it!"

"No, Father," Blake said, laughing. "Alwayna did it."

"No," Alwayna said, flushing. "Our love did it."

Creighton Farewell only shook his head. "Don't matter to me, any which way. All I know is I'm glad I won't be a servant to any fairy. I told you I was too old for that."

"And we are too young," Blake said, laughing.

"Excuse me," a voice interrupted. Father MacKenzie stumbled over to them. "Wh-where am I? Wh-what am I doing here?"

"You are here to perform a wedding ceremony, Father," Sarabeth said kindly. "Do you remember?"

"I do," Father MacKenzie nodded, starting to smile. A sudden look of horror crossed his face. "But I remember I'm supposed to join a woman and . . . a cat."

"That won't be necessary anymore," Damian said quickly.

"Praise the Lord," Father MacKenzie said. "I knew I must be dreaming."

"Perhaps," Blake said. "Do let us proceed. I am anxious to, er, receive the church's blessing on our union as well."

Blake's father guffawed. "A diplomatic way of phrasing it, son."

Everyone laughed and they quickly took their places. Alwayna looked to Blake as good Father MacKenzie began the ceremony. A pure joy entered her. Blake was real and human. He would not disappear. She spoke her vows loudly and clearly, without fear. Blake's deeply voiced response was as sure and strong. When he looked at her now, she could only see the dreams promised within his eyes.

Father MacKenzie pronounced them husband and wife. Blake kissed Alwayna once more. The cheers and applause from the inhabitants of Chancellorville rang in her ears. It was such a warm, mortal sound.

Blake drew back. He smiled down at her. "I told you we were destined to love each other."

"Yes," Alwayna said, her eyes glistening with sudden tears. "In a way, we have Trillion to thank for that."

"Perhaps," Blake said. He held her close. "But I promise we will live very happily without that fairy."

Alwayna thrilled to feel his strong arms about her. "Or the tail."

"Yes," Blake said, laughing. His eyes glowed in sudden mischief.

Instantly, roses in every hue of blue imaginable showered down on the people in the great hall. Midnight blue. Turquoise Blue. Cerulean Blue. Alwayna gasped in delight as did all the onlookers.

We'll dance under many a blue sky, Alwayna," Blake said softly. "From now on."

"And forever after." Alwayna nodded.

She knew it to be true. Time was theirs now. Time for the growing and sharing and belonging. Time for the magic and the love.

Time. Which, after all, is eternal.

A BEWITCHING
MINX

by

Nancy Lawrence

ONE

Sebastian Camerford, Lord Byefield, looked into her eyes and knew he could not resist her. He had never been able to refuse her anything—not when she looked at him just so, with the light of anticipation in her eyes; not when she looked at him with that soft expression of pleading that had the power to melt his resolve as nothing else on earth could.

He should have scolded her. He should have explained to her in no uncertain terms that no female of his acquaintance was ever allowed to disrupt the solitude of his library. He should have told her how audacious and unladylike she was for daring to sit on his desktop, bringing her head level with his, looking him straight in the eye, as if she thought by doing so she could bend him to her will.

He should have done all those things, but he didn't. Instead, his stern gray eyes met her blue eyes and he forced his brows together in a slight frown. "A kitten?" he repeated, discouragingly.

His gruff demeanor didn't fool her for a moment. She smiled slightly and returned his gaze with wide, unblinking eyes. "Yes, Uncle."

"And what, may I ask, makes you think I wish to spend my afternoon looking for a stray kitten?"

"Because it is the dearest little thing," she responded with all the reasoning of a ten year old. "I found it in your garden earlier and Mama said I might keep it, but when

I tried to dress it properly for tea, it scampered away and I cannot find it anywhere!"

Since Sebastian was well acquainted with his niece's penchant for dressing in human attire any animal unfortunate enough to come within her orbit, it came as no surprise to him that one of the poor creatures had tried to escape. "The kitten sounds like a very ill-mannered guest. Perhaps you should consider having your tea without it, Mary."

"No, Uncle, I cannot." There was the merest trace of a pout about her lips. "Truly, it is the prettiest little kitten I have ever seen, with white hair and blue eyes. I've never seen a kitten with blue eyes before, so I know it must be very special. Please help me find it. Please?"

Her voice held that pleading tone again—the same tone that, in one fell swoop, held the power to make him abandon all his plans for the afternoon and believe with all his heart that nothing was as important at that very moment as finding a kitten possessed of white hair and blue eyes.

"Mary, if I help you find the kitten—"

She gasped with delight.

"I said *if* I help you find the kitten—will you be a good little girl and be kind to it?"

She nodded vigorously.

"You mustn't force it to wear your stockings and shawls if it doesn't wish to. Do I have your promise?"

"I promise, Uncle!"

The last of his resolve melted away. "Very well, I shall help you find your kitten—" He stopped short as Mary threw her chubby arms about his neck and almost choked him with affection. He held her briefly, then stepped back to wag an admonishing finger at her. "If you find the kitten before I do, you must take care not to frighten it. Do you understand?"

"Oh, yes, for frightened kittens scratch. Mama told me so."

"Your mother is correct. Now where was the kitten when last you saw it?"

"I was trying to carry it up the stairs but it jumped out

of my arms as quick as lightning! It ran toward the blue salon, I think."

The blue salon boasted several pairs of tall glass doors that gave out onto a small terrace at the back of the house. That autumn afternoon the doors had been left open to allow the room to air. Sebastian frowned slightly. "I fear your kitten could be anywhere. I suggest you search the house while I search the gardens."

"Could we not find the kitten together?" asked Mary, slipping her small hand hopefully into his.

"We could, but I think we shall find it that much sooner if we divide our efforts."

"Very well," said Mary, releasing her hold on him. She hopped down from her perch upon his desk and went to the library door, but paused just before opening it. "I shall search the old schoolroom. The kitten might be there playing with the toys."

He smothered a smile and said, with perfect sincerity, "A logical course of action."

She flashed him a bright smile. "Very well. I shall call to you if I find her before you!"

She was gone in an instant, leaving behind only the sound of her shoes beating a soft tattoo against the hardwood floors as she scampered down the hall toward the stairs.

Sebastian, too, left the library, and made his way in the opposite direction, toward the back of the house, where the blue salon was situated. A footman ushered him into the room and he entered to discover that the salon was curiously bereft of furniture and that the doors leading out to the terrace were still standing open. He went through them and stepped out into the late autumn afternoon.

His sister was there, seated quite comfortably and taking a dish of tea at a suite of furniture that he immediately recognized as belonging to the blue salon. It had long been her way to try to reorganize his bachelor existence to her liking whenever she chanced to visit him; pilfering his furniture was, he judged, simply the latest crack start she had taken. At times, he took genuine exception to her interference in his life; other times, he merely pretended to so as not to encourage her in future.

He eyed the furniture ominously. "Ella! I see you have once again managed to rearrange my household without asking my permission."

She looked up and saw that his expression was quite serious, but since his tone held no trace of anger or annoyance, she merely smiled back at him. "Was it not clever of me? We're enjoying such fine blackberry summer weather, I thought it would be a shame not to take advantage of it while it lasted, so I had Barrows serve tea out here. Come sit down," she invited with a wave of her hand toward another of the silk upholstered chairs she had pirated from the house. "I've finished my tea, but I should be glad to pour out a dish for you."

He shook his head. "Not now, I think. I have something of a mission to accomplish first."

"Don't tell me," she begged with the sudden light of amusement in her eyes, "that Mary convinced you to help her find the kitten! I told her I would help her look for the animal. I begged her not to bother you in your library, Sebastian—truly I did!"

"As it happens, she was no bother at all," he said, evenly.

"Indeed? I recall a time when I once dared to encroach upon your precious library, and you threatened to have me flogged!" said Ella with a laugh as she stood and gave her skirts a shake.

"Mary does not interrupt on the merest of pretexts," he said seriously. "There can be no comparison."

She laughed again and started for the door of the salon, saying, "No, Mary only interrupts you for important matters, like kitten hunts and begging you to judge which of your hunting dogs looks more fetching dressed in pantalettes."

He scowled slightly. "Nonsense. I treat your daughter

no differently from the way I treat any of my other nieces and nephews."

Ella paused at the door to the salon and turned back to smile softly at him. "I know it is your way to be sane and sensible and not given to flights of emotion. Still, you've been very sweet to Mary and me since my husband died. Mary quite adores you, you know."

He wasn't sure he was at all comfortable with the direction in which their conversation had turned, and he retreated behind a scowl. "I thought you were going to help Mary find her kitten."

"I am—as are you, I suspect. You spoil her shamefully, Sebastian!" She paused a moment, then added, with a hint of a knowing smile, "I see you do not try to deny it."

His scowl increased. "Would it do any good if I did?"

Ella laughed again and went into the house.

Sebastian dismissed his sister's words with little effort. Down the terrace steps to the garden he went. He set a slow pace along the path, his gray eyes searching for any sign of the white kitten with the blue eyes. Only for Mary would he have sacrificed his afternoon thus; only for Mary would he have walked his garden lane, clucking his tongue and calling out in a ridiculously high voice to an animal he would have had no desire, under any other circumstance, to bring into his home.

He was near the garden wall at the far end of the property when he saw a flash of white dart across the path. He heard a slight rustling sound as his quarry scaled the trunk of the maple tree and disappeared within its leafy branches. Beneath that tree was placed a wrought-iron bench and Sebastian stepped up on it.

The tree had not yet begun to shed its autumn-colored leaves and he could not see past them to discover if the kitten was hidden among the branches. Blindly, Sebastian reached up through the branches and leaves. His strong fingers immediately came in contact with something soft and slim and furry.

He wrapped his fingers about the creature, but when

he gave it a tug, his prisoner let out not a kittenish mew, as he had expected, but a very feminine yelp.

He was surprised, but not surprised enough to let loose his hold. He notched the toe of his boot against a low branch and hiked himself up farther. His head poked through the branches, and he saw that instead of holding a kitten, he was holding the fur-trimmed cuff of a lady's boot top.

His gray eyes traveled upward. He saw a shapely thigh over which clung buff-colored breeches. Higher still, he saw a richly embroidered brocade waistcoat fitted over the curving contours of a feminine form. From there it was natural for his eye to travel still farther, past the white shirt open at the collar, revealing the slender column of a woman's neck, and on up to his captive's face.

She was young, of perhaps twenty summers, and she was looking back at him with brown eyes gone slightly wide with a look of guilty surprise. Her lips were parted as if she wanted to speak, but could not hit upon any sensible thing to say. She was clutching to her bosom a small white kitten with blue eyes; both creatures—the lady and the cat—blinked slowly at him.

What such an attractive young woman was doing in his tree, Sebastian could not guess. Why she was dressed in breeches and boots, he could not fathom. He thought at first she might be one of the street urchins that abounded in London, but a closer inspection revealed that her hands were soft and neatly manicured and her chestnut hair, although not cut short in the latest style, was dressed nevertheless atop her head in an array of fashionable curls.

His gray eyes locked with hers and he said, with perfect composure, "Perhaps, madam, you might explain what you are doing in my tree."

She favored him with another slow cat blink and repeated, *"Your* tree? Do you live here?"

"Yes, I do and you, I fear, are trespassing."

He gave her his most disapproving look, which had not the least effect upon her. She said, quite genially, "I was merely fetching my kitten. Truly, I was in my garden with her when I heard her begin to cry and discovered she had climbed into your tree by way of one of the branches that hangs over our garden wall. The poor little creature was so frightened, I simply had to try to rescue her."

"Our garden wall?" repeated Sebastian, trying to delve to the roots of the young woman's rambling explanation.

"I am Miss Amelia Merriweather." She let loose her hold on the branch upon which she was perched with the full intention of extending her hand toward him in a most ladylike fashion. Instead, she succeeded merely in playing havoc with her balance.

She let out a little *eek* of terror as she wobbled precariously upon the tree branch.

Sebastian quickly reached up and wrapped his hands about her waist, steadying her. When he was certain she was in no danger of toppling to the ground, he relaxed his hold upon her long enough to clasp her finely tapered fingers in his and say, simply, "Byefield. At your service, madam."

She smiled at him in a way that was both friendly and assessing. Her brown eyes traveled quickly over him, taking in his aristocratic nose, his solid chin, and his oh-so-properly squared shoulders. "You are not at all as I imagined you would be. You see, I have been very curious about you ever since my aunt and I became your neighbors. Tell me, do you live in this big house all by yourself?"

For some reason, he was reluctant to let loose his hold on her. He was also having a difficult time making logical sense of anything she had yet said and found himself repeating, stupidly, "My neighbors?"

"Yes, indeed. You see, my aunt and I have moved into the town house next door." With a graceful wave of her hand toward the garden wall, she indicated the fashionable residence that abutted his. She also set her balance to wavering again, prompting Sebastian to reestablish his hold about her waist.

He favored her with a thoughtful, measuring look. So

this was his new neighbor! He had been quite curious about the new occupants of the house next door, for since their arrival, Sebastian's sleep had been disrupted each night by strange noises coming through the wall that divided his town house from the next. He was having a difficult time believing that this pert, petite woman could be responsible for such mischief.

"*You* live next door?"

"Yes, with my aunt. We decided to take a house in town until my uncle returns from his travels abroad." She cocked her head to one side and peered at him quizzingly. "What is it? Why do you stare at me so?"

There had to be some mistake, he judged, as he peered up into her lovely face with its expression of utter innocence. There had to be some logical cause for those nightly, disruptive noises other than this young woman. He ignored her question and said simply, "Perhaps, madam, I should assist you down."

She accepted this suggestion with a smile of relief. "Thank you! I was rather wondering how I should manage to get down on my own. It didn't seem so difficult to get up here, but once I had settled myself in and had hold of Jelly, I realized I had climbed much higher than I had thought!"

He had been about to begin the task of lowering himself down from the tree, but at her words, he paused and looked back up at her in a rather exasperated way. "Jelly?" he repeated.

She smiled at him and nodded. "Jelly is my kitten. She is so sweet and loving that, when it came time to name her, I tried to think of the sweetest thing I knew. Jelly!"

"I see," he said discouragingly, for he had no intention of promoting a conversation along that vein. But when he looked up at her and saw the friendly and rather artless smile that touched the corners of her lips, and noticed the way the autumn-colored leaves framed a perfect backdrop for her brown eyes and chestnut hair, the scowl faded from his expression and he found himself rather charmed.

How long he stared up at her, at the pleasing picture she made, he had no idea, but his attention was recalled to the matter at hand when she said quite prettily, "Please, sir, will you help me down now?"

Amelia Merriweather cradled her kitten against her breast and, with Sebastian's strong hands about her waist, began to scoot her way across the branch. A moment later she was in Sebastian's arms as he very gently set her booted feet down upon the walking path.

She looked up in his eyes. She saw dark lashes that were more lush than any man's should be. She saw the ring of pale blue that merged like a kaleidoscope with the gray of his irises. She saw detachment, aloofness in those eyes, and she saw a gentleness there, deep down where it could remain well hidden from casual observers.

"Thank you!" she said, smiling. "I am much more comfortable now that I am upon solid ground again."

He released his hold on her and had to make a conscious effort to school his gaze upon her face rather than upon the enticing outline of her legs and hips encased in snug breeches. "Not at all. However, I would suggest you find a way to keep your kitten on your side of the garden wall. My niece had plans to claim it as her own."

"Did she? I hope she won't be too disappointed and will understand if I mean to keep the dear little thing for myself."

"I shall explain it to her. She has a great deal of understanding for a ten year old."

She cocked her head to one side. "Much like her uncle, I daresay. You may tell your niece she is welcome to visit Jelly whenever she likes. I shall look forward to making her acquaintance."

"I shall tell her so," he said cordially. He set his hand to her elbow and began to guide her toward the garden gate that divided his property from that belonging to the house next door.

"And you must call upon us very soon, as well," she continued on as she fell into step beside him, "for I am certain my aunt would very much like to make your acquaintance."

"If the occasion presents itself," he answered, with a distinct lack of commitment.

At the garden gate, Amelia shifted her hold upon the kitten so that she might extend her hand once again to Sebastian. "Thank you for your assistance, sir. I fear I should still be sitting in your tree had you not happened along to help me."

There were many things he might have said, but he was feeling a trifle bemused by Miss Amelia Merriweather. It wasn't until she had gone through the gate and he had pulled it closed behind her that he realized he had missed a golden opportunity. He should have spoken to the young woman about the nightly rumpus she was kicking up; he should have explained to her that she was disrupting his sleep and that such a circumstance could not be allowed to continue. Instead, Miss Merriweather's happy chatter and outrageous clothes had thrown him a little off his usual, temperate stride to the point that he had barely been able to follow the thread of their conversation.

Never again, he vowed. Never again would he miss an opportunity to tell Miss Merriweather exactly what he thought of her nocturnal shenanigans. Never again would he allow her nighttime noises to disturb his sleep; and never again would he allow one look into those pansy brown eyes of hers to distract him from his course.

Amelia waited only long enough for her neighbor to swing the old wooden gate closed before she set her kitten back down on its feet and ran full tilt into the house, calling, "Aunt? Aunt! Where are you?"

She found her aunt, Mrs. Ginevra Merriweather, in the front hall of the house, where she was surrounded by trunks and boxes, cashes of linens, and baskets of odd household knickknacks. A footman, two maids, and a handful of deliverymen were scurrying about under her direction. As Amelia burst into the room, her aunt turned and said in a softly scolding voice, "Amelia dearest, how naughty of you! You promised you would help me set this house to rights if only I allowed you to dress as comfortably as you did in the country. Instead, it has been an hour or more since last I saw you!"

"It couldn't be helped, truly! And only wait until I have told you my news!" Amelia paused dramatically and said, "I have met our neighbor!"

Aunt Ginevra was engaged in sorting through a basket of linens to determine its proper destination in the household, but at her niece's announcement, she stopped and looked up at her niece. "Have you? How extraordinary! Tell me, is he—?" She stopped short as she realized that the servants and deliverymen had ceased tending their business for the more entertaining prospect of listening to Amelia's tale of her encounter with the neighbor.

Aunt Ginevra threw open the nearest door and ushered her niece into a small salon. "Come in here, my dear, and do be careful where you step. We are so disorganized, I fear it is simply a matter of time until one of us shall tread upon something fragile!"

Amelia waited only until her aunt had closed the door upon the servants in the hall before saying, in a rush, "Oh, bother the mess, Aunt, for I shall help you with it presently! But first, I must tell you about our neighbor, for he is not at all as I expected he would be!"

Having learned long ago that it was very near impossible to curb her niece's enthusiasms, Ginevra Merriweather twitched a Holland cover back from an upholstered chair and sat down, saying, "Then you must tell me all about him. But first, how is it you came to meet him, my dear?"

"Jelly climbed over the garden wall into our neighbor's tree. I merely climbed up to fetch her and realized from up in the tree I could see very well into some of the windows of the house next door."

Aunt Ginevra gave a short gasp. "My dear, you didn't spy on our neighbor, I hope!"

"I simply wanted to see what manner of person could make so much noise in the middle of the night. Aunt, I have been awakened by our neighbor's rackets every night since we have lived in this house. I was very well convinced there was something rather sinister going on or, at the very least, something quite depraved. I simply had to see for myself if my suspicions were correct."

"I fear your imagination has got the best of you, dear. Tell me, did any of your suspicions bear fruit?"

"I don't think so. Lord Byefield is not at all the sort of Bacchus figure I thought he would be. Instead, he was very polite and quite gentlemanly. He's somewhat older—in his thirties, I should think—and rather handsome."

Her aunt absorbed this information a moment. "How fortuitous! We have moved into a house next door to a man who is gentlemanly, mature, and handsome. I daresay we could not have asked for a better neighbor. He must be an altogether pleasant man."

"I'm sure he could be so, if he wished it. He had the most magnificent gray eyes, which he made frown a good deal. In fact, he didn't seem the least bit pleased to make my acquaintance."

"Why would he not wish to do so?"

"I don't know," said Amelia, giving the question a great deal of thought. "It was almost as if he had already decided to dislike me before ever having met me."

"How very peculiar. Even more peculiar is the manner in which he keeps you up at night with his incessant noises. My dear, did you chance to speak to him about that? Did you ask him to show a little consideration for your rest?"

Amelia shook her head slightly. "I didn't and I cannot think why I let such an opportunity go by. I had begun to think there were nightly bacchanals going on next door. Aunt, those noises I hear every night coming through the wall cannot, I assure you, result from any normal, decent activity!"

"So you have said, my dear. And I've often wondered if you haven't let your imagination run away with you a bit."

"Having met Lord Byefield, I must admit he doesn't at all seem the bacchanal sort I thought he would be."

"It seems a shame you did not seize the opportunity to speak most strongly to Lord Byefield when you had the chance. I'm certain you could clear up the entire business with a simple conversation."

"You're right, of course. When next I meet our neighbor, I shall speak to him straight away. I shall be polite, but stern, and I shall insist that he cease engaging in whatever activity causes such horrid noises. Believe me, Aunt, I shall not again be dissuaded by a pair of gentle gray eyes!"

TWO

Amelia was given an opportunity to do just so the very next morning. She was assisting her aunt in setting the house to rights when she discovered that a bundle of kitchen linens had somehow found their way into one of the bedchambers. She gathered up the wayward bundle and made her way down the stairs; and gained the front entry hall in time to see her aunt's very proper butler admit Lord Byefield to the house.

He handed the butler his hat, stick, and gloves, and his gray eyes swept over the spacious entry hall. The room was bright and spacious and not at all shabby, but it was still bare of any furnishings or personal touches that might have made it truly welcoming.

His eyes traveled up the imposing staircase, and on the landing, he spied Amelia. She stood poised there above him, staring down with her brown eyes gone wide with surprise. Her hair was styled once again upon her head, but several tendrils had come loose from their pins and brushed lightly against her forehead and neck. Her cheeks were flushed with the delicate color of one who had just recently engaged in a mild exertion. Her arms were laden with the kitchen linens and she was again clad in distracting, figure-revealing breeches. All in all, she looked charmingly disheveled and it took every bit of his lordship's resolve to keep his mind on the purpose of his visit.

Needlessly, the butler intoned Sebastian's name. Amelia

fixed a smile of polite welcome upon her lips and began a slow descent down the stairs, fully intending to make as dignified an entrance as she possibly could with a pile of table linens in her arms.

"Good morning, Lord Byefield. I am glad you've called, for I wish to speak to you on a matter of some importance."

"And I to you," he said in a tone that was far from genial. "In fact, I've come to give you a lesson on being a good neighbor."

Her descent came to a sudden stop. There was something about his tone that immediately set her hackles up. There was something in his voice that was a trifle angry, a bit condescending.

She had planned to be pleasant, to be polite; but in the face of this rather rude pronouncement, she decided to abandon all pretext to courtesy. Her temper flared. From halfway down the stairs, she said, *"You're* going to give *me* a lesson? When next I am interested in attending a school that teaches thoughtlessness, sir, I shall most certainly come to you for lessons."

He cast her a sharp look, his attention arrested. "What are you talking about?"

"I'm talking about you and your incivilities," she said, drawing herself up. "I am speaking of whatever horrid things you do in your home that keep me awake half the night!"

"Keep *you* awake?" he repeated. His temper had been simmering when first he had entered the house. Now it rose slightly in degree. "My dear young woman, it is you who keeps me awake at night. I have called here today to express to you, in no uncertain terms, that your behavior is unacceptable. I cannot imagine what sort of activity you are engaged in that should kick up such a riot and rumpus every evening, but I should hazard a guess it is not of the educational variety."

Amelia felt a hot flush of anger mantle her cheeks as she started to descend the remaining stairs. She intended to ask that he leave. No, she intended to *demand* that he leave. She intended to explain, in a firm yet civil tone, that she had no time for such games and that he simply could not continue to disrupt her sleep each and every night. She intended to say such things and more, but in the end, no such words were spoken.

She had very nearly completed her descent when her kitten appeared and chose that very moment in which to express its affection for her. Jelly tangled her body and tail about Amelia's booted ankles just as she gained the bottom of the stair.

Amelia tried to avoid treading upon her kitten, and doing so proved her undoing. One of her booted feet slipped from the step as she rose up on the toes of her other foot to a precarious height. For a moment she teetered on the brink of catastrophe, balancing uncertainly upon the step, the linens still clutched in her arms.

Vainly did she struggle to maintain her dignity and her balance. In the end, the linens went flying, the kitten let out a yowl and streaked back up the stair, and Amelia pitched forward, straight into the arms of Lord Byefield.

He caught her securely against him. His arms slipped about her shoulders and waist, and she flung her hands about his neck and held on. How long she remained in such a position, she had no idea, but she rather thought she might have been content to stay in his arms forever.

"My God, Miss Merriweather, are you all right?" he asked in a voice of satisfying concern.

She looked up into his eyes and was rather disconcerted by how near they were to hers. "I believe so. It was silly of me to pitch down the stairs, but my kitten—"

"I saw it," he said grimly. "The animal picked a deucedly poor time to wrap itself about your legs before it scampered away. You could have been killed!"

Amelia thought this only a slight exaggeration, but she chose not to argue the point. She was content merely to remain in Sebastian's arms, and she would have done exactly so had not the merest of sounds caught her attention. She turned her head slightly and saw that her aunt had entered the hall and was regarding them curiously as they stood wrapped in each other's embrace.

"Amelia?" said her aunt in a kindly voice "How splendid for you! You have made a friend already and we have been in this house less than a week! Perhaps you would be so good as to introduce him to me."

Amelia drew her arms from about Sebastian's neck as a flush of embarrassment crept over her face. "Dear Aunt, it is not as you think!" she said, a good deal flustered. "I was merely—I had kitchen linens in my arms, you see, and I daresay I would have caught my own fall but— Oh, this is Lord Byefield, Aunt!" she uttered at last in great confusion.

By contrast, his lordship appeared not the least bit perturbed, even after being assailed by table linens. He slowly drew his strong arms from about Amelia and favored her aunt with a bow of great composure, as if catching young women in midair was a regular part of his daily routine.

"Your servant, madam," he said in his deep voice, "and I hope you will make no hasty judgment for having come upon us thus. I only just arrived when I took upon myself the very pleasant task of catching your niece before she tumbled down the stair."

"Very prettily said," pronounced Aunt Ginevra approvingly. "You seem to be a very accommodating gentleman. I wonder, then, if you would be so good as to have a bit more consideration for my niece. She needs her rest, you see, and I'm afraid you're guilty of keeping poor Amelia awake half the night."

Sebastian's jaw tightened. Had everyone in the house gone mad? He said with measured patience, "I fear, Mrs. Merriweather, that you have it all wrong. Rather, it is your niece who is keeping me up at night. In fact, after the din I suffered through last evening, I felt I had no choice but to call upon you first thing to demand you stop whatever it is you are doing to interrupt my sleep!"

"But the noises are coming from *your* house," insisted

Amelia, "not ours. I can assure you, Lord Byefield, our home is quite serene in the extreme!"

No sooner did those words leave her lips than a loud crash sounded from overhead. She started visibly and cast a look at Lord Byefield.

"What was that?" he asked. One of his dark brows shot skyward as if he had caught her in some kind of falsehood.

"I-I don't know." She could only hope that whatever had fallen and caused such a horrid racket wasn't about to come crashing through the ceiling.

"Don't you think we should investigate?"

"Yes, but—but I can't imagine it was anything to worry over," she said, willing him to believe that such occurrences were rare. That soaring eyebrow told her he was forming the opposite opinion. "Very well, I shall see what happened, but I assure you, there is nothing to worry about."

But once Amelia chanced to considered it, there was something to worry about after all. That loud crash they'd heard had come from the room directly above the entry hall, and that, she realized, was curious indeed.

She made haste up the stairs and didn't stop, even when Sebastian called after her, "Wait! Miss Merriweather, I'm coming with you!"

"No need!" she called back over her shoulder, her pace never slackening. "I assure you, nothing is amiss!"

He took to the stairs two at a time and caught up to her at the second landing. "Then you shall not object if I come with you."

Her course never altered. "You don't understand. You see, there is nothing in that room—nothing there at all—that could have made such a commotion!" They reached the chamber that was situated just above the entry hall. Amelia flung the door open, saying in a rather agitated way, "Only see for yourself!"

Sebastian's gray eyes swept from one corner of the room to another. He had expected to discover something of importance. He had expect to find at last the cause behind those nightly sounds that Miss Merriweather was doing her best to hide. Instead, he found nothing.

Not one stick of furniture rested upon the polished floor. No draperies hung at the windows. No mirrors or artwork adorned the walls. Only Amelia's kitten was there, watching them from her place on the sill of an open window.

He frowned slightly as he slowly stepped across the threshold. "I don't understand. From all the riot that was kicked up, I would have thought half the room had turned on its side!"

Amelia followed him. "I told you there was nothing here. What, I wonder, could have caused such a commotion?"

"There can be only one explanation," he said very reasonably. "It can only mean that the sound we heard didn't come from this room."

Amelia cast him a look of surprise. "How can you think so? We both heard the noise from downstairs. It was directly above us as we stood in the hall."

"We must have been mistaken. We must have only *thought* the sound we heard was directly above us."

"I assure you, Lord Byefield," said Amelia, drawing himself up a bit, "my hearing is in perfect order, as is my judgment. The crash we heard came from this room."

"Then what made the noise?"

"I daresay we shall never know," she replied quite simply as Jelly jumped down from the window to twine herself about her mistress's legs. "I suppose what happened in this room shall remain just another of life's delicious mysteries."

His dark brow danced again. "Mysteries? I don't believe in them. In my experience, every occurrence has a logical explanation, Miss Merriweather."

She answered his challenging tone with a smile. "Indeed? Then tell me, please, what occurred in this room?"

His eyes again scanned the bare walls. There was a strong autumn breeze blowing through the open window, ruffling the kitten's hair, as it sat once again upon the sill. Sebastian shooed the kitten away and drew the window shut. "I would hazard a guess that the wind simply blew the sash open and the crashing sound we heard downstairs was simply the windowframe blowing back against the wall."

"Perhaps." It did seem like a logical explanation, but Amelia wasn't ready to admit it. She cast him a doubtful look.

Under any other circumstance he might have been offended or, at the very least, annoyed that his learned and logical explanation of a situation had not been readily accepted. But he saw the mulish set to her chin and found, almost to his own surprise, that he was rather more charmed than vexed. He watched her a moment and said rather gently, "It is, I assure you, the only reasonable and logical explanation."

It may have been a reasonable explanation, but Amelia clung to the belief that a hundred open windows together could not have made such a racket. Even worse, she had a niggling suspicion that the noise she and Lord Byefield had chased up the stair was curiously similar to the noise that awakened her every night—the same noise she heard each evening from the other side of the common wall that separated her bedchamber from Byefield house.

That recollection put her in mind of her previous complaint. She said, with what she hoped was a great deal of dignity, "Not everything can be explained with logic, Lord Byefield. I hope you will remember that when next you take it into your head to accuse neighbors of unseemly activities."

"Is that so?" he asked, far from cowed. In fact, his brow went up ever so slightly in question and she had the distinct impression that he was somewhat amused. "Then in return, I suppose, you shall do the same? I would hate to leave here knowing you think me capable of doing—how did you say it?—*horrid things* that keep you up at night."

She dipped her head a moment, hoping that by doing so he wouldn't see the guilty flush on her face. "I'm sorry to have said such a thing, but you made me angry, you know!"

His expression softened a bit. "Forgive me. It was wrong of me to storm in here like a runaway mail coach."

"And I am sorry, too," she said handsomely, "for I did rather think the worst of you. After hearing those dreadful noises every night since we moved into this house, I was quite convinced there was something wholly sinister going on in your house. Of course, I no longer think so now that I have met you and seen how stuffy you are."

The words were out before she had a chance to consider them; and so mortified was she to have uttered such a thing that, for a moment, she couldn't quite bring herself to look at him.

When at last she raised her eyes to his, she saw there was an odd expression on his face, dark and disquieting.

He smiled slightly, in a way that held no warmth, and he said very evenly, "I have been called a good many things in my life, Miss Merriweather, but I don't believe I have ever been described so before."

"I beg your pardon, sir! I swear I didn't mean that the way it sounded," she said in utter misery.

"No harm, Miss Merriweather," he said in that same even tone. "Come, let me return you to your aunt. I'm certain the poor woman is wondering by now what has become of us."

When the very same noises emanated again that night through the wall that divided Byefield House from the house next door, Sebastian was furious. The hour was well past midnight, and while he was not yet asleep, he had retired to his bed with a book and a glass of port. No sooner had he settled himself quite comfortably in his bed than the noises began and his temper rose to boiling point. It was time, he decided, to teach Miss Merriweather a lesson.

Donning a dressing gown, he stomped downstairs and out into the garden. A cool autumn breeze was blowing, rustling the trees and scattering dried leaves along the path in front of him. The breeze did nothing to cool his temper, however, and he pushed with unnecessary force through the garden gate that divided his property from that next door. No sooner did he advance pell-mell into the neighboring garden than he promptly collided with Miss Amelia Merriweather.

Instinctively, his hands came up to steady her. A hearty oath escaped his lips at the same time he heard her let out a soft whoosh of startled breath. His arms circled about her and her small hands clutched at the lapels of his dressing gown.

"What the devil are you doing out here?" he demanded in a voice mixed of exasperation and anger.

"I might ask the same question of you!" she said, and while the expression on her face was accusing, her voice was possessed of a breathy quality that told him she was even more surprised than he to find herself once again in his arms.

He loosened his hold about her and looked down to examine her in the moonlight. "Have I hurt you? Good God, what the devil were you thinking . . . ?"

The words died away as he realized she was clad in little more than a nightdress over which she had drawn a pale pink satin wrapper. Her hair was loose and fell past her shoulders in a cloud of chestnut waves that the wind caught and set to dancing against her face and neck.

She ignored his scrutiny and countered, "A better question would be, what are *you* doing here, sir? How is it I find you on this side of the gate?"

"I was on my way to ask—no, to *demand*—that you cease that infernal racket you were making!"

"Me? But *you* were the one making those dreadful noises!" she insisted although she was finding it difficult indeed to scold the man at the same time she was supremely conscious of the feel of his arms about her. "You woke me from a very restful sleep—and not for the first time, I might add. I have had enough, Lord Byefield, and

I was on my way to rap at your door—to break in, if I must—and confront you once and for all."

He drew a deep breath for patience. "My dear Miss Merriweather, I assure you my house is as quiet as a church."

"It cannot be. I distinctly heard those horrid crashing sounds coming through the wall—the very wall that divides your house from mine."

"Nonsense. The sounds were coming from your side of the wall—I am certain of it."

Amelia drew a deep breath for patience. "Very well then. If neither I nor you are responsible for making those dreadful noises, where are they coming from?"

It was a question Sebastian was having a devil of a time considering. In fact, he was having difficulty considering anything but the fact that he was holding a rather lovely young woman in his arms. She, on the other hand, didn't seem the least confounded to find herself in the arms of a relative stranger. She didn't struggle against him or demand that he set her free. Instead, she merely stood within the circle of his arms, looking up at him with a slight frown of concentration, which he found somehow disarming. In the dim light of the moon, her eyes were little more than deep pools of black. He would have preferred to see her eyes as they had been in the full light of day—expressive and candid. He would also have preferred concentrating on the feel of her satin wrapper as it slid beneath the pads of his fingers, or on the way her chestnut hair would feel if he scooped a handful of it up off her shoulders and twined it between his fingers.

Instead, he forced himself to concentrate on the matter at hand. "I don't know, although I am certain there must be some logical explanation. Miss Merriweather, are you certain there is nothing—"

He stopped short as a loud clatter sounded through an upper-story open window of Merriweather house.

"That's *my* bedchamber!" breathed Amelia. "I am certain of it!"

At last Sebastian drew his arms from about her. "Stay here."

"No, I'm coming with you."

He should have argued with her. He should have insisted that she remain where she was, in the relative safety of the garden, while he investigated what he deeply suspected to be the works of a burglar. Instead he found, almost before he knew it, that Amelia was following close behind him as he made his way through the quiet dark of the house. As he climbed the stair to the second floor, she slipped her small hand in his. Instinctively, he tightened his fingers over hers.

"Which chamber is yours?" he asked in a hushed tone.

She led the way down the dark corridor and paused beside a heavy oak door. "Do be careful," she whispered as he turned the knob.

The old door swung noiselessly back on its hinges and Sebastian peered into the blackness that was Amelia's bed-chamber. Amelia made a move to step around him into the room, and he shoved her back with one hand.

It took only a moment or two for his eyes to adjust to the darkness. The moon cast a pale shaft of light through the window, enough light for him to make out the outline of a bed, a wardrobe against the far wall, and a dressing table and mirror.

He crossed the threshold and knew, before he even felt her clutch at his arm, that Amelia was following less than a step behind him. She grabbed hold of his sleeve and held on, determined to stay with him, determined to miss nothing. She matched him step for step, her body pressed against his back. Together, they advanced into the room.

A movement along the far wall, so faint that it might have been nothing but his imagination, made Sebastian stiffen slightly. He drew his arm back to shield Amelia where she stood behind him and he felt her tighten her hold on his sleeve.

"There's a lamp on the table by the bed," she hissed, trying to be helpful.

Sebastian struck the lamp and held it aloft, sending an arc of light across the room. He fully expected to discover a thief cowering in a corner or, at the very least, a recalcitrant servant bent on pilfering some of Amelia's trinkets or jewelry. He found, instead, nothing.

No other person was present in the room. Only Amelia's kitten purred contentedly at them from its place on top of the bedcovers.

Amelia stepped out from behind Sebastian and surveyed the dimly lit chamber. "There's no one here but us."

"Whoever was in this room must have been frightened off by all the noise he made."

"But there's nothing amiss in the room," she said as she examined her orderly possessions in the faint light. "No chairs have been overturned or vases shattered. Where is the damage an intruder would have caused?"

"It's possible you were mistaken when you thought the noise you heard came from this room. There are other rooms that face out over the garden, aren't there?"

She shook her head slightly, and even in the pale light of the candle, her chestnut curls danced with color. "There was no mistake. The noise we heard came from my bedchamber, I am certain of it."

He set the candle down on a table and drew his hand through his hair. "There must be some other explanation, some other logical reason behind what we heard tonight."

She cocked her head to one side. "Must everything be logical?"

"Yes," he said without hesitation.

She gave a light laugh. "Then I daresay you don't wish to hear my opinion on the matter!"

"You mistake. If you have any information or theories that might help sort through this situation, I, for one, should like to hear them."

"You shall not think my notions at all logical."

He smiled slightly. "I consider myself forewarned!"

"Very well." She sat down on the edge of the bed and her kitten immediately availed itself of her lap. Amelia ab-

sently stroked its soft fur and the animal purred contentedly. "I think the noise we heard when we were down in
the garden is the very same crashing sound that has awakened me every night this week since my aunt and I moved
into their house."

Her words took him a bit by surprise—not because he
found her statement to be preposterous, but because her
words made perfect sense. She was right; there *had* been
a similarity between the noise they'd heard from the garden and the noise he had come to both expect and dread
every evening. Had he not been so distracted by a pair of
brown eyes and a cloud of chestnut hair, he might have
realized that fact for himself.

After a moment she asked, "What do you think?"

"I'm ashamed to say I didn't think of that myself," he
answered simply, "for now that you have mentioned it, I
do recognize the similarity. The noise we heard in the garden is very much like the noise that comes through my
wall at night."

"You cannot know how relieved I am to hear you say
so! I was beginning to think myself a Bedlamite for believing in ghosts and things that go bump in the night!"

One of his dark brows shot up. "Ghosts? I assure you,
Miss Merriweather, no mention has been made of ghosts
or goblins or any other such nonsense!"

"It's not nonsense," she defended. "And if a ghost is
not to blame for the strange things that have occurred,
what is, pray?"

"I may not have an answer to your question, but I certainly know there are no ghosts involved. As a matter of
logic, Miss Merriweather, spirits and specters cannot exist."

"Is that so?" There was something about the self-assured
way he spoke that set her back up. She leaned across the
bed and thumped on the wall behind the headboard. "The
noises I hear every night come from the other side of this
wall."

Sebastian's glance swept the room again. He had the

impression that the layout of the Merriweather house was the mirror image of his own home, and if that were the case, the only thing on the other side of that wall was his own bedchamber.

"That's impossible," he said. "I assure you I am not responsible for the noises you hear at night."

"But that is exactly my point, for I am not responsible for those horrid sounds either. Where, then, are they coming from?"

Again he ran his hand through his hair in a rather exasperated fashion. He wasn't at all used to working puzzles he couldn't solve and Amelia Merriweather's enthusiastic, if absurd explanations weren't helping matters. "I think we might come up with a reasonable answer," he said, "but not now. Not tonight. The hour is late and I daresay you wish for your bed."

No sooner did the words leave his mouth than he was supremely conscious of their situation. His eyes scanned the bed—the very same bed that she had obviously been sleeping in before she had rushed down to the garden. The very same bed that served as an acute, if rumpled reminder that he was quite alone in a bedchamber with a most attractive young lady.

He thrust his hands into the pockets of his dressing gown. "I think we would be best served to discuss this matter tomorrow," he said, feeling like an uncomfortable schoolboy for the first time in a long time.

Amelia noticed the change in him. His gaze no longer lingered over her, but faltered, then shifted away. She had seen the way his eyes had traveled down the length of her bed, and in an instant, she was just as uncomfortable as he. A hot flush crept over her, caused not by embarrassment, but by a sudden awareness.

She set her kitten aside and got up from the bed. "I'll go down with you," she said, and she claimed the candlestick on her way to the door.

He didn't follow her, but remained for a moment in the

middle of the room, as if he weren't sure it was safe to move. "There's no need, Miss Merriweather."

"Amelia," she said, pausing and turning to look up at him.

He frowned, not at all certain of her meaning.

"Please call me Amelia," she said, removing any doubt. It seemed like a simple request, to her way of thinking. After all, if she were going to have a gentleman in her bedroom in the middle of the night, it seemed a matter of good form to at least be on a first-name basis with the man.

In the dim light of the candle, she saw Sebastian's stern expression soften a little. Certainly, his tone was much more gentle as he said, "Very well, Amelia. But you stay here. I shall find my way out."

He reached out to take the candle from her. His fingers brushed hers and she felt an odd quiver of feeling snake through her.

"Good night, Amelia," he said, and slowly, he left her bedchamber, closing the door behind him.

THREE

The next morning Sebastian entered the small family dining room at the back of the house to find Ella and Mary there before him.

Mary paused in her consumption of a slice of toast to greet him with a bright smile. "Good morning, Uncle 'Bastian," she said through butter-coated lips.

He gave one of her curls a light pull. "Good morning, Mary. And which of my animals have you selected to practice your mothering skills upon today?"

"Oh, I should like to have a new pet, so I've put out traps in the garden to catch a bird," she said with a note of excitement to her voice. "In the tree yesterday I saw a bird with a white tuft right here,"—she pointed to her breastbone—"and it sang ever so sweetly. Mama said if I catch him, I may keep him."

"And since she has baited her trap with bits of lace and a bowl of her morning porridge, I don't think we shall have to worry about an addition to the family anytime soon," said Ella with a wink at her brother.

She poured out a cup of coffee and passed it to him. "You had a late evening," she remarked conversationally. "It must have been well past midnight this morning when I heard you walk past my room."

"It was indeed late, but I wasn't out reveling and raising deviltry, if that is your meaning."

"I never thought so for a moment!" she replied

promptly. "After all, it's not as if you spend your evenings as other young men do."

His eyes flew to hers, his attention arrested. "What do you mean?"

"Mean?" she repeated, a little bewildered. "Why, nothing, I assure you!"

"Ella, do you think I am dull?"

She let out a small choking sound of surprise. "Not at all!"

"Stuffy?"

"Sebastian! Whatever are you talking about?"

"Nothing, except I was merely wondering if you think I'm less than exciting for a man of my age."

"Other men of your age haven't had to go through what you've endured these past years. But tell me, what has caused you to ask such questions?"

"No reason in particular," he said quite casually.

He hoped that he had heard the last of that subject, but after a moment, his sister asked in a voice of deep suspicion, "Just what *were* you doing in the middle of last night, pray?"

"As it happened, I was assisting my neighbor."

Since Ella knew it had long been her brother's notion that a good neighbor was an absent neighbor, this remark piqued her interest. "Indeed? Tell me, how much possible assistance could your neighbor require at one o'clock in the morning?"

He hesitated. His sister's curiosity was boundless and that, coupled with an arsenal of well-intentioned but meddling ways, caused Sebastian to hedge his answer. "She— that is, I—*we* thought we heard an unusual noise coming through an upper window, which was a cause of no small concern to my neighbor. I merely lent my assistance in the investigation," he finished, wishing he were a much better liar.

"Did you?" She regarded him in silent interest. "Tell me what you discovered. A burglar perhaps?"

"No."

"A naughty servant who had learned the hiding place for the key to the wine cellar?"

"No."

"Then what, may I ask, made enough noise to cause such concern?"

"I don't know. Perhaps it was a ghost."

Startled, Ella's eyes flew to his. "Sebastian, you cannot be serious!"

He laughed then, something his sister hadn't seen him do in some time. "To tell you the truth, I don't know if I'm serious or not. But my neighbor is most serious and remains heartily convinced that the town house next door is haunted."

Mary's blue eyes widened. "Will the ghosts come to this house, Mama?"

"No, dear," said Ella firmly, "for there is no such thing as ghosts and it is most cruel of your Uncle 'Bastian to tease you so. You mustn't pay the least heed to what he says. Are you finished with your breakfast? Good, then run along now. Perhaps you might look to see if you have caught a bird in the splendid trap you set in the garden."

Mary hopped down from her chair, and no sooner did the door close upon her than Ella turned to stare at her brother.

"When, pray, did you develop a belief in ghosts and noises in the night?"

"I haven't, I assure you."

"But you just said—"

"I said my *neighbor* believes a ghost caused the commotion we investigated last night. I said nothing that would indicate I shared that belief."

"Thank goodness for that!" she said with some relief. "You have always been the only truly sane and sensible member of this family and I should hate to see you change now! I suppose you gave your neighbor one of your crushing set downs for having uttered such nonsense."

He sipped at his coffee. "It isn't nonsense to her," he said quietly.

Ella did her best to keep her countenance, for she realized that in that simple sentence, her brother had betrayed very much more than he had intended.

So Sebastian's neighbor was a female, was she? A female, Ella judged, of marriageable age and a certain amount of physical attraction, else Sebastian, an intelligent man and hardened bachelor, wouldn't have been quite so tolerant of her espousing a subject upon which he had often heaped a good deal of derision. Ghosts, indeed!

She was suddenly filled with a strong desire to make the acquaintance of the young lady responsible for causing her ever rational brother to speak with perfect gravity of ghosts and noises in the night.

Looking across the breakfast table at him, she was careful not to show any curiosity, but said simply, "Perhaps during my visit I shall have the opportunity to meet your neighbor." She waited, hoping he would offer to make the necessary introductions. She waited in vain.

"Perhaps."

She tried again. "I must confess, I am most curious to make the acquaintance of anyone who can speak to you of ghosts and spirits and exit the conversation unscathed."

He cocked one dark brow her direction. "You make me sound intolerant, Ella."

"Just logical in the extreme," she answered, smiling brightly at him.

She left the breakfast table soon afterward, and he did not see her again that morning. He went about his daily routine, but found he had no interest in the matters with which he usually dealt. Instead of concentrating on the business before him, he found that his attention kept wandering back to Miss Amelia Merriweather's beguiling pair of brown eyes.

He wasn't sure what to believe where she was concerned. The well-developed skeptical side of his temperament told him that she was playing some kind of deep game, that she was making those ungodly sounds at night, then denying any knowledge of them, for what purpose he could not guess.

Yet he was also possessed of some small ability to trust; and in that trusting mind-set, he could almost convince himself that Amelia Merriweather truly did believe in ghosts and spirits and phantoms of the night. She probably also believed in forest elves and gothic romances, but that didn't necessarily mean that such things were real and true.

What Amelia Merriweather needed was a good dose of reality—a good lesson in the true way of the world. Then she'd abandon her ridiculous notions and flights of fancy. Then she'd have to learn to deal with the reality of a rather cruel world, just as he had learned to do years ago. Then she'd be as sensible and logical as he was.

But then he'd have to watch the light go out of those perfect brown eyes of hers and that fate, he realized, was one he simply did not want to consider.

Ella arrived at the Merriweather doorstep with a single purpose in mind: to discover what manner of woman could cause her sane, sensible brother to forget himself so completely as to utter—with perfect sincerity—references to ghosts and haunted houses. Such behavior was most unlike Sebastian and she was determined to root out the cause of it.

If her brother was to learn of her meddling, she knew he would be vexed in the extreme, but she gave more weight to satisfying her curiosity than to suffering Sebastian's temper.

She anticipated that her brother's neighbor must be an exceptional woman. It had, after all, been some years since Sebastian had last allowed himself to be smitten by a female, and that episode had ended so disastrously that she had begun to doubt he would ever allow himself to feel affection for a woman again. Only she knew how extraordinary it was for her brother to trust his heart once again to a woman.

Curiosity drove her to discover if the woman next door was deserving of such an honor.

Sisterly instinct drove her to hope this woman would prove to be kinder with his affections than the last one had been.

Her name was announced and she was conducted into a stylishly appointed drawing room. Mrs. Ginevra Merriweather greeted her quite warmly and in the first few minutes of conversation, confirmed that she was, indeed, the new occupant of the house.

As her hostess busied herself with the ordering of refreshments, Ella felt her heart sink. Mrs. Merriweather seemed a very pleasant sort of woman, possessed of a kind disposition and a gentleness of spirit, but if Ella were any judge, the woman was also on the shady side of forty. Her figure was plump, the corners of her eyes sported the fine lines of a woman past her prime, and beneath her cap Ella saw the suspicion of graying hairs. Even worse, a wedding ring adorned the woman's finger. What, Ella wondered, could Sebastian possibly be thinking to take up with such a woman?

They exchanged simple pleasantries, and after a few moments of conversation, Ella was fully convinced that Sebastian could not possibly have anything in common with Mrs. Merriweather. Certainly, she could not match Sebastian in mind; her education was limited, and her understanding was far from keen. Ella was beginning to feel quite discouraged, indeed, when the door opened and a servant entered the room, bearing a laden tea tray.

A moment later, a young lady entered, followed by a kitten, which mewed softly and clung close to her skirts. She paused a moment to instruct the servant in laying out the refreshments, but abandoned that task when Mrs. Merriweather extended her hand toward her, saying, "Ah, Amelia. Do leave all that and come here. I should like to introduce you to our neighbor. Amelia is my husband's niece, you see, and she is staying with me until my husband returns."

Ella's spirits brightened. In Amelia she saw a very pretty girl, possessed of a natural manner that was quite pleasing. She watched as Amelia dipped an elegant little curtsy. In her brown eyes, Ella detected a hint of friendly candor. In all, she thought the girl was charming.

She said, "Miss Merriweather, I cannot tell you how pleased I am to make your acquaintance. I was just telling your aunt that since my husband's passing, I have made it my habit to visit my brother two times a year. He tolerates my intruding upon his bachelor existence very well!"

Amelia sat down upon a small settee and her kitten claimed the cushion beside her. "I cannot believe he would think so where his own sister is concerned!" she said. "As for his neighbors— Well! I have met him three times before, and—forgive me!—each time he has been alternately courteous, imperious, and far from kind!"

Ella's dark brows flew up. "You don't think my brother is kind?"

"I am certain he is kind to those for whom he holds an affection," Amelia answered quickly.

"But he holds no affection for you—is that it? I am sorry to hear you say so, for I think oftentimes Sebastian gives a wrong impression. I hope you will give him another chance. He is truly not as some people think: stuffy and rather cold of heart."

Amelia regarded her a thoughtful moment, then said quite candidly, "Shall I confess to you? I was one of those people. When I first saw your brother staring up at me between the tree branches, he was rather forbidding and not the least friendly. But then I detected a certain—how shall I say it exactly?—a certain gentleness about him that was quite appealing. And he was very gallant when he helped me climb down from the tree."

These innocent words held the power to send Ella's mind reeling. What kind of a meeting had taken place between them that would compel Amelia to climb a tree, she could not imagine; what possessed her ever rational brother to do the same was something her dazed mind dared not contemplate.

Before she had the opportunity to voice any of the many questions that plagued her, the door opened and Sebastian's name was announced. He entered the room. A startled silence fell upon the ladies, which was broken when Amelia went to him, her hand extended, saying, "Lord Byefield! I am glad you have called. You see we are already entertaining your sister!"

He took Amelia's hand in his and smiled at her, a fact that caused Ella to stare. There was, indeed, a gentleness in his eyes as he looked down upon Amelia—a gentleness Ella had not seen in some time.

Sebastian looked up then and caused a guilty flush to rise in Ella's cheek. "Ella! You've had a busy morning," he said, but in such a genial tone that she had to believe he was not entirely vexed with her for what he would undoubtedly look upon as interference in his life. He held a chair for Amelia, then seated himself close beside her.

Ella cast him a quizzing look. "I hope you will do me the courtesy of not scolding me in front of your neighbors, Sebastian."

"Never in front of the neighbors, Ella," he said with a shadow of a smile. He directed his attention to Mrs. Merriweather, saying, "Ma'am, I shall not stay long. I merely came to satisfy myself that you and your niece were well and not suffering from the strange goings-on that have plagued this house."

"And your house, too, I understand," said Mrs. Merriweather sympathetically. "Amelia has told me everything, you know. Such a mystery! I dare not think what may be causing such an uncomfortable situation."

Ella shifted her gaze toward Amelia, saying, "I know all about those horrid noises, for they have fired my brother's temper every night for the past week. I understand you have a rather interesting theory about it, my dear."

Amelia laughed slightly and said, as she poured out a

cup of tea and passed it to her aunt, "It is not interesting to your brother, I assure you!"

"You mustn't pay any heed to Sebastian. He left his imagination by the wayside years ago. Tell me!"

"Very well." Amelia passed a cup of tea to Sebastian at the same time she cast him a defiant look. Then she said, "I think it would be ever so interesting, and much more exciting, if our troubles were caused by a ghost!"

Mrs. Merriweather looked at her in some alarm. "My dear, you cannot mean such a thing!"

"But, Aunt, there is no other explanation. Even Lord Byefield—who, I am certain, is a very intelligent and learned man—can offer no other account for such strange goings-on."

"Not yet, at any rate," said Sebastian. "But merely because a logical answer is not readily apparent does not mean that a nonsensical answer is acceptable."

"I think I like your notion better, my dear," pronounced Ella, "and you mustn't pay my brother the least heed."

"I cannot disregard Lord Byefield's ideas entirely," Amelia said with a nod to that gentleman, "for my head tells me he must be correct. But at the same time, I have a feeling—a premonition of sorts—about this whole affair that I simply cannot ignore."

"Womanly intuition," pronounced Ella, "is rarely wrong."

"I was thinking that we might discover something of importance if we spoke with previous residents of the house," suggested Amelia, and she was immediately rewarded with Sebastian's quick look of approval.

"An excellent notion," he said. "There must be some way to question others who have lived here and discover if they, too, heard the same strange noises we have."

Ella's smooth brow furrowed in thought. "Now that I think on it, I recall that this house was once owned by Lord and Lady Talboy."

Mrs. Merriweather nodded. "I recognize the name. They reside in Gloucester now, do they not?"

Ella shook her head slightly. "That would be the grandson and his wife. No, I am speaking of Lord and Lady Talboy of perhaps thirty years ago. They were deeply in love and remained inseparable throughout their many years of marriage."

"Isn't it refreshing to hear of such devotion in this day and age!" remarked Mrs. Merriweather, swirling her spoon in her teacup. "It sounds almost like a fairy tale."

"Except that this fairy tale did not have a happy ending, I fear. Lord Talboy passed on, you see, and after her husband's death, poor Lady Katherine Talboy continued to live here, in this town house, cherishing her husband's memory. I'm told it was her dying wish that no unmarried woman should ever be allowed to live in the same house where she enjoyed so many years of wedded bliss."

"What a charming story!" exclaimed Amelia.

"Charming perhaps," said Ella as she leaned over to cover one of Amelia's hands with her own, "but were you truly listening, my dear? You are, after all, a single woman."

Amelia suddenly knew herself to be the center of attention. Every eye was fixed upon her and she gave a short, nervous laugh. "You cannot mean it! Are you telling me this house is cursed? Are you saying I cannot live here because I am an unmarried woman?"

"So it would seem," said Ella quietly.

"What utter rubbish!" injected Sebastian. "Amelia, I beg you will not listen to my sister. She is a romantic in the extreme, and this particular story is tailor-made to her liking."

"Indeed?" asked Ella with feigned imperiousness. "Then explain how it happens that only married women have occupied this house ever since Lady Katherine Talboy's passing?"

"Ella, you're talking nonsense!" said her brother in some disgust. "You are trying to turn coincidence into design!"

"Am I? Then how do you explain those nightly noises? You never complained of them until Amelia moved into this house."

"I cannot explain them other than to say that there must be some sensible explanation. It might be creaking floorboards or a piece of furniture the Merriweathers possess that somehow causes the noises to occur."

"Tell me, Mrs. Merriweather," appealed Ella, "do *you* think the nightly noises could be caused by a wardrobe or a floorboard?"

Mrs. Merriweather blushed slightly and averted her gaze. "I cannot say, for, you see, *I* have never heard the noises." She saw that both Amelia and Sebastian were regarding her incredulously, and she said quickly, "It's true! Never once have I been awakened in the night! In fact, I must confess that I have slept quite peacefully since the day we arrived in this house. So you see, I fear I can be no help to you at all."

"Aunt, you've never breathed a word of this to me before!" exclaimed Amelia.

"I simply didn't wish to upset you, my dear. Oftentimes you have been so distraught and so adamant that no one could possibly sleep through such a din, I couldn't quite bring myself to confess that I slept most soundly."

"Well, if this isn't a curl," breathed Amelia, thoroughly bemused.

Ella made a slight sound in her throat. "As long as Mrs. Merriweather has confessed, perhaps I should, too."

"Don't tell me," said Sebastian in awful calm, "that you've never heard the noises either."

"I haven't, but I merely assumed it was because my bedchamber is on the opposite side of the house."

"Are you telling me the truth?"

Her fingers traced a crossing pattern over her heart. "Upon my honor." She gave him a moment to digest this bit of information, then said, "You realize what this means? It means that the only two people who have heard the noises at night are the only two people who are unmarried. That, in my opinion, is more than mere coincidence, brother!"

"But what would cause such sounds?" asked Amelia,

thoroughly intrigued. "I refuse to believe they can be caused by furniture positioned incorrectly in a room."

"The sounds are caused by Lady Talboy," said Ella firmly.

Sebastian set his teacup clattering down upon the table. "Ella, I refuse to listen to such utter rot. Next you shall be telling us that this Talboy woman is haunting the place and is no doubt right here among us even as we speak!"

"And why not?" countered his sister.

Amelia's brown eyes widened with excitement. "Perhaps that is the answer. I recall reading once that spirits often communicate with the living through the bodies of people or objects that are familiar to us."

"And in what authoritative text did you read that, Amelia? In a gothic romance published by the Minerva Press!"

Ella cast him a look of reproach. "Now, Sebastian, don't scoff. Only think for a moment of the significance of what Miss Merriweather has said!"

There was silence in the room for a short time; then Mrs. Merriweather asked in a rather small voice, "I believe you said earlier that Lady Talboy's given name was Katherine, did you not?"

Ella nodded. "I did indeed."

"I see. She hesitated a moment. Then, with a great deal of reluctance, she said, "Isn't Kitty a typical nickname for Katherine?"

Another moment of silence ensued. Then four pairs of eyes turned toward Amelia's kitten, nestled comfortably on the settee cushion.

Amelia was the first to find her voice. "Goodness! You don't suppose it could be true?" she breathed, her eyes sparking with excitement.

"Amelia, don't listen to them," said Sebastian severely. "You might do better to believe in the man in the moon than to believe the ghost of an old woman has taken up residence in your cat!"

"But it makes perfect sense," she said, giving the matter

no small amount of thought. "What an extraordinary thing to have a kitten possessed by a matchmaking spirit!" She scooped the kitten up in her arms. It nuzzled affectionately against her chin and touched one soft white paw to her cheek.

"It's preposterous, is what it is," Sebastian insisted, and he watched Amelia as she cooed words of endearment at the kitten.

She looked up at him and smiled slightly. "Perhaps not of so preposterous, for now that I think of it, I recall that Jelly has been present at every encounter between us."

Her words struck him with a ring of truth although he remained unwilling to admit it. He shook his head slightly. "I do not think you can be right."

"But I am. Only think of it. Jelly was there when you and I first met. In fact, I recall that you were following her when you found me in your tree. And Jelly has been present on every other occasion you and I have been together. Remember? When we searched the room above the entry hall, the only thing we found was Jelly."

"Yes, that's true, but . . ."

"And when we chased that horrid sound in my bed-chamber, we discovered only Jelly there."

Words failed him, for how could he argue with something so preposterous? Yet, now that he considered it, Amelia's kitten had indeed somehow figured in every episode in which he had found himself alone with Amelia; and on more than one occasion, the blasted animal had somehow contrived to place Amelia in his arms. He fought against the notion. After all, just because such coincidences couldn't be explained with logic didn't mean they had to be explained with foolishness.

He wasn't quite sure how he was going to do it, but he had to somehow convince her that she was uttering impossibilities. "Amelia—" he began, only to have her interrupt.

Still holding the kitten, she leaned over and placed her hand over Ella's fingers and asked with enthusiasm, "Do you think, ma'am, there might be something here in the house that could tell us a little about Lady Talboy? Some trinkets that belonged to her perhaps or maybe a small likeness?"

"I don't know, my dear. But I think it would be very well worth the search."

Amelia was on her feet in an instant. "I could not agree more! Sir, if you will accompany me on my search, I daresay we shall discover some item that shall convince you at long last there is something quite supernatural occurring in this house!"

Common sense told him to refuse. Instead, he found himself saying, "Very well! I shall come with you, but only so I shall be present when you discover nothing at all untoward!"

She laughed, quite unperturbed by his challenging tone. With Jelly in her arms, she led the way into the front hall. Then she asked, "Where, I wonder, would be the best place to begin our search?"

"The portrait gallery in this house was once very fine. If you're wishing to see what a ghost looks like, I suggest you look there for a portrait."

His words were curt, his tone, sarcastic, and he immediately regretted speaking to her in such a manner.

But Amelia was not the least bit offended. Instead, she smiled up at him, adjusted her hold on the kitten, and led the way up the stairs to the portrait gallery.

Sebastian opened the door and ushered her inside. The walls of the long room were adorned with a myriad of portraits of various shapes and sizes.

"Wonderful!" she exclaimed. "Only see how many portraits were left behind by previous owners of this house. I am certain there must be an old likeness of Lady Katherine Talboy here somewhere." She set her kitten down on its feet and gazed with wonder at the framed portraits up on the wall.

Sebastian closed the door and watched with appreciation as Amelia began a slow progress down the gallery. It was the first time he had seen her in a gown, and he had to admit that, much as he liked seeing her in breeches and top boots, he enjoyed even more seeing her in wispy skirts of muslin and lace. Her movements were graceful and not the least bit self-conscious, and the low neckline of her gown afforded him a clear view of the elegant curve of her neck.

Had she not recalled his attention and beckoned him to join her, he might have stood there gazing at her from the doorway for the rest of the afternoon.

"Do come and see what I have found!" she called to him from halfway down the gallery.

She was examining a portrait of an elderly woman, and when he reached her side, she said eagerly, "There! Do you see the similarity?"

"Mm-hmm." Since he was much more interested in guessing how it would feel to tangle his fingers in her rich chestnut curls, he paid little heed to the portrait.

"Look again," she urged him. "I am certain there is a likeness."

At last he looked up and gazed upon the portrait of an elderly woman of obvious noble birth. From her manner of dress, he would have guessed that the portrait had been done many years before. The woman's hair was dressed high upon her head, and it was the color of freshly fallen snow. Her face was kindly, and it bore the fine lines of age. Her blue eyes mirrored the color of the richly woven gown she wore. Her nose was pert, and beneath it, her pink bow lips were closed and poised in the merest of smiles.

Amelia looked up at him, her brown eyes alight. "Do you see the similarity?"

"Similarity to what?" he asked, quite unsure where Amelia was leading him.

"The white hair, the blue eyes—you must see the woman in this portrait looks exactly like my kitten."

One of Sebastian's dark brows shot up in skeptical warning. "Amelia, don't start *that* business again. . . ."

"There can be no other explanation for all the strange

goings-on," she said in a perfectly sensible tone. "Don't you believe in spirits?"

"No, I do not," he said most emphatically. "Nor do I believe in ghosts inhabiting the bodies of kittens or in domesticated pets that can hatch matchmaking schemes!"

"You cannot mean that!" she said with a slight laugh. "This is, after all, England. The countryside is bloated with ghosts. They leak out of every country estate from here to the sea."

"You are confusing folklore with fact," he said with considerable patience.

"What about Westminster Abbey? It is a known fact that the Abbey is home to several royal ghosts."

He cocked one brow. "And where did you come by such a fact?"

"I read it in a guidebook I purchased when I first arrived in London."

He almost choked. In the end, he demanded in a rather exasperated fashion, "Amelia, you cannot possibly be that naive!"

A spark of resentment fanned to life within her. "I'm not naive," she protested, but it was it was a weak protest at best.

"Yes, you are, and deplorably credulous, as well. Tell me, do you make it a habit to believe every bit of nonsense put before you? Or do you merely believe everything you read in the pages of a *Traveler's Guide?*"

Resentment flamed. Looking up at him, she saw that his gray eyes were gleaming with mockery and no small amount of irritation. Goaded, she retorted, "Perhaps I am naive, but I would much prefer to be thought a gullible girl than to be thought a practical man lacking in any imagination whatsoever!"

"Upon my word—" he began angrily, but his words halted when he saw her tilt her chin up, as one who intended to take a blow with courage. The gesture disarmed him somewhat and he said, in a much more even tone than he had thought possible, "I think you do me an injustice, Amelia."

"Maybe I do, but you"—her gaze fell away—"you laughed at me." When next she looked up at him, she saw that he was regarding her with an oddly penetrating look.

He said abruptly, "It was wrong to do so. Forgive me."

"No, no, it is I who should apologize to you," she said, feeling suddenly penitent. "I should never have spoken so and I—I'm sorry!"

Those brown eyes of hers were his undoing. In their depths he saw sincerity and softness, and he realized it had been a long time since last he had seen such tenderness in a woman's eyes. Some dormant instinct to protect came to the fore and he said in a gentle tone, "Shall we cry truce, Amelia? Shall we agree that in this instance, at least, we shall forever disagree?"

She hadn't realized she had been holding her breath, but at this request, she gave a sigh of relief. "Yes, let's do. Besides, I don't think I could stay angry with you for any great length of time."

She saw that odd expression had once again crept into his eyes, but it lingered only an instant and was replaced by a smile. It was the first time she had seen a smile on his lips, and she found herself wholly enchanted.

"I think we have a new understanding of each other," he said in a deep and gentle voice.

Certainly, Amelia had a new understanding of her neighbor. And when he placed his hand upon her elbow, she had the sudden feeling of having suffered a small electric shock.

"I think it's time I escorted you back to your aunt," he said as he drew her toward the door.

He gave a tug at the knob, but the door didn't budge. Although he turned the knob again and pulled, the door still wouldn't open.

"I don't understand it. A few minutes ago this door opened without so much as a whimper."

"Perhaps it's locked," offered Amelia.

"There's no key. In fact, there's no locking mechanism at all."

"That's curious. Why, then, won't the door open?"

Sebastian rattled the knob again, and when it again failed to open the door, he muttered a curse.

Amelia turned toward her kitten, which had hopped upon the fireplace mantel and was regarding them through half-closed eyes. "Jelly, are you responsible for this?"

Sebastian cast Amelia a look of exasperation. "For God's sake, don't start talking to that cat as if it could understand you!"

She cast him a quizzing look. "We called a truce, remember?"

He controlled his temper with an effort. "You're right. Forgive me. But I hate to hear such a lovely girl as you speaking such nonsense."

She cocked her head to one side. "Why are you so very reluctant to see the truth? Every bit of information we have learned so far has pointed to Jelly."

"Amelia, there are no facts, no information. The only thing you have is coincidence!"

"There are men in prison who have been convicted of crimes based on fewer coincidences than we have seen in this house."

He ran his hand through his hair in a gesture of exasperation. Was it his imagination, or was she starting to make sense? He decided to try again. "Amelia, don't you see? It's nonsensical to believe that the spirit of a dead woman could suddenly reside in a kitten. You didn't think your cat was possessed before you moved into this house, did you?"

"But Jelly wasn't my cat before," she said quietly. "Jelly was here in the house when my aunt and I moved in. I merely assumed the poor little thing had been abandoned by the previous tenants and I adopted it as my own. The kitten came with the house, sir."

He stared at her. No more arguments came to mind; no

admonishments passed through his lips. He could only look at her sweet face and wonder how on earth a slip of a girl could so shake him from his usually sensible course. When, he wondered, had her arguments become more logical than his? At what point had her nonsense turned to reasonableness?

"Amelia, are you certain?"

"Of course!" she answered promptly and with the slightest of smiles. As Sebastian digested this bit of intelligence, Amelia dragged a chair over against the wall, right beneath the portrait of the white-haired lady.

Sebastian watched her climb up on the chair and frowned. "What are you doing?"

"I'm taking the portrait down. I want to show it to your sister and Aunt Ginevra."

"Are you sure you should? That chair is looking a bit wobbly. Allow me to ring for a servant to do that for you, Amelia."

She flashed him a quick smile. "The door is stuck, remember? A servant won't be able to get in."

He was about to remind her that a stuck door also meant that she couldn't get out with the portrait, but the words died away as he watched her struggle to pull the portrait from the wall. She wiggled the frame but succeeded more in sending her skirts to swaying than dislodging the portrait from the wall.

The movement of her swinging skirts proved distracting and more than a little beguiling. Sebastian could see the faint silhouette of her legs through the thin material of her gown, and as she reached up to grasp the edges of the frame, her skirts rose slightly, enough to allow him a teasing glimpse of a very nicely turned ankle.

He gave another halfhearted pull at the door. It didn't open. This time, instead of cursing the door, he leaned against it, quite at his ease, and thrust his hands in his pockets, content to merely enjoy the view of Amelia on the chair.

She felt his gaze upon her and felt, too, the heat of a

blush creeping over her cheeks. She stole a sideways glance at him. He didn't seem to be angry any longer. He didn't stand regarding her with a look of stunned exasperation, as if she had just sprouted a second head, as he often did whenever she said something with which he disagreed.

No, the expression she saw now on his face was one she had never seen before: watchful and measuring, almost as if he were seeing her for the first time. His constant regard left her feeling a bit unnerved, a trifle breathless.

Recklessly, Amelia tugged at the portrait with more force than she had intended. The chair wobbled perilously under her feet.

Sebastian tensed. "Amelia, let me help you," he said, striding toward her down the length of the room.

He had almost reached her when she gave another tug at the portrait. This time, her sudden, jerking movement rocked the unstable little chair from four legs onto two. She let loose her hold on the frame and flailed her hands in a vain effort to maintain her balance.

Instead, it was Sebastian who kept her from toppling over. In one swift movement, he scooped her up in his arms and held her high against his chest. His experience with her in the tree had already prepared him for the fact that she was light and easy to hold. He wasn't prepared, however, for the realization that she molded very easily in his arms, as if she were designed by some master plan to fit perfectly against him. He had to force himself to think sensibly. "Are you all right?"

She turned her large, soft eyes upon him and he thought he saw, for just the fleetest of moments, a spark of laughter in their brown depths. "I'm quite fine indeed," she said. "And you?"

He recalled what he had been thinking before Amelia had so fortuitously dropped into his arms. "Never better."

He bent down slightly and pulled his arm from beneath her knees, allowing her feet to slide to the floor. Then he adjusted his hold on her, keeping her close against him, watchful for any sign that he had overstepped, that he had assumed too much.

Amelia gave no such indication. Instead, she stood there in the circle of his arms, soft and welcoming, the merest hint of a smile touching the corners of her lips, her eyes never leaving his face.

It would have been so easy for him to kiss her then and there. It would have been easy to claim her lips and forget everything else in the world—the noises in the bedroom, his sister downstairs, even the cat on the mantel.

So beguiled was he by the prospect of holding Amelia in his arms and lowering his lips toward hers that, at first, he didn't even hear the soft mew of the kitten. He didn't pay any attention when the kitten got up and stretched languidly. But when the kitten jumped down and began to affectionately rub its body against his ankles, he did take notice.

As did Amelia. "Jelly dear, stop that!" she ordered to no avail. The kitten shifted its attention toward her leg and rubbed against her, punctuating its display of affection with a commanding mew.

"What the devil is that animal doing?" Sebastian let go his hold on Amelia long enough to reach down and shoo the kitten away. But no sooner had he taken Amelia once again in his arms than the kitten came right back and arched its back against Sebastian's leg.

"I think Jelly just wants to be petted," offered Amelia helpfully.

"Petting a cat isn't what I had in mind right now. I had rather planned to kiss you." He heard the sharp surprise of her breath, and her sweet brown eyes opened just a bit wider.

"You did? And has your plan changed?" She was entering dangerous territory by urging a man to kiss her, but she didn't care. She knew only that she wanted Sebastian to kiss her, right here and now. Perhaps he needed encouragement? She felt her kitten nudge against the backs of her legs, as if it were urging her to step even closer within the circle of Sebastian's arms.

"That kitten of yours is extremely distracting."

"Please don't pay her any heed. I think she is simply trying to tell us she approves."

Sebastian's dark brows came together. "Approves of what?"

"Our being together."

He looked at her for a long moment. His arms fell away. "Amelia, is that what you think? That the only reason I took you in my arms is because *your cat* wished it?"

The sudden change in him left Amelia a little bewildered. Only a moment ago he had been gentle and commanding; he had left her feeling breathless with nothing more than his simple touch. All of that was gone. Now he was frowning, and there was a harsh note to his voice she had never heard before.

"But you heard the stories," she said, a little bewildered. "You heard what your sister and my aunt said downstairs."

Sebastian smothered a heartfelt oath. "Amelia, when I kiss you, it will be because I want to, not because some supernatural force makes me do so. No furry matchmaker can compel me to do anything I don't wish to do."

He took a step away from her then and clasped her hand. "Come with me," he commanded, pulling Amelia inexorably toward the door as her kitten scampered after them.

"Where are we going?"

"Back downstairs."

"But the door is stuck, remember? We'll have to wait for someone to come and let us out."

He turned the doorknob. The door swung open. Sebastian caught himself before another oath of frustration escaped his lips.

Amelia stepped out into the corridor and swung about to face him. She wanted to ask what she had done that was so wrong; she wanted to ask what it would take for him to hold her in his arms again and make her feel just as she had a few moments ago.

Sebastian didn't give her the opportunity. "I think it's time you returned to your aunt, Amelia."

Even in the dim light of the paneled corridor, he could see the questions in her eyes. He could tell that she was blaming herself, wondering what she had done to make him change his mind about kissing her. He hated to see those brown eyes of hers filled with worry; he would much rather see them filled with laughter as they usually were, as they were when first he found himself attracted to her.

It was those brown eyes of hers that drew him. In Amelia's case, the poets were right: Her eyes were a mirror to her soul. And when he looked in her eyes, he saw honesty and sweetness. And when she smiled, it was like opening a door into a room filled with sunlight.

He hadn't felt so in years, for he hadn't allowed himself to get close to any woman. But he had felt a closeness to Amelia from the moment he had first discovered her sitting with absurd dignity in the branches of his tree. Since then she hadn't once strayed far from his thoughts.

But now those magnificent eyes of hers were filled with worry, uncertainty, and doubt; and he knew he was the cause of it. He reached out and gently touched his fingers against the soft blush of her cheek.

That simple gesture transformed her. She took a deep breath and smiled. When he smiled back, she knew she was forgiven. She knew he wasn't angry with her and that they could go on as before.

"Come along," he said softly. "I'll take you back." He reached behind him for the door, intending to pull it closed. His fingers brushed nothing but air.

He turned slightly, searching for the doorknob; instead he saw a flash of white as Amelia's kitten reared up on its hind legs on the other side of the door. In the next moment, the heavy oak door—the very same door that had once held them prisoners in the gallery—slammed against his back, launching him right at Amelia.

He grabbed for her and tried to soften the impact. Together they hit the opposite wall of the corridor as if they had been shot from a cannon.

"Are you all right?" asked Sebastian for the second time in less than an hour.

Amelia fought to regain her breath. Her back was mashed against the wall, her face was against Sebastian's shoulder, and she was supremely conscious of his arms again about her, holding her tightly, securely. Her mind was racing, as was her breath, and her heart was pounding in a manner that she didn't think was caused by the wall hitting against her back. "What happened?"

"I'm not certain but I think that blasted cat of yours slammed the door on us." He looked down to find Amelia regarding him with amusement.

"Jelly? Don't be silly. Jelly is only a kitten. She's much too small to ever shut a door that hard."

"Now who is being sensible and logical?" he demanded, but there was no censure in his tone. Instead, his voice was deliciously deep, almost a whisper, and she could hear it rumble up from deep within his chest.

Amelia wasn't sure what to do. Her arms were around Sebastian and she imagined she could feel, even through his coat, every muscle in his broad back. She felt his breath dance against the curls on top of her head, and a curious quiver snaked through her. "You aren't hurt, are you?" she asked and marveled over how low her own voice had become.

Sebastian's elbows had suffered the most from their impact against the wood paneling, but he rather thought he would have bruised his arms a hundred times if it meant he could hold her so. She was trapped between him and the wall, her softness pressed against him. He had only to dip his head to see that slight, tentative smile on her lips or to see her beautiful eyes looking questioningly up at him.

Then she blinked. It was that same slow cat blink that had caught his attention when they'd first met. The same blink that caused her lush dark lashes to sweep slowly across the tender rise of her cheek.

That blink was his undoing; it wore away the last of his control. Slowly, he lowered his head and kissed her.

Her lips were soft and oh so sweet beneath his. Many times in his mind he had imagined kissing her, but he'd never imagined that her lips would be so addictive. Like a fine, dark wine, she filled his senses and he drank her in.

His arms folded so tightly about Amelia she could hardly breathe, and she clung to him, tasting the flavor of tea on his breath, feeling the smooth pressure of his lips against hers.

At last he raised his head a bit. "Amelia, you know very well your cat caused none of this," he said firmly.

She couldn't speak, not with her breath coming in short bursts and her heart lodged up in her throat. She didn't care if it was her kitten or the man in the moon who finally compelled Sebastian to kiss her; she was just happy that he finally was doing so. He was waiting for her to say something but she could manage nothing more than a very contented sigh.

"And you know I kissed you only because I wanted to, not because of some supernatural force or any other crazy reason that may have popped into that beautiful head of yours."

"Yes," she sighed again, and she was immediately rewarded by Sebastian bending down to kiss her again.

The next time he raised his head, he drew his arms from around her. He grasped her shoulders and held her a little way away from him, steadying himself.

It was all Amelia could do to hold herself in check, to keep from flinging herself against his chest and holding on. A moment ago she had been lost in his touch; now he had moved ever so subtly away from her. She could still see the soft gray of his eyes as he looked down at her, but she would much rather have seen his eyes as they were a moment ago, when there had been a dark light shining in their depths that both frightened and intrigued her.

"I should take you back to your aunt," he said, wishing he were the type of man who could blithely ignore his conscience upon demand. "She's no doubt wondering what's become of us."

He would much rather have stayed there in the hall, kissing Amelia, feeling the pulse of her heart beating against him, and exploring the feel of her body against his. But that reasonable side to his personality—the sane streak that had always stood him in good stead—took over.

Without another word, he gently tucked her hand in the crook of his arm and led her back down the stairs, back down to her aunt.

FOUR

Sebastian Camerford was a practical man. He prided himself on his good judgment and he rarely made mistakes. Oh, there had been that one instance a few years back when he had pledged his heart to the wrong woman, but that mistake had been remedied soon enough when she had taken her affections, and her quest for a rich husband, and moved on. He was not the kind of man who made it a habit to spend an entire night thinking of an unconventional miss who believed in ghosts and considered her cat a supernatural matchmaker. He wasn't the sort to lie awake in his bed remembering every last nuance of a kiss or recalling how it felt to hold a woman in his arms. He was too practical for such things. Or so he thought.

He stepped out onto his terrace, into the cold morning breeze, knowing full well that a vision of Amelia Merriweather had haunted him all night. She had haunted him as thoroughly as any specter or spirit her lively imagination could have conjured.

He had hoped the bracing air would bring him back to his senses; he had hoped the crispness of the autumn wind would clear his head and allow him to think of something—anything—but Amelia Merriweather.

He was destined for disappointment. She filled his thoughts, and without so much as a whimper of protest, he gave up and allowed his memory of her to overtake him.

From the other side of the wall that separated his property from the house next door, he heard the sound of footsteps. Some sixth sense told him it was Amelia.

He opened the old wooden gate. She was there just as he knew she would be, walking slowly through the garden, a thoughtful frown marring her smooth forehead. She was dressed in a pelisse of deep red trimmed with fur, and a small bonnet with similar trim allowed him a tantalizing peek at a few of her chestnut curls.

At the sound of the gate opening, she looked up and saw Sebastian striding purposefully toward her. In a rush of feeling, she recalled the kiss they had shared, and an odd weakness seized her. "Good morning!" she managed to say with tolerable calm. "How do you fare this morning?"

"Tolerably well, considering that I had nary a wink of sleep last night."

"The noises?" she asked sympathetically.

"They've become too much of a familiar nightly ritual to keep me awake for long. No, it was thoughts of you that prevented my sleeping."

She blushed adorably. "I hope they weren't angry thoughts. I know I've tried your patience considerably with talk of spirits and ghosts. You don't believe in such things, but I do."

"I wouldn't have you believe anything else," he said simply.

Her eyes flew to his with an impish light. "I don't believe it! Can it be that sensible Lord Byefield has changed his mind about the existence of certain supernatural forces?"

"I wouldn't go so far as to say I've changed my mind. Let us merely agree that I am more receptive to the notion."

"I shall test you," she warned. "I shall tell you stories of my kitten's magical abilities and watch you for signs of skepticism."

"You won't see any, for, you see, I believe wholeheartedly in the magic of your cat."

Her eyes opened wider. "I never thought to hear you speak so!"

"Nor did I, but it's perfectly true. Whether or not your kitten is possessed of a matchmaking spirit, I have to admit it alone is responsible for bringing us together."

For a moment she thought her heart had stopped beating in her chest. "Bringing us together?" she repeated, hoping—no, praying—that she had heard right.

He took her gloved hand in his. "Amelia, would you be very much surprised if I were to confess that I am attracted to you?"

She hadn't expected him to speak so, and his question threw her a little off balance. "Are you? But how can you be? We've known each other less than a week," she said, more out of caution than out of disbelief.

"I don't know. Maybe because the last thing I expected when I embarked upon a kitten hunt in the garden was that I would find you. But then I pulled you from my tree, and from the moment your booted feet touched the ground, I haven't been the same. I'm more alive now than I have been in years."

She was having a difficult time breathing again, thanks in large part to that flicker of sparks she saw lurking in the depths of his gray eyes. "Because of me?"

He smiled slightly. "Because of you."

She felt as if she were in the middle of a wonderful dream that was too good to be true. "But you know so little about me and I know nothing about you!"

"What would you like to know?"

"Everything! Tell me anything! Tell me how the same man who conducts kitten hunts can insist upon being so practical."

"It's not an interesting story," he said dismissively.

"It is to me."

He straightened up slightly and clasped his hands behind his back. "Very well. I was very nearly married once.

Ah, you're surprised, but it's true. Some years ago I was betrothed to a young woman, a beauty of some renown. She could have had her pick of any bachelor, and she chose me.''

"Did you love her?'' Amelia hated to ask the question, but she had to know.

"I thought I did at the time. But I was young and foolish and dazzled by the prospect of starting a family of my own with a beautiful wife at my side.''

"But you didn't marry her, did you?''

"No. My father died and it happened that his affairs were not quite in the order I had thought. The fortune my family once possessed was virtually gone. And once my betrothed discovered it, she was gone, too.''

He stopped speaking. Indeed, there was no more to say. The story was over, and Amelia thought she could guess the rest of it.

"So you retreated behind a wall of logic and reason,'' she said gently. "That way, you wouldn't run the risk of being hurt again.''

His gaze fell away and settled on the colored leaves scattered along the garden path. "Something like that.''

She took a step closer to him. "I won't hurt you. I promise.''

When next he looked at her, that odd expression was back in his eyes—the same expression that had caused her to catch her breath in the portrait gallery. The same expression that now sent a tremor of exhilaration through her limbs.

"I'm falling in love with you, Amelia, and I can't seem to stop myself.''

She drew a deep breath. "In that case, I shouldn't try.''

He smiled then, a slight, almost knowing smile, and he grasped her hand to draw her to him.

"I'm not rich.''

"Nor am I.''

"And I'm practical in the extreme.''

"I wouldn't have you any other way.''

His smile increased as he looked down at her tenderly, exultantly. Then he did the only sensible thing he could think of: He kissed her.

It was an exhilarating feeling to be kissed in a garden, thought Amelia as she raised her arm to circle Sebastian's neck. The touch of his hand at the back of her waist sent a quiver of sensation through her, and she responded by drawing his dark head down, closer to her own.

When at last his lips left hers, he looked at her, his brow flying skyward. "Do you mind very much being kissed by a practical man void of any imagination?"

She blushed mightily. "How wicked I was to you! I'm surprised you ever considered *speaking* to me again, to say nothing of kissing me!"

"On the contrary. I find that when you're being kissed, it's impossible for you to talk."

"Wretch!" she said in a most loverlike fashion. "I assure you I can speak most sensibly when I am in the proper mood."

"I'd rather you weren't sensible when you are in my arms, if it's all the same to you."

"Then stop talking and kiss me again," she commanded daringly.

He was about to comply when his attention was caught by a movement in a nearby window of the house. He looked up and saw Amelia's kitten sitting on the sill, its languid gazed fixed upon the two them. "Is that blasted cat of yours watching us?"

Amelia turned her head just far enough to see. "I think she is. And I think she has a very approving look about her."

"I don't care if that animal approves or not," said Sebastian grimly. "I'm going to kiss you again."

And he did just that.

THE BLACK CAT

by

Hayley Ann Solomon

ONE

Not a glimmer of a moonbeam brightened the velvety black night as Lord Santana muttered a curse under his breath and squinted to look at the sky. The winds were wild and stormy, but the dark rider in the elegant greatcoat of Bath superfine urged his horses onward.

He did not stop to check that his carriage and outriders and footmen and grooms were in slow attendance several waterlogged miles behind him. That he took for granted. What he *did* do was spur his animals ever forward, grim determination etching faint lines across his sardonically handsome features.

"Likely get a wetting," he thought as the first telltale drops of rain brushed against buckskins. Again he cursed the necessity to be out on such an unpromising night. Just his luck that the evening should be moonless, blessed with thousands of stars but not *one* bright enough to act as a guide or luminary.

Foolhardy, he'd been called, but that was him all over. He was needed in London and nothing—certainly nothing so paltry as inclement weather and a midnight sky—would stop him from getting there.

He transferred the reins lightly from one hand to the other, for he was a notable whip and would have *scorned* to allow the constraints of a brewing storm to hinder his handling. Indeed, even now, two frisky but perfectly matched chestnut bays trotted quite steadily into deepening mist. When the twinkling stars seemed suddenly to all but vanish, the dark was even thicker than the earl had first thought.

He adjusted the collar of his greatcoat so that perfectly starched shirt points crept ever closer to his skin. For an instant, he wished he'd brought a scarf; then he thought the better of it. A scarf could be the very devil with a cravat and he was in sufficient trouble with his valet not to care for another dressing down.

The problem was his household still thought of him as a child in small clothes rather than the strapping, war-weary, worldly elegant and supremely bored young noble-man that he was. It amused him, at times, to allow their illusions to continue, for there was no doubting the kind-ness behind their regularly issued scoldings, nor the fond-ness behind their endless cosseting.

Of course, the *newer* staff looked up to him as a demigod and would never *dream* of addressing him in the terms of his butler, his valet, his nurse, and his rather plainspoken head groom, but then they had only ever seen the hand-some ape leader of the Four Horse Club, the elegant ar-biter of fashion, the select young gentleman who was at once mentor to the Prince of Wales and the headstrong champion of such noxious causes as the plight of chimney sweeps.

A flash of lightning interrupted his stray thoughts. He eased the reins ever so gently, for the animals were prone to be restive. They'd require skillful reassurance if the thunder sounded any closer. He listened, alert for the loud, heavy drumrolls that followed every dangerous flash of light. He did not have to wait long, for now that the clouds had burst, the sky was a ferment of activity, dark and haunting and illuminated in patches by sheets of light rendered slightly opaque by the mists.

He uttered a soothing, gentle gabble of words to the horses, one of which—the left—had stumbled slightly in fright. He tightened his hold to communicate control and prayed that she had not sprained a fetlock. The superfine was now saturated. Wet, wild water sprayed down the nape of his neck and trickled under his collars and cuffs. My lord did not care. For an instant, he knew a moment's pure exultation as lightning split the sky in two.

The instant passed as exultation turned to fear and urgency and a deathly, ghastly transition from sitting to standing, a loud scream at the horses, a desperate whinnying as reins wrenched and a thundering heartbeat pounded mercilessly in his ears. The world was once more plunged back into an inky black, but *this* time his lordship knew of a certainty he was not alone in the storm. He drew a cautious halt and leaped down, cursing, from his high perch.

Somewhere out there, the glistening emerald eyes of an animal had been reflected in the lightning flash. It had sprung from the branches overhead and vanished into the mists. My lord did not concern himself with such a paltry thing. This was England, after all. He was, however, perturbed and more than a trifling displeased that the animal had been closely followed by a wisp of a girl. His heart still pounding, he felt his devastating horror turn instantly to violent fury as he realised that his horses had not, as he had first feared, trampled her to death. The sketchiest glimpse he'd caught in the sudden, split light suggested that the lady had not even *thought* of his oncoming chaise as she'd chased after the animal. Even in the dark and pelting rain, she surely must have been aware of his approach. As his warmly booted feet touched the ground, he stared into the fog, hoping his eyes would adjust.

Common sense urged him to continue on his way, but unwilling chivalry coupled with serious fury forced him to remain. If there was a stranger out there in the mists, she might have need of his help or shelter or . . . a good whipping. The earl whirled around as he heard a soft chuckle behind him.

The wild beast of the great green eyes had apparently *not* vanished into the storm as he'd first imagined. Instead, he was even now being cradled. A kitten resting soulfully in creamy, sultry, *defiant* arms of satin white. The sky lit up once more and Lord Santana was dazzled by the unexpected magnificence of that which he glimpsed. Even as darkness descended yet again, the earl could tell that the young woman was as rain drenched as the cat, her mane of tousled hair loose to her waist and her gown—if such it can be called—shockingly damp. He drew in his breath, for subsequent lightning revealed his initial impression to be correct. She was more beautiful by far than even his wildest imaginings.

"You could have been killed!" The anger in his voice was unmistakable, for the very *thought* of crushing such a creature under his wheels shook him to his impeccable core.

The maiden, far from being cowed, looked directly into his eyes and laughed. Her lips were invitingly red, her throat appearing a perfect cream against the remote and unlikely backdrop. From the recesses of his consciousness, Santana became aware of the faint strumming of a lute and a Spanish guitar. The flicker of a circle of lanterns momentarily caught his attention. He turned back to the girl.

"You ought to be horsewhipped! If you have not a care for your *own* life, think, at least, upon my beasts! Even now, they are sweating from fright."

The girl looked at him impishly. "They will recover, my lord—faster, I am sad to say, than your lamentable temper!"

Santana's eyes narrowed. He was unused to being treated so cavalierly, and this by a little slip of a girl with no business being out on a cold and dangerous night. Smugglers were abroad. That was one of the reasons for his recall to London. His concern for her deepened his sense of outrage. He drew himself up to his full—and not inconsiderable—height.

"I take leave to tell you, my dear, that you have not yet *witnessed* the full splendour of my wicked temper. I have it very well in check right now and you may be thankful for that, for I assure you that your curvaceous little rear end would even now be smarting had I not."

The cat ceased licking its paws and impaled his lordship with a glare that seemed to be almost luminous in its intensity. Santana had the faintest glimpse of unsheathed claws before it relaxed back into its comfortable position and resumed its artless posture.

The woman's vexing retort transformed itself to a slight giggle as she noted the gentleman's *own* clinging shirt and magnificent torso beneath. Sad to say, she did not avert her eyes in maidenly confusion. She allowed them to rest quite provocatively upon his frame before placing her splendidly ungloved hands upon a trim, delectable waist.

"Temper, temper, my dear sir! No need to be so odiously stuffy! All is well and you may continue on your precious way. I daresay a night like this would not suit *all* of England's beaux!"

Her tone was mocking and slightly—ever so slightly—provocative. Santana cursed and did what he had sworn he would never do on English soil again: He took her in his arms and kissed her with the abandon the night deserved.

When he had done, the laughter had fled entirely from the young girl's gaze.

"I am not what you think me, my lord."

"No? What *are* you then, my little gypsy queen?"

She looked at him strangely, almost tenderly, and answered him with faraway eyes and a voice that was hardly her own.

"I, my lord, am your destiny."

Santana fought the uncomfortable hammering of his heart with a light, slightly mocking riposte.

The mists seemed to close in around them, and when he looked up, she was gone. The night was faintly disturbed by the clatter of coach wheels in the distance. His carriage and outriders and footmen and grooms, no doubt. Shrugging rather dazedly, he called out in the pouring midnight rain. There was no answer, save for the cheery voice of Patterson, his head groom.

"Child, I think you know you are different." Laura Rose cast beseeching eyes at Melinda, the only anchor she acknowledged in her carefree, will-o'-the-wisp existence. Now that Lord Henry was dead, there was nothing keeping her from returning fully to her roots—to the delicious, exotic, semimystic world of the Romanies.

"I am a gypsy, mother! Born one, bred one!"

"Born a *lady*, bred a gypsy. A strange mix, my child, but you were never one to laugh off destiny."

Melinda shrugged her expressive shoulders. Wild hair tumbled to her knees and she brushed it back crossly.

"Am I no longer to share in your existence then? Never again to dance to the moon, never to lute with abandon, never to feel soft sand under my feet and sleet in my hair?"

A tear played at the back of Laura Rose's eyes. She smiled brightly, however, and assured her daughter that becoming a lady did not necessarily mean being shielded from the elements.

"Come, Mother! You know what I mean! What about passion?"

"What *about* passion?"

Mother regarded daughter keenly. Melinda felt a soft blush suffuse her being. It was true that she had never before experienced passion as incarnate as the night before, when she had entered the half world of a lady rather than the more familiar one of a gypsy. She wondered, when she entered society, if she would ever encounter that particular gentleman again. Her heart gave a strange lurch at the thought. Her mother, keen to sense these things, pushed her point home.

"Fate, Melinda, is an uncontrollable force. It drives one and empowers one if one has the vision to allow it. I believe you *have* that vision, my dear. It is one of the gifts I have bestowed upon you—just as the gift your *father* bestowed is the legacy I now wish you to fulfill."

"You do?"

Laura Rose nodded firmly. "The marquis is a strange man but a kind one despite his bellicose way. Ignore his exterior and seek his hidden depth. Though born to the world of society, he is simpatico with the Romanies. I would not entrust you to his care if I did not feel him to be worthy."

"Worthy? He is a notorious scoundrel!"

"Look beyond you, Melinda! Always seek deeper than appearances. *You* know that! Still waters flow deep and your grandfather is as complex and as wily a man as ever there was."

"You will stay with me?"

"You know that I cannot, Melinda! Your birth is irreproachable and I fancy I have taught you to speak with the manners and intonations of a lady. But *my* presence will cast a blight on that. Go out into the world you belong to unfettered by these gypsy chains."

"They are not *chains*, mama! They are invisible strands of angel dust, and light and gossamer as—"

"Melinda!" The voice was faintly stern.

"You will visit me?"

"I will visit your grandfather. It is not fitting that I see *you.*" The words were uncompromising and the daughter opened her mouth to protest. She was silenced by a delicate wave of the hand. "Once a year, on St. Agnes's eve, I shall visit you. We will dance to the stars and sing ballads until our throats are hoarse. You shall *have* your passion, but I predict, Melinda, that you shall not need it."

"No?"

"No! You were born to passion far greater than any you shall get roaming the earth with our people."

Melinda opened her lips to argue, but something in her heart stopped her. Instead, she yielded to the murmuring of her soul and laughed instead. The sound tinkled tremulously in the air as she changed key, of a sudden, and began to sing.

That was almost a year ago and the lure of the little baggage in crimson had almost ceased to haunt Lord Santana's dreams and waking moments. If he still chose to puzzle over the incident in the odd, contemplative moment, none was more annoyed by these stray thoughts than the earl himself. He had admirably completed his little mission for the home office—and several more of the same kind in the interim—with the result that even now, a band of particularly unsavoury smugglers were awaiting trial at the assizes.

My lord sighed as his eyes flicked over yet another dinner card from Lady Darcy. He hesitated for an instant before dropping it unceremoniously into the *regrets etc.* pile. Sedgewick would see to it in the morning.

To his indignation, his services were no longer to be called upon. Some bright young sprig at the home office had decreed that his title and rank placed him a little too far above their touch. It was useless to argue that this had been of little consideration during the war, when he'd risked life and limb on a daily basis for king and country. The impossible little man in drooping shirt points and a singularly poor cravat had merely blinked, executed a *ridiculously* elaborate bow, and stubbornly refused to see reason.

Lord Guy Santana, the third Earl of Camden, scowled prodigiously. He grappled with the rebellious notion of consigning his entire correspondence into the cosy fire flickering before him, then thought better of it. Instead, he dutifully scanned the waiting heap of calling cards and gilt-edged invitations for anything vaguely of interest. He found nothing that might arouse his spirits in the slightest and dropped them *all* into the *regrets etc.* pile. Then he poured himself his fourth drink of the day. An excellent cognac, but sadly unappreciated.

"Damn that woman!" The gypsy incident was still in his blood, hovering dangerously in his thoughts. He tried not to admit that the little widgeon's *hellishly* intoxicating aura held him in its thrall, but it was useless to lie to himself. It was an undeniable fact that, since that fateful ride, my lord was bored with every female that he encountered. So irritated was he with their simpering ways, their modish blond ringlets, and their limpid blue eyes, that his temper was fast gaining the wicked reputation he'd boasted of that wet, storm-driven night.

Quite *apart* from all this was the vow he'd taken on the Peninsula. No more dabbling with womankind—he'd had more than his fill of them and they did nothing but cause expense and disillusionment on both sides despite a few moments' passion. *He*, of course, refused to be married; *they*, on the other hand, could become quite irksome in their wiles to accomplish this very thing. After several close shaves, two duels, and a great deal of bother, my lord had taken the unprecedented decision to set aside lust, avoid all lures, and generally play the monk in his dealings with the gentler sex.

His lordship now prided himself, amongst his confidants, of being the most wily of bachelors. He was awake to every suit and not above discomposing the most *pretentious* of dowagers—not to *mention* tender young things— with cold conversation and stiff, haughty manners.

Nonetheless, his wealth was so prodigious that he could not be ignored. Nor could his rank. Guy Santana continued to receive invitation after invitation, card after card. His credibility was set as impossibly high—almost legendary—when he'd arrived at Almack's in pantaloons and gained admittance. The occurrence was sufficiently unusual for the patronesses to bend their rigid dress code for such an auspicious occasion, causing the Duke of Wellington himself to scowl and remark that *he* had not been treated with such civility!

The Earl of Camden had never spent a duller evening and had resolved not to repeat his mistake in the future.

Now, as he gazed out of his thirteenth-century castle window, he saw not a thing. In truth, there was a hive of activity, for gardeners were trimming the hedges and several carriages were drawn up alongside the servants' entrance bearing—though he did not know these details—such essentials as sealing wax, flint, ice for the icehouse, and wheat from his country estate. Flour in London was close to inedible and Cook insisted on this luxury at least.

Trifles. All trifles. Life was intolerably dull. The sun just caught the gleam of his signet against long, slender fingers. They were not used to being idle and he did not like it. Two kitchenmaids looked up, caught sight of him, and giggled. My lord was intolerably handsome with his lean frame and firm, tightly clad chest. His black hair was cropped short—unfashionable, perhaps, but intoxicatingly sensuous to the silly young maidens casting sheep's eyes at him from below. He returned inside. He had ceased noticing such things.

TWO

"Camden, I insist you avenge my honour!"

"Insist, Lady Leigh?" The words were polite but the tones were insulting. Lady Lavinia Leigh contemplated throwing the half-full decanter of wine about his person, then thought better of it. There was something about Santana . . . something about the firm set of his mouth and his lithe, sinewy body that did not auger well for feminine wiles of this sort. She twirled around the room, a delicate confection of organza and pearls, and tried a different tack. Fluttering her eyelashes, she allowed a small tear to overflow from her limpid green eyes, then licked her lips tentatively.

"Please, my dear sir! You can have no *notion* how odious it is having half the *ton* turn its back on me whenever I enter a concert chamber or visit Covent Gardens or—"

"You should have thought of that *before* you consented to elope with the Marquis of Fotheringham!" My lord's tone was hard. His hand reached for the bellpull.

"No!"

"Yes, my lady! It passes comprehension why you should have chosen to grace *my* chamber with this sad tale, but believe me, I am not up to it before breakfast. And I assure you, your own credit will not stand for being caught alone in a gentleman's chamber at this—or indeed any other—hour. Go, I beg you, before it is too late and half of London sees your hackney coach drawn up outside. I would be loath to further besmirch your *already* impugned reputation!"

He glanced at the voluptuous curves that spilled artfully from the crest of the low, square-necked bodice. He was certain she'd chosen the dress with care, and that the faint shadows he could detect just beneath the thin muslin were for his benefit exclusively. The lady noted the direction of his glance and moved just a little closer. A faint smile played about her deliciously painted lips. Men found her irresistible. The earl, no doubt, would find her so, too.

"My lord, you do not understand! If you could vouchsafe for me, my credit would be *restored!* Only *you* have that power, for I am sure you are not unaware of your influence on society! Oh *do,* I beg you, spare me a thought!" She licked her lips entrancingly and his lordship thought with fleeting admiration that the lady was accomplished. Were his heart not solidly bound up elsewhere, he might have found himself tempted. As it was, he did the only gentlemanly thing he could do under such circumstances. He stifled his sardonic amusement at the lady's pitifully obvious wiles and kissed her hand.

"You will do it?"

My lord caught a genuine inflection of despair in the lady's tone. He dropped the hand and sighed. True, she deserved every bit of censure for allowing herself to be gulled by an old dotard like Fotheringham—no doubt the lure of a title and riches had been too great to resist—but still, she appeared, now, to be *genuinely* close to tears. My lord's heart softened infinitesimally, for he was not, by nature, unkind or vindictive.

He thought of the hours of boredom ahead and decided that it would possibly *not* be a bad thing to challenge Fotheringham to a duel that might restore the fallen woman's credit. If marriage was out of the question, he could at least see to it that she was housed respectably and paid a decent annuity. That, as he understood it, had always been the price of virtue among gentleman.

He nodded curtly at the woman, then bade her dry her

tears—for he could not abide watering pots—and present herself to his housekeeper for refreshment. She looked bemused, at first, fully expecting a little licentious interlude as payment for the earl's trouble. In truth, there was a slight twinge of disappointment as he rang for Sedgewick and she realised that she was not, after all, to sample his renowned—and much whispered of—caresses. Instead, she listened with half an ear as the butler was apprised briefly of the necessity of paying off the hack and otherwise accommodating the unexpected houseguest. Despite a perfunctory nod when Lord Camden shortly took his leave, the lady had the most lowering suspicion that she had just suffered two slights. She had not only been neglected, but she had actually been forgotten.

A small stop at Whitehall was enough to inform him of Fotheringham's present whereabouts. *Not* his country seat or any other of his several palatial residences. The marquis was to be found a mere fifteen miles from London, along a dirt track that was as unused as it was unfamiliar. Rumour had it that he was becoming decidedly quirky in his old age.

Only the revelation of his latest fling with the lovely Lady Leigh reassured his contemporaries that he was still sane at least. If he could deflower the famous Lavinia, he was not quite in his dotage yet! The very act that had ruined one reputation had been the saving of another. Guy smiled cynically at the irony as he urged his snowy Arabian onwards through the cold, icy wind. The trip would be invigorating for the beast, if not productive for poor, downcast Lavinia. Thank heavens, at least, the sun had chosen to show itself.

The earl was growing faintly impatient as the stallion skipped over the small pebbles. Ahead of him, there appeared to be nothing more than endless long grass interspersed with heather and clover. He fleetingly noticed the bees and the odd rabbit racing across the footpath, but his mind was more on his destination. Had the directions he'd been given been credible?

He was fast thinking himself the victim of some practical joke when faint flickers of smoke indicted the presence of a small establishment in the clearing beyond. My lord patted the Arabian before easing him expertly into a trot. By the time he'd leaped down from his saddle and walked round to the heavy oak door, he was whistling a merry—if not entirely edifying—tune under his breath. He regarded the rusting iron knocker with quizzical amusement before unrepentantly rapping loudly upon the frame.

Lord Danvers Fotheringham was within, though the woman at the door denied him. My lord pushed past the person of questionable virtue and strode into the damp, dimly lit parlour.

"Come out, Lord Danvers, for I shall have my satisfaction!"

The marquis emerged, pasty faced and wild-eyed for all his years of dissipation.

"I am an old man, Lord Santana! Leave me be!"

"As you left poor Lady Leigh? She is disgraced, you know. Though I might endeavour to save her shame, the scandal is not to be denied. I blame you. I demand revenge!"

"Demand, Lord Santana? Very high-handed of you I am sure, but also rather stupid. You must know that society will look askance at a man prepared to draw his cork with a gentleman twice his age! And whatever you may think, the delicious Lady Leigh went quite willingly, I assure you. It is *wonderful* what wealth and position can buy these days."

"You hardly look *rich* in these environs!"

"Fortunately the . . . ah . . . modest style has more to do with *convenience* than the state of my purse!" The marquis licked his lips assessingly and a cunning smile crossed his fleshy features. He was irritated with the earl's lofty attitude, but decided, for the moment, to placate him.

"If you harbour any misgivings on this subject, Santana,

you may call upon my bankers Messrs. Barton, Ridgebeck and Co. I trust they will satisfy you on that score. As for my reasons for occupying *this* particular neighbourhood and in *this* particular manner, they are entirely my own."

Lord Santana curled his lips in scorn. He'd heard rumours of the Marquis's strange association with the gypsies, but had never bothered overmuch with them. Instead, he allowed his eyes to rove over the bright, tasselled silk shawl that lay negligently across the worn, expensive sofa. For an instant, his eyes met those of the woman's and he was intrigued to find them watching him avidly, almost with an arrested interest that sent faint, highly involuntary shivers down his immaculately clad spine. Not insolent, exactly, but . . . *Bother* it! If Fotheringham wanted to bed a gypsy woman it was none of his concern. He gave the woman his back and turned again on the master.

"As if I cared one way or another! If you are as rich as they say, then we are merely evenly matched. And I repeat again—if you malign Lady Leigh I shall have my revenge."

"You show a remarkable interest in the lady. Are you sure that it is not simply a fit of *pique* that drives you?" Lord Danvers smiled and his yellowing teeth looked particularly disturbing in the half-light.

Rain dripped from Santana's greatcoat and rolled onto the floor. His eyes flashed in a manner that his friends knew to be dangerous indeed. "You are perilously close to being milled down right on your own hearth!"

"Pshaw! Talk, Lord Santana! Idle talk! If you want satisfaction, be a *man!* Challenge me to a game of wits, not a duel! *Then* I shall show you who is the better adversary!"

"I want nothing but your blood, Lord Danvers! Golden guineas do not tempt me and as for your exulted position . . . Well, by birth, it may be mildly superior to mine, but rank counts little with me."

Lord Danvers set down his glass and his eyes sparkled with a certain cunning. There was nothing he liked more than a well-matched challenge and the young hothead before him looked like excellent game.

"I do not seek to barter *riches,* Lord Santana! I am far too worldly wise to tempt you with such trifles."

"What, then?"

"If I win, you shall leave me be. You will send me the key to your *very* fine cellars, and you shall walk out of this cottage, never again darkening my door with your virtuous prosing. If I seek to abduct some *other* young lady in the future, you shall not intervene. I find I have no taste for the self-righteous ramblings of green young bucks."

Santana yawned. "But I am hardly *green,* Lord Danvers. And the inducement shall have to be *incalculable* for me to accept your offer."

"It *is.* You shall have two of my greatest treasures: my granddaughter and the last born progeny of Hera, my cat."

There was a moment's stunned silence. Lord Santana raised a pair of angry brows in the gloom, but then his mood, strangely, altered to an amused cynicism.

"I accept, Lord Danvers." He offered no explanation for this sudden whimsicality, but his eyes turned toward the table set neatly for one in the corner. "Shall we? I intend to teach you a lesson you shall surely never forget. By the by, is that mangy cat the great treasure of which we speak?" He pointed to the corner, where a pitch-black cat was just putting the finishing touches to her grooming.

Since she ignored them both with equal disdain, Lord Danvers was forced to point out the excellence of her fur and the singularly luminous lustre of her eyes. "Very unusual, Lord Santana! Very unusual!"

His lordship refrained from commenting that since he could not actually *see* her eyes, he was gambling away his cellars and a woman's honour purely on hearsay. It *did* cross his rather sardonic mind, however, that if the granddaughter were in as poor a shape as the cat, Lord Danvers would be welcome to her. More a liability than a treasure, he would wryly imagine. He made a mental note not to get saddled with the chit should he win.

Just as he was smugly congratulating himself on his decision, something tingling at the back of his neck caused him to look at the creature once more. This time, her uninterested air was replaced with something so piercingly familiar that Santana was startled. The eyes were indeed green, and they gleamed from the midnight coat in a way that only one other cat had ever done before. Santana was filled with a slight foreboding, for the cat seemed an omen to him, and for all his pragmatic wit and cynical demeanour, he could neither discern nor decipher what the creature was an omen *for.*

He turned his back on it disdainfully, but the cat's eyes seemed to bore into him as he dealt the first three cards of commerce. Lord Danvers's luck was in and his lordship knew a moment's hesitation as the three-card flush was followed by a cunning win on points. A little less jaunty, the earl suggested a change, since his eyes had alighted on an aging faro box on the mantelpiece. The marquis's yellowing teeth grinned an acquiescence as the younger man fetched the box. It vaguely irritated Santana that the woman remained, seemingly quite intent on the spectacle. He said as much to the marquis, who chuckled throatily and announced that, whilst she was often a dashed nuisance, there was to be no turning his daughter-in-law from her only fixed place of residence.

"Daughter—in-law? You are funning me!"

"Laura Rose? *Surely,* Lord Santana, you have been privy to the gossip and rumour and insatiable speculation. I would have expected Laura Rose to be the most talked-about young bride of the century! Of course, it was all slightly before your time."

"What was?"

Miss Laura Rose, or whoever she was, eyed the earl speculatively, then nodded silently in the earl's direction. Without so much as a by-your-leave or a simple, honest-to-goodness curtsy, she gathered up the shawl, bright on her shoulders, abundant greying hair spilling wispily from gaudy clips, and was gone—into the howling winds, the earl noted in fleeting astonishment.

When Santana pursed up his lips and inquired why the marquis did not go after her and closet her in her chamber for a fool, Fotheringham merely guffawed throatily and nastily remarked that Laura Rose would be more able to hold her own with the elements than a cosseted young sprig like himself.

The Earl of Camden was not used to being treated in this manner. Angrily, he took up the faro box and called the order of the cards. He hardly noticed when he was correct, merely repeating the process like a man possessed, his eyes fixed frostily on Fotheringham.

Fotheringham, clearly enjoying himself, did not appear to *mind* the debts mounting up his side of the table. In between calls, he regaled the earl with the story of Laura Rose's life. Born a gypsy, bred a gypsy, wild, free and unfettered. Until she had been tamed, that is, by Henry, Lord Fotheringham, his youngest and favourite son.

The marquis's eyes became moist and surprisingly faraway as he related the tale. Santana found his fingers relaxing as he listened to the age-old saga of star-crossed lovers, the divide of cultures, of a clandestine marriage and the inevitable birth of a baby girl. Fotheringham's voice was so strangely poignant as the wind whistled through the grates that the earl ceased his fidgeting and gave the man his full attention. The black cat prowled closer, eyeing Santana up and down before leaping with unerring grace upon his lap.

Startled, he nearly cursed the creature to perdition, but before the words were out his mouth, a strange peace settled over him, and the compelling, luminous green eyes soothed his impatient nerves to the point where he could settle back and allow Danvers to expound at length about the cruelty of society—no news to Santana—and the subsequent death of Lord Henry in a confounded curricle race.

Laura Rose had simply vanished into the mists, taking with her nothing but the lock of hair Henry had teasingly cut for her one day and the little bundle that was his eternal legacy. Baby girl and mother had disappeared completely, leaving the marquis bereft and inclined to some of the greater vices to which he'd become accustomed and renowned.

He never defiled young maidens, but the likes of Lady Leigh were a challenge and a distraction to him. Fair game in a world tawdry with iniquity. He did not *say* as much, but Santana, reading between the lines, was silenced. A piece of dirt hit the windowpane and the cat looked up inquiringly. Sensing nothing more, he allowed his head to sink gently back into the unwilling lap.

Unconsciously, Camden found himself stroking the animal, and while it did not precisely purr, the action must have found favour, for its claws retracted visibly and the lithe body relaxed, almost imperceptibly, at his touch.

It did not occur to Santana to ask what had become of the girl. When Fotheringham sank back into companionable silence, broken only by the offering of snuff, the earl roused himself from his unusually sedentary state and took stock of the game. How unlike him to come searching for an adventure and settle for something almost as tame as whist or . . . or . . . yes, dammit, cribbage! Faro was only marginally better than either of these miserable pursuits, and as for allowing himself to be bested at commerce . . .

The notion galled the young earl. He pushed his chair back and eyed the mountain of paper debts facing them. Clearly, by a quite vast margin, he was the winner. He swallowed in satisfaction. Devil take it! At least *that* part of the wind-spoiled day had not gone awry.

"You made the correct choice, my lord."

Fotheringham looked at the debts stacked before him and raised a brow.

"How so, Santana?"

"If those debts were incurred in the flesh rather than on paper, you would have need of *more* than just an apothecary."

"Very true. I pride myself on being sagacious enough

to avoid all such encounters that would redound to my cost."

"*This* one has, however! You owe me a great deal by the looks of those markers."

"Pshaw! Not a farthing! My granddaughter and the cat. Mind you, the loss of the prospect of your wine cellars is not insignificant. Lady Leigh may consider her honour avenged."

"You seem remarkably sanguine under the circumstances. Do you intend to produce this granddaughter or do I merely take an IOU?" Santana's lips twitched humorously.

For an instant, Fotheringham's old eyes flashed, but only moments later, they were hooded once more.

"You may take the cat. I shall have the girl delivered to Camden Court on the morrow."

"Good gracious, man. You cannot be serious!"

"Can I not?" Brown eyes met blue.

"You cannot dispose of your kin as if they were no more than three pieces of silverware or a basket of fruit!"

"You agreed to the terms, Lord Santana."

Santana's eyes narrowed. "So! This is merely another ploy to foist the marriage state onto me. I might have guessed, Lord Fotheringham! You are a wily old creature, but I tell you, you shan't cozen me this way."

"We had an agreement. . . ."

"Very true. But nothing, I may say, made mention of *nuptials*. If your granddaughter comes to me, it will be in the unwedded state or not at all. Ouch! What was that?"

Blood seeped through the earl's elegant white kidskin gloves. He looked suspiciously at the cat, but she was stretched innocently across his lap and hardly looked guilty of inflicting such an unexpectedly painful injury.

"What the devil . . . ?"

"Do not, I pray you, curse in my home, Lord Santana!"

"As far as I am aware, Dewhurst *Castle* is your home, my lord! Besides, I shall curse where I please. No! No! Take the blasted handkerchief away. The blood seems to have staunched itself. I will take the cat, your apologies, and no more."

"Very well, Lord Santana. You shall take the cat. As for apologies, I am not in the habit of making them, and on the eve of my eighty-second birthday, I do not intend changing my ways for a fledgling like *you!* You may consider Lady Leigh's honour—such that it is—avenged. I shall set up some small pension for her and maintain her house in Richmond. Who knows? For such largesse she may *willingly* choose to furnish me further with her favours." He cackled a little maliciously at the disgust that was evident on the earl's face. He continued with a little less levity. "If you remain adamant on the point, we shall say no more, for the moment, about my granddaughter."

"I remain adamant."

Lord Fotheringham's eyes shuttered for a moment. "I hope it is not an obstinacy you shall live to regret, Lord Santana. I shall pray you then good day."

Santana allowed a breathtaking grin to stretch across his intense, darkly handsome features.

"Good day to you, *too,* my lord! By the by, what does this mangy scrap eat?"

"She adores turtle soup in the shell. A little turbot on the side is always pleasing, though I believe a bowlful of buttered lobster and some fresh sea oysters are regarded as her particular favourites."

"Indeed?" Lord Santana's brows arched. "Perhaps the creature is better off with you then, for I assure you my chef will balk at serving even *preserved* turtle to a mere feline!"

"I do not believe the creature will have a problem with that. To be sure, fresh is best, but you will find her not an *unreasonable* companion, I assure you."

Since the cat chose that moment to mew pitifully and look up at Santana with its piercing, knowing eyes, the earl was silenced. He merely scooped up his bundle, marched from the parlour, and made his way to the waiting stallion. He pocketed the animal in his capacious, elegantly cut

greatcoat as if she were of no more account than a
ha'penny coin, untethered the beast, and edged into an
invigorating gallop guaranteed to shake the cobwebs from
his addled mind. If he continued due west, he might find
himself closer to a modicum of civilisation. The winds were
too gusty to turn back and head home. He heartily prayed
that the little town of Northumbleton was not too far a
distance. The inn's culinary repute was now, unexpectedly,
occupying his full attention.

THREE

"Patterson, I *implore* you not to poke your head so disapprovingly at me! Pretend, I beg you, the animal is a horse. A little mangier, perhaps, than you are used to, but a sound animal nonetheless. You have only to groom it and feed it, and I am tolerably certain you shall deal well together. Come, come, desist from that Friday face of yours! Cats need *far* less attention than your average pony—by all accounts they practically clean *themselves!* It shall not be such an unbearable addition to your stable duties I assure you!"

The head groom did not, in any way, appear mollified by these words of autocratic comfort. Since he was one of the select few who had known his lordship since childhood and been privy to all his bumps and scrapes in the past, he now viewed it as his prerogative—indeed duty—to remind the earl of what benefitted his rank. Clearly, an inky black feline of uncertain origin did not rank high on this list.

"Don't you go bamming me, savin' yer lor'ship! A 'orse be 'orse and a puff of fur ball be somethin' very different, mind! Give over wiv vis nonsense, me lor'! I be takin' the animal all right and tight down to Annie Ludlaw I be! *She* be knowing what to do wiv it—like as not she's drownded a fair few in 'er time. . . ."

His voice trailed off as cat and master simultaneously afforded him a glare of intense displeasure.

"All right, all right, guv! I be takin' her but don' say I didn' warn yer—"

"Thank you, Patterson! You relieve me greatly! Now if you will be so good . . ."

He extended his arm and tried to extricate the cat from his shoulder. To no avail. She dug her little claws in tenaciously and refused to budge.

If Patterson snickered, the earl, particularly forbearing under the circumstances, chose to ignore him. He tried yet again and *again* the cat refused to dislodge.

"Curses! You are not a *cat*—you are a little vixen!" The creature purred and stretched luxuriously upon the tip of his immaculate epaulette.

"Don't stand there gaping, Patterson! I see I shall have to allow the scrawny little thing indoors. Perhaps Mrs. *Farrow* can make the little she-devil see reason."

Apparently not. Mrs. Farrow, it must be said, was more inclined than Patterson to adopt the creature. She tempted it with little saucers of milk and heavenly tidbits of salted pork from the cellars, but to no avail. The cat stubbornly refused to leave the earl's presence for more than a few moments at a time.

His lordship, it may be said, found his new associate to be annoying, willfull, and excessively vain. Since being presented into the earl's dignified household, she was looking a lot less scrawny and altogether rather pleased with herself. She preened incessantly and he wondered, several times, what *severe* aberration of fate was now leading him to serve his tormenter turtle soup in a tureen of solid silver. That he caused this repast to be followed up with seasoned oysters and some particularly tasty salmon from his streams did nothing to improve his temper or discourage the belief that he must have finally lost his wits.

Only the emerald eyes of the little creature gave him pause. So like those *other* cat's eyes! And of course, there was the girl. Strange that he had not *noticed* the colour of her eyes—only the strange, slanted shapes and the dark lashes so thick that they curled. . . . He shook himself from his reveries. *She,* of course, was *just* as annoying, willfull, and vain! Not for the first time, he wished he'd at least exchanged names with his midnight siren. Who was she? Who, who, who? He'd returned to the spot several times, but of course, gypsies being what they were, she'd moved on. Perhaps forever. My lord sighed. He must do something before lethargy crept into his blood and tainted it entirely.

He glanced at the cat, who was looking very satisfied with itself as it licked its paws and prepared to stretch out upon the marble statue of Venus Santana had imported especially from Europe.

He contemplated it for a moment, then allowed a slow, mischievous smile to creep across his masculine lips. "So! I see I am saddled with you, my precious! Since your mother's name was legendary and you are looking rather more beautiful than mangy, I shall hereby name you after the god you seem so happy to repose upon. From now on, you are *Venus,* my pet, the goddess of love and beauty. Quite an elevation, wouldn't you say? Come, come, we shall have to garb you in attire that is fitting." Suddenly energised, he allowed Venus to trail after him as he made his way directly to the chamber he'd selected exclusively for his use.

It was rather more stark than the rest of his elaborate castle, but functional, elegant, and supremely tasteful nonetheless. His desk, as always, stood bare but for a handful of blooms he had himself selected that morning. Apart from this deference to aestheticism, there was little in the chamber that revealed a softer side to his personality. The books arrayed across the whole of one wall, while well read, were nonetheless perfectly shelved and immaculately in place. None of the portraits that were abundant through the galleries and hallways hung here. To the right of his desk stood a high-backed chair, lined in blue velvet a shade deeper than the damask drapes just behind him. There were many round beaded windows with thin, artfully wrought glazing bars that he'd had fitted for increased light, but they were severely plain and unadorned by any of the Gothic extravagances that appeared, currently, to be the fashion.

Whilst the panes looked out on a courtyard and traditional rose garden below, the writing chair was placed *away* from them. A tall, bronze candelabra and a colza oil lamp offered further functionality to the chamber, which boasted several mahogany cabinets, a large map, and two life-size marble statues the earl particularly admired for their smooth, simple lines and subtle symmetry. The furnishings were complete with a single chaise longue in mottled hues of blue, gold, and dusty pink. The item, though charming, was a concession to comfort rather than prevailing trends, which dictated canary yellow or burnished red as colours of consequence.

The earl, now, ignored these features as he opened his drawer and fetched out a key. Striding purposefully to one of the mahogany cabinets, he fitted the key and unlatched a drawer that pulled out entirely. He reached his hand behind the panel as Venus watched from a distance, vaguely disdainful of the proceedings.

"Yes, turn up your nose, my little goddess! I will wager a sovereign that not many *other* females will appear as uninterested!"

The earl finally found what he was looking for. He nodded in satisfaction as he drew out an old satin-clad box. When he opened it, the sunlight danced on its contents and caused little flashes of light to filter across the small male preserve.

"Ah yes, my Venus! Come see what I have for you." It was fortunate that his lordship was not superstitious, for he could *swear* the sleek creature understood every one of his silky, half-playful words. She leaped upon the writing table, gracefully avoiding knocking over the peonies.

"Miaow!"

"I should say so! Come here, you little vixen!"

Obediently, the cat took a pace forward and extended a sleek, shimmering black neck. Her eyes appeared very green as the earl removed the bracelet of ice-white diamonds surrounding a single, luminous, and utterly lovely cabochon-cut emerald.

"Will it fit? Excellent, Venus. It was meant to be! I now brand you my personal page. Wherever I go, you shall go, too. We shall be excellent friends, shall we not?"

The cat did not deign to reply. It seemed, to her, that the earl merely spoke the obvious. Instead, she leaped up upon his shoulder and rubbed her soft head just beneath his lordship's chin.

His lordship did not appear to mind being scratched by the jewels. He laughed shortly and rang for Sedgewick.

Lady Aurelia Callum looked as if her face had been slapped. How *dared* the man have the effrontery to appear in her drawing room with a . . . a . . . *cat* upon his shoulder! Was he mocking her? The cat appeared to be wearing *exactly* the type of bracelet that she most coveted. She grew crimson when she remembered hinting, a little, during the dance at Richmond.

My lord had attended as a duty, since the occasion was the betrothal of his good friend Lord Soames, and he had, much to her delight, been introduced to her as an eligible partner. His conversation had been disappointingly distant and *appallingly* noncommittal despite her *very* best efforts. And now this!

She would be the laughingstock of the *ton,* allowing him to ruin her gathering in this disgraceful fashion. She could picture it: no mention in the *Morning Post* of the elite get-together she'd slaved over for weeks, only pages and pages on Lord Santana's latest flight of fancy. It was sickening! There'd be speculation, snickering. . . . Perhaps she should, after all, give him the cut direct. She quivered a little and did not quite like the polite sneer upon her guest's amused countenance.

"May I share the jest, my lord?"

"Jest? I assure you, Lady Aurelia, there *is* none!"

She laughed a little nervously. "The cat . . ."

"Venus? Do not put yourself out on *her* behalf, I beg! A selection from that interesting-looking cold collation over there shall do perfectly. *Shan't* it, Venus?"

The cat looked approving and leaped from shoulder to table with such grace that his lordship could not quite resist pointing out her particular lightness of feet and delicateness of movement.

Her ladyship paled and Santana did not, somehow, think it was from admiration.

"Hartshorn, my lady? Here, allow me!" He pulled the stopper from her trembling hands and waved the vile substance in front of her nose. "The very thing, do not you think? You shall be all right in a trice, unless you prefer to repair to your chamber?" The lady gave an anguished moan that, sad to say, greatly satisfied the world-weary earl. With a cheerful nod, he allowed several lackeys to dance attendance upon their mistress before strolling, nonchalantly, into the supper room.

"Oh, my lord! What a perfectly *charming* animal! Amabel simply *adores* pets! Don't you, Amabel?" A disgustingly huge fan was fluttered in the earl's face before a limpid sigh was detected from beyond.

"Indeed I do, Mama. I would not for the *world* wish to push myself forward, but I do believe I have a special bond with all living creatures. I daresay *you,* my lord, *share* it!" The lady—a vision in a heavy pink creation of muslin and lace—pushed past the fan and extended her satin clad hand to pat the evening's social sensation.

The earl had just been concocting, in his head, a suitably dampening response to this *simpering* outpouring, when the cat did something he had not previously seen her do. The fur rose upon her back and she crouched threateningly against Santana's immaculate shirt points. He could *feel* her power, for her claws unsheathed and he had an uncomfortable, pricking sensation through his snowy, excellently folded cravat.

She hissed at first, then spat. She comprehensively spat-tered Miss Amabel Rutherford-Smythe's expensive gloves before emitting a slight snarl and relaxing back, innocently, upon my lord's shoulder.

The earl had the most lowering sensation that he was about to laugh. Instead, he cleared his throat, but the amusement lurking behind his limpid brown eyes was unmistakable. Miss Rutherford-Smythe smothered a most unladylike curse and allowed herself to be led to the powder room by her indignant mama. Unfortunately for her, the scene had not gone unnoticed, and it was the inspiration for a rather unseemly limerick published by the *Post* the following day.

For the first time in a long time, Guy Santana found himself actually *entertained* at these gatherings. He found himself discarding less and less mail into the *regrets etc.* pile and placing several rather key invitations into the *gratefully accept* basket. It was not long before Venus was an adept part of the social scene. Hostesses came to understand the inevitable. If they desired Lord Guy's attendance at their soirees, routs, and balls, then they must, quite naturally, expect and resign themselves to the ubiquitous presence of his goddess, Venus.

Some of the nastier spinsters—and indeed, some more elevated personages like the Countess Lieven and the Princess Esterhazy—withheld their judgment, but their very silence caused talk and gave certain circles to understand that there was still a lurking question mark behind the suitability of the third Earl of Camden's latest whim.

If it had been a *chère d'amour* or some such thing, it would have been quite different, for young ladies could feign no knowledge of the circumstance or, at the very least, did not have to come into regular confrontation with it. But an animal at an elegant rout? The social implications were enormous and rather too difficult to entirely condone.

The matter was settled, once and for all, by a rather pompous, hand-inscribed invitation from the Prince of Wales himself. This in itself was not remarkable, for Santana was known to be a particular intimate of the prince. What *was* remarkable was that it was to be one of his royal highness's fabled balls and *that,* everyone knew, was something the prince took very seriously indeed.

Would he countenance the admittance of Venus? London was abuzz with speculation and several of the very de rigeur gentleman's clubs set up a cautious bet on the issue. Odds were *not* in favour of Venus—few thought Santana had the gumption to appear with a cat creasing his elegant Weston-tailored pockets—but doubt still prevailed. Alas for some of the loftier noblemen! Several gold guineas were lost as the little goddess strutted in on a leash, quite at ease with her sumptuous environs and *equally* sumptuous master.

Santana, in a blaze of rubies, looked remarkably elegant as neckerchief, finger and shirt cuffs glittered in a shade that exactly matched the rich thread running through his tight, superbly fitting superfine coat. The sumptuous satin of his knee breeches were, to the discerning, of a slightly *darker* hue, but a tolerable match nonetheless.

The lackeys hardly blinked as they took my lord's card and announced him in ringing tones that caused a hush all through the ball room.

"His lordship Guy Santana, third Earl of Camden, Viscount Lansborough and his . . . and . . . well, and . . . *Venus,* your highness."

There was a general gasp as the prince plodded jovially across the room. He eyed the cat warily—for in the past, she had shown a discomforting propensity to hiss at him. Tonight, however, she was apparently prepared to be perfectly graceful. Accordingly, the prince decided it would be churlish—not to mention downright rude—not to return the favour.

In a rather loud undertone that was guaranteed to be overheard by the most auspicious of his guests, he politely regretted that Venus had not received an invitation herself, hence the rather clumsy announcement by his manservant.

"Be assured, my fair Venus, the mistake shall not again occur." He grinned wickedly at Santana and accorded him an unregal wink that spoke volumes for their friendship and secured Venus's place in society forever more.

Guy Santana, though he was loath to admit it, was now rather fond of his feline. He liked her loyalty, he liked her startlingly intelligent eyes, and above all, he liked her perspicacity. When she hissed at Colonel Bridgewater and purred at the ancient and charming Miss Denby, his lordship was heard to utter, in tones of astonishment, that the little vixen was "the most discerning creature alive."

Thus it was that the strange alliance progressed. If it seemed, at times, that the cat repined, the earl set it down to ill humour. After all, did he not, himself, have fits of the dismals?

A clear image of the glorious gypsy girl flitted like lightning in his mind. In that moment, he could sense her keenly, taste those cherry lips, smell her wild, untamed gypsy scent, which mingled with the rain in tantalising profusion. When he closed his eyes, he could almost hear her mocking laughter. He burned from her goading eyes. If he knew that his pet could—and did—conjure up those self-same images, he might have been shocked out of his habitual complacency. Fortunately for him, he had no notion of the circumstance. It was left to Venus—goddess of beauty and love—to watch and wait.

FOUR

Mr. Daniel Pelliat murmured quietly under his breath. The earl—alerted to the fact that his lawyer must have something of great moment to discuss with him, since that gentleman did not *habitually* interrupt his morning's review of the House speeches—set down the rather tedious paperwork and bade him enter with a smile.

"Come in, Pelliat! Shall I ring for tea?"

The lawyer shook his head emphatically. "Indeed not, my lord! It is merely that I wish—"

"Boring legal documents, Pelliat?"

Pelliat nodded, though he was not certain that boring was the correct description for the documents he carried.

"My lord . . ."

"Guy, Pelliat! Or if you must, *Santana* will do! I cannot *abide* niceties in my own home."

This was obviously not a new matter to the very correct Pelliat, who merely bowed rather gruffly and endeavoured not to bring his lordship's name into the conversation again.

"Uh . . ."

"Yes, Pelliat?"

"I feel certain that you shall wish to see this yourself."

"What is it?"

"It is a last will and testament, my lord."

"Indeed? How very exciting, Pelliat! Not my own, I hope?"

Pelliat could never *quite* detect the twinkle in the third earl's mischievous eyes, so he almost always failed to note when the earl was funning.

"No, indeed, my lord! In a manner of speaking, my— that is, Santana, ahem."

He concluded on a choke that caused his employer to chuckle in amused sympathy.

"Manner of speaking? How cryptic, Pelliat! So tell me— if it is not mine, have I been left a worldly fortune?"

"No . . ."

"No? You disappoint me. A watch then? A keepsake?"

Pelliat shook his head.

"Come, Daniel Pelliat! Do not seek to slumguzzle me, I beg! If that is a testament you are waving in my face, there must be something bequeathed. Not so?"

The lawyer nodded.

The earl was patient. "Exactly *what*, Mr Pelliat, have I inherited?"

"You appear to have inherited, my lord, a debt of honour."

The earl's face, for the first time, clouded slightly.

"Beg pardon?"

Patterson cleared his throat a trifle nervously and wished himself outside on the castle lawns. Even, if necessary, in the well-tended moat—anywhere, in fact, other than where he now found himself.

"Cut to the quick, Daniel! Or better yet, give me that damn paper!"

The earl stretched out his hand and unceremoniously removed the document from his lawyer's hand.

"Good God! I cannot be reading this correctly!"

"I am afraid you are, my lord."

"The gall of the man! Even in death he is the wiliest, most unscrupulous . . ."

"Quite, my lord."

"What is to be done, Pelliat?"

"Are the contents veracious, my lord?"

The earl glared at him. "You are not actually contemplating *upholding* this drivel?"

The lawyer shifted uneasily onto the other foot.

"Well, my lord . . . It is just—well . . . Venus, you know, is famous!"

"Venus is a *cat*, Pelliat! I fail to see any material connection."

"No, but . . . Well, it seems a remarkable coincidence that you acquired the feline at the very time that the marquis specifies in his testament."

"I am not disputing the origins of Venus, Pelliat! I am quite happy to admit that Fotheringham ceded her to me in payment of a gambling debt."

"And the girl?"

The earl frowned. "Gracious, my good man! Do you think me a *monster*? I won her, it is true, but I *immediately* waived my right to the prize! I am not so desperate to get myself leg shackled that I must needs throw a dice to acquire a wife! Why, I do not like to boast of it, but I daresay there might be any *number* of young women willing to oblige me on this score."

Pelliat did not dispute this. He would have been a veritable greenhorn if he had tried to do so. The earl's eligibility was obvious and not a matter of contention, as he rather sternly tried to point out.

"What troubles me, your lordship, is what is to become of the chit?"

"Heavens, I have not the foggiest notion! It is not, after all, my concern, and I refuse to marry on grounds as flimsy as these. Old man Fotheringham evidently took a gamble from his grave and it has not paid off. There is an end to it. For I assure you, if I sponsor her in any *other* way, I shall be guaranteeing her ruination. I am not so abominable as that."

"You would not consider acting as her guardian, my lord? The terms of the marquis's will are sufficiently vague, I feel—"

"No, I will not!"

"You will not even meet with her . . . ?"

"Jumping Juniper, Pelliat! How many times do I have to spell out the same thing? If the wench is out of pocket—and I cannot imagine that she *can* be—I can possibly help out in some entirely anonymous manner. Beyond that, my goodwill and tolerance has been stretched far enough for one morning, I believe."

Pelliat bowed. "Very good, my lord. I only inquired because there is no question of the young lady being an adventuress. She has been left *all* of Fotheringham's unentailed fortune, which, as I understand it, is far from inconsiderable."

"Excellent, Pelliat, you relieve my mind, for I now no longer have to act as benefactor. And now, if you please, I suggest you return to your rooms in town. *I* should like very much to return to these speeches."

Daniel Pelliat knew when he was beaten. He bowed perfunctorily and stepped with great precision out of the chamber. The earl had just thrown away the catch of a lifetime. Miss Melinda St. Jardine was worth a cool forty thousand pounds a year. He sighed. Such matters, he knew, would not weigh with the likes of Guy Santana.

In an office not too far from the one where Daniel Pelliat's plaque gleamed gold in the morning sunlight, another man of law was soothing a ruffled client that morning. Miss Melinda St. Jardine was elegance itself in a dark merino morning dress with long sleeves and only a very narrow flounce visible on the petticoat. The simple, but stylish, attire was finished by a sash of deep black, tan gloves, and a filmy gauze veil that obscured the eyes yet somehow presented, to the town-weary solicitor, a certain mystique that he had hitherto found lacking in his female clients.

Of course, the garb could not *quite* be considered full mourning and the spectacled man at the chestnut work desk had to frown, slightly, at this show of whimsicality—he hoped not levity—on the part of Miss St. Jardine.

True, though, her fortune would no doubt compensate for this slight lapse in traditional etiquette. Besides, she looked *charming* in her garb. Yes, he would describe it as half mourning, even if a little unconventional in style. He smiled.

"Miss St. Jardine, his lordship was most specific on this point. He requires you, if possible, to fulfill the terms of his wager. He believed that his honour was quite grounded in this point and I am certain, my dear, you would not wish to disrespect a man who has bequeathed you so much."

"No, indeed." Miss St. Jardine's tone tinkled with precisely the correct amount of humility. Her eyes, however, were flashing ominously. It was fortunate that the man at the desk was too shortsighted to notice.

"What kind of a person, I wonder, would accept such stakes? I am a *person*, not a chattel!"

The lawyer firmly shut his mouth. He would *not* retort with the obvious corollary. What kind of a grandfather would *offer* such stakes? He merely shook his head mournfully and suggested that there was not much to be gained by pursuing this lugubrious line of thought.

"Ah, but I think, perhaps, that there is." Melinda looked thoughtfully at the lawyer. "Is he handsome—this paragon I am supposed to be betrothed to?"

Mr. Pendleton set down his quill pen and eyed her thoughtfully. "You really know very little about society, Miss St. Jardine!"

"My upbringing was unusual, as you know, sir. I have spent the last year adjusting to my new life and becoming . . . accustomed." A tear sprang suddenly into her strange, rather beautiful eyes. She brushed it away fiercely before remembering her black embroidered handkerchief and dabbing in a more civilised manner.

"My grandfather thought it wise to delay my presentation at Court for at least a year. I was privately presented last fall, but what with the season at an end and the marquis rather housebound . . ." She did not need to finish her sentence. The gentleman understood her perfectly. Whilst Miss St. Jardine was officially out, she was, as yet, an unknown quantity to the *ton*. He wondered how she would take, then smiled. The combination of her beauty, wealth, and unconscious charm would undoubtedly stand her in good stead, even with the high sticklers.

His thoughts clouded, suddenly, with the notion that an innocent like her was bound to become the target of every fortune hunter in the book. He relaxed, suddenly, as he finally understood the intention behind the marquis's bequest. Wily old fox! By marrying her off to Santana, he was at once providing for her safety, her reputation, and the perpetuation of her wealth and lineage. He only hoped the earl would fall gracefully into the trap. By all accounts, he was a wily one himself.

Miss St. Jardine leaned forward curiously across the desk and repeated the question. "What is he like, then, this wagering wastrel?"

"Wagering wastrel?" Certainly, he would not *himself* have referred to the third Earl of Camden in those terms, but under the circumstances, he could understand why the *lady* did.

He cleared his throat portentously. It was not for him to enlighten her as to the manner in which the earl was circumstanced. If Fotheringham had desired her to know the extent of the earl's fortune, he no doubt would have told her so at length himself.

Melinda politely repeated the question, though Mr. Pendleton, accustomed to human foibles, could see that she was slightly impatient.

"His lordship is excessively fortunate in his features, ma'am. I would be hard-pressed to describe him to you precisely, but since I am in regular correspondence with my colleague Mr. Daniel Pelliat, his lordship's own council, I believe I might be able to secure a miniature likeness of him if you so desire."

Miss Melinda St. Jardine suppressed a passionate snort. Likeness! The man should be presenting himself to her door at the very least! A little piqued at his obvious negligence in this matter, she tilted her chin ever slightly and declared she could have no possible interest either in a miniature or in the original itself.

Mr. Pendleton was not deceived. He could see his client burning with a natural feminine curiosity and pressed his lips together in a complacent smile. All, then, was as it should be. When she stood up, he was wise enough not to press the point. It was in this precise manner that the whole singular interview was brought to a close.

Much, much later, in the stillness of the canary room—a little salon set aside exclusively for the comfort of the Marchionesses of Fotheringham—she allowed her thoughts to wander to that *other* gentleman that destiny had decreed peculiarly her own. She had felt it in her heart, in her wild, intuitive soul, though there could be no reason or logic attached to the instinctive belief.

And now, she was ordered to ally her fate to one Guy Santana on not so much as a *meeting*, let alone a chance encounter in a storm. She smiled, for the inclement weather had only been *half* as violent as the tumultuous sensations she'd experienced in that other man's arms.

It made perfect sense—her cool English blood told her so. Marriages of convenience were commonplace—almost *expected* in her proper new world. If Fotheringham had ceded her to Santana she had no doubt he had a reason. In the year Melinda had come to know him, she knew that her grandfather by blood did not make mistakes.

If she were a gambling debt, it was a debt the marquis had undoubtedly intended to incur. She wondered yet again what kind of a man would agree to such stakes. She closed her eyes but her thoughts were not helpful. They led her directly as always, to the mocking, amused, passionate, and blazingly angry gaze of . . . She knew not whom.

Perhaps, when she took her place in society, she would come across him. That had always been her hope—her one reason for submitting to the transition that had been foisted upon her. Her eyes fluttered gently closed and the book lying open upon her lap slid to the floor unnoticed. When her breathing had deepened considerably, the shadow at the window slipped silently from sight. Laura Rose was certain her daughter would make the right choice. Destiny, after all, was no small thing.

Miss Melinda St. Jardine looked with bemusement at the many greetings and flowers that cluttered Dewhurst Manor's two large receiving rooms in a profusion of colour, card, and scent that certainly had not been precedented in the marquis's lifetime. She had inherited her grandfather's shrewdness along with her mother's intuition, so she was neither gratified by this show of favour nor particularly relieved by the understanding that she was now regarded as a diamond of the first water by London's celebrated *ton*.

She was more than passing certain her sudden fortune had a helping hand in this state of affairs. In this, she was correct, of course. She would have been astonished to learn, however, that her beauty was *also* fast becoming a byword. In truth, her mocking gypsy heart would have chuckled uproariously at the fashionable love sonnets that even now were issuing from the pens of every sprig worth his salt.

Her half mourning was proclaimed as more than "fitting" under the circumstances, though the "circumstances" were always whispered about under gloved hands. Where any lesser endowed individual would have been shunned for not donning black for the requisite period, Melinda's muted pinks and dusty lilacs were considered "all the crack" and eminently suitable.

Melinda herself, however, found them a sad trial, used as she was to gay canary yellows, saffrons, emerald greens aglitter with rich cerises, azure blues, and crystal whites.

She bit her nails now, as she paced the room, waiting word from her betrothed. Try as she might, she could conjure up no mental image of him, for every time she drifted off into her trancelike world of spirits, the annoying image of her stranger of the mists arose to replace any alternate thought.

How provoking! And it was not as if the man were not insufferably overbearing! She wondered what the Earl of Camden would be like. Stuffy, no doubt, with a little mustache trimmed exactly so and elegantly gloved hands placed ever so properly behind his back in the bluff military manner she found hard to take. The English and their muted, understated mannerisms! Almost as though they were embarrassed at having any feeling at all . . . Heavens, she was doing it herself now: submerging her grief in a listless, lackluster stroll toward the herb gardens. She could hardly remember the last time she had cried with true abandon.

Oh yes . . . She did. Grandfather Fotheringham had rid himself, finally, of her cat. As if Aphrodite had been some morbid link to her spiritual past rather than an extension of her soul itself. And yet . . . yet he had been a wise man.

She'd sobbed unashamedly at his breakfast table. She remembered vividly how he had cast her an odd, secretive, knowing look and admonished her quietly never to fear. The spirits had a strange way of looking after their own. She wondered, not for the first time, if he was right.

Outdoors, the chill air was brisk enough to revive her lagging thoughts and cause a renewed briskness to creep into her step. She placed her hands firmly back into their gloves and then into her thin, feather-light muff. If she did not watch out, her fingernails would be chewed down to the bone and *that*, she knew, would be a social folly. Or would it? Her ridiculous fortune, she supposed, made *anything* forgivable.

Suddenly, her delightful, impossibly beautiful mouth curved into something very like her former gypsy smile. By George, she was hellishly bored and she would test the theory out. She'd *give* the little chittter chats something to exercise their tongues about! She didn't care a ha'penny for society's approval. And if Lord High and Mighty Camden should consider her an unfit bride, so be it.

With an irrepressible chuckle, the delectable Miss St. Jardine disappointed *several* waiting beaux by claiming a head cold. They would have been alternately surprised, disapproving, and downright outraged if they had subsequently caught sight of a swathe of petticoats ably shinnying a drainpipe and descending with ease onto one of the roofs of the servants' quarters. From there it was a mere matter of a jump, but Miss St. Jardine, though she had jumped worse in her time, cannily decided to make use of some of the creeping vines upon the manor walls. It was a small matter of moments before she was down, her brown velvet gloves slightly—ever so slightly—the worse for wear, but otherwise completely and *charmingly* intact.

"And where do you think you are off too, ma'am?"

"Jane!"

The abigail who had been assigned to properly chaperon her and attend to her needs looked grim. "It be a fit you be givin' me, ma'am, and I take leave to tell you that you scared me 'alf out o' me senses!"

Miss St. Jardine, alight with mischief for a change, chuckled merrily.

"Poor Jane! I am a sore trial, am I not?"

The maid, who was exceedingly fond of her young mistress, gypsy blood or not, grudgingly agreed.

"Now don't take a pet, missy! You been brought up unconventional like! Just you be creepin' back up the backstairs and I'll see to it none is the wiser." Melinda nodded briskly.

"Leastaways," she added musingly, "I shall see to it that folks around here mind their tongues. Stop yer gawkin', Hawkins! You go mind yer vegytables for a change!" This last on a slightly fiercer note, for the under gardener's eyes were nigh on popping from his head. Obviously, he had managed an *excellent* view of the spectacle.

"Jane, I shall not retreat! I have a severe fit of the dismals, and if you do not wish me to altogether sink into a decline . . ."

The maid looked alarmed. "That I do not, missy! Still, his lor'ship was most *particular* in his instructions. You were to be treated *exactly* like a lady, ma'am, and I reckon as 'e'd turn in 'is grave if 'e was to see yer climbin' in that 'umble-tumble way."

"Fortunately, Jane, he shall *not* see me. Oh, do stop lecturing me! My mind is all set up, so you might just as well take yourself off to Mrs. Gantry in the kitchens. You go have a nice comfortable coze and I'll shake the cobwebs from my brain. I reckon I have had my fill with ladying for a while. I need to think and I cannot think whilst I am dressed up like a prissy little china doll receiving heaven knows how many 'Ladies this' and 'Lords that'." She stopped for a moment to catch her breath.

The maid was looking a trifle uncertain, so Melinda pressed home her advantage. "Jane, I am mistress now. I am *ordering* you to go have a cup of tea! And do be a dear and see if there are any of those delicious French fancies left. I have a mind for a few when I return."

Jane stared at her blankly, growing horror dawning on her pretty features. "Return?"

Miss St. Jardine stood her ground. "Return, Jane! Go on then! I am only taking Bosun for a spin."

It was fortunate that Miss Jane Dantry knew nothing of horses, or her mouth would have gaped open even further and she might have fallen into a swoon merely to protect her mistress from such folly. Fortunately, she had never been one to hobnob with the grooms, and so she had no notion that Bosun was a large stallion, largely untamed and tolerated in the stables only for its nobility of birth and its potential for stud.

As for a sidesaddle . . . Well, the proud stallion would have scorned the impertinence.

FIVE

Miss Melinda swung herself up with ease. Her table manners might still, at times, be frowned upon, but none in the stables could ever deny that this granddaughter of a marquis had a regular way with animals.

The cheery smile she bestowed on Smithers almost blinded him to the stark reality that it was Bosun, not Starlight, who bore her weight. True, she was sitting astride, but that did not weigh with Smithers, who knew little of etiquette and wished he knew even less. What mattered, after all, was that Miss Melinda was a bruising rider and a credit to his stables. Pity she was a mere wisp of a girl, but there, one could not have everything.

He cast a seasoned eye over her defiant bearing, then looked to the horse. "Not sure that be the correct beast for you, milady," he mumbled, for he avoided, at most costs, the necessity of talking with the gentry.

"Nonsense, Smithers! He is the very thing for me on a beautiful spring day like this. Is it not true that Starlight has cast her shoe and Albany has his hands full with Dancer and Chance?" The head groom nodded, wondering where the wee lass came by her knowledge.

"Excellent, then, for there is no one to exercise Bosun and I feel certain that he can do with the gallop. Besides, the Viscount of Brinkley is interested in his purchase and I'd like to take him through his paces before making a decision."

Smithers nodded. It was not his place to brangle with gentlefolk and like or not the little miss knew what she was doing. She had as shrewd a head on her shoulder, like the late marquis and her father before her and that was a fact.

A tear wet the stable hand's eye as he thought of Lord Henry. Mighty fond of him he'd been and now here was his daughter, right as a trivet and ready to take over control. Well, she had earned his respect, and if she wanted to take on the flighty beast, there was nought he would do to stop her. A trifle headstrong were the Fotheringhams and that was a fact, but he'd not change that for the world.

"Jane will have me scalp for this!"

"Jane is not coming."

The old man nodded sagely. "Aye. Like as not, like as not." Then he turned and made his way back to the warmth of the stalls. It was time for his morning pipe of tobacco and the hay needed tending.

Dewhurst Manor was near the gates of Richmond Park, so it was not so very unsurprising that Miss St. Jardine's unladylike gallop to the entrance went unremarked except by the most lowly of tradesmen, unlikely to cast much social slur upon her person.

Once in, she allowed her mood to subtly alter to that of the stallion, so that horse and rider were united as one. She gave Bosun his length and the great distances afforded him by the park were spanned in moments, the beast cantering so swiftly that Melinda was breathless with a wild, unstoppable excitement. There were so many paths to choose from, so many unroamed avenues, huge vistas of fields that seemed quite unattended but for the odd solitary rider seen here and there upon the horizon. To the left there was a bank of primroses and dandelions that Melinda found quite heavenly, but beyond that still there was a stream.

Melinda could just hear the tinkling of champagne glasses and the loud, unmistakable chink of china. She made a most unladylike face as she pulled Bosun up and veered off to the right. An al fresco picnic was not something she was wishful of encountering—especially in her defiant, cross-grained state.

The path she selected seemed satisfactorily solitary. How different from Hyde Park, where she had consistently refused to take out so much as a *tilbury* never mind a frisky animal yearning for exercise. The crowds there were perfectly amazing and had little, she knew, to do with an honest ride. Seen and be seen. Miss St. Jardine was only just entering that world, yet she was already heartily sick of it. St. Agnes's Eve was an aeon away. There was no respite, except on this green, green turf on this brilliant—almost summery—sunny day.

She muttered something of the sort to Bosun, who must have taken offence, for he reared his haunches and bucked wildly, quite out of keeping with Melinda's expectations. A breathless surge of anticipation coursed through her being as she strove to gain control of the strong, half-tamed beast. *Like me!* she thought defiantly as she clung on to the immense creature, clutching at the mane in a vain attempt not to lose all dignity and tumble in a heap to the ground. False hope!

The thud of hard earth against her ears came as a shock. Likewise, the familiar galloping of hooves coupled with an unmistakable neighing of horseflesh. Then there was the angry, biting tone of a gentleman directly above her. She closed her eyes and hoped that if she sank into a swoon it would go away. It did not.

"Are you mad? Are you quite, quite mad?"

The question was too pointless for her to vouchsafe an answer. She kept her eyes closed and determined, very hard, not to peek. All of a sudden her heart was hammering profoundly in her chest and it had nothing, she knew, to do with the fall.

She heard the thud of boots as the rider's feet slipped from the saddle and firmly onto the hard earth close to her cheek. Then a heavy step as she felt some magnificent presence tower over her assessingly. She managed a faint moan as her lips parted, but he was not deceived.

"I promised once to horsewhip you. Perhaps now is an excellent time." The tone was grim and her eyes popped open at once. How *dared* he?

She caught a faint glimmer of amusement in the eyes before they were shuttered, once more, by a facade of possibly well deserved fury.

"Good. You are awake. I suspected the threat might act as a greater reviver than hartshorn!"

"You are a beast!"

"How very fitting, for you are a beauty!"

There seemed nothing to say to this sally, so Melinda sat up, brushed off her morning dress, and glared at the impeccable gentleman before her. He *would*, of course, be entirely immaculate, in a riding coat of deep blue trimmed with silver buttons. His doeskin breeches fitted more perfectly than Melinda could quite care to contemplate, so she looked up. Straight into eyes of flint.

"Do you care nothing for your livestock that you ride pell-mell across public gardens?" The tone was conversational, but the gypsy in her was not deceived. The words bit into her like the lash he had promised.

Melinda could think of no biting enough retort, so she said nothing, merely allowing her swath of dark hair to curl about her defiantly. He moved toward her and she stood up at once, grabbing hold of Bosun's saddle. Unfortunately, the animal was so large that, without a box or at least the willing hands of Smithers, she could not remount him without some considerable loss of dignity.

"So! You seek to run away. Possibly wise, for as I think I have mentioned once before, my temper is prodigious."

"Indeed it is, sir! Faith, you are no more than a bully, for it is not as if I ride through Bond Street or even through your precious Hyde Park or Covent Gardens! I ride merely in a place respectably designated for such an activity, and if others are too hen hearted to give their mounts their head—well I, sir, am not!"

Her eyes glittered with a mixture of fury and tears. She had yearned, dreamed, *longed* for this moment, but now that it had come to pass, she wanted to do nothing more than flee to the wilds and sob her eyes out with the passion she was born to.

The gentleman was unyielding. "Beyond that bend there is a curricle that has lost its wheel. Two of my good friends are getting ready to allow a team of high-stepping grays test out their paces. Think, woman! This place may be quieter than some of the *other* London haunts, but it is not entirely uninhabited. Besides"—he eyed Bosun with a practiced eye—"that animal is too big for you. Your groom should have his head read, allowing you to mount it. And *astride!* I shall spare your blushes and say nothing on that head, but where, may I ask, are your servants? You are *surely* not jaunting about unattended?"

Melinda scowled. She was a gypsy born, unused to being fettered by society's odious constraints. A groom indeed! Why should she need a groom when she could fly swifter than the wind, bareback, upon Appaloosas from the West and Arabians from the East?

True enough, she had grown fond of the marquis and did not wish to allow disgrace to fall upon his name, but surely this was the outside of enough? A complete stranger to roundly berate her in a public place? Perhaps she should slap his face.

She lifted a delicate, slender hand to do just that but the earl was swifter and far stronger than she had given him credit for.

"Oh, no, no, no, my pretty!"

"Let me go!"

The earl might have done just that, but he suddenly found the little velvet gloved hand quite intoxicating, so he retained it smugly and chose to look into steaming, glowering eyes.

"You are not a gentleman, sir!"

"Then we are well matched, for *you,* if I recall, are not a lady!"

"Oh!" The outrage was voiced as a squeak. Melinda wrenched her hand from the stranger's grasp and turned to Bosun, who was mildly chewing the grass for all the world as though he had *not* just thrown his mistress off without a by-your-leave.

"No, don't go!" The words were genuine, which surprised Miss St. Jardine. She fumbled, for a moment, with the long, leather reins. Then she looked up. Her eyes were enormous pools of vivid blue in a perfect, expressive, adorable face.

"I have searched all of London for you!" The words were seductively soft. Melinda felt herself shiver from the mental caress. She blinked, then turned her nose up scornfully.

"Why? To dress me down in public?" She hoped her tone was suitably disdainful, despite the wistful hammering of her traitorous heart.

"This is hardly in public, my dear. When I wish to deliver a public set down, be assured I shall do so with more audience than one willful, disobedient stallion and an equally willful mistress!" The words were spoken more with amused irony than malice, but Melinda felt herself colouring nonetheless. How *could* she be discovered in this bumble bath by the very object of her spirit dreams?

Miss St. Jardine felt slightly faint with confusion. It did not help that the man towering above her was grinning widely and regarding her with a stare destined to upset even the *hardiest* maiden's composure. To cover her confusion, she allowed cold reason to intervene.

"I do believe I hear someone on the footpath!"

"*Do* you? My point exactly! You can't go haring around the countryside on an oversize beast when half the population is taking a stroll through the gardens! It is neither wise nor comme il faut!"

"A year ago I would not have thought you cared a *jot* for such trifles! You appeared, to me, to be a *man*, not a lily-livered mouse talking about convention! Comme il faut, comme il faut! Was our little tryst in the storm *comme il faut?*"

Miss St. Jardine spat out the words, for she was confused, overset, and more than a little angry. The cherished moment she had dreamed of all this tedious time in exile— nether gypsy queen nor lady born—was spoiled.

She'd imagined a reunion of sentiment, of surprise, of ecstasy. Not a dispassionate discourse on etiquette preceded by the undignified threat of a spanking. She wished she could bring herself to despise those twinkling dark eyes, but to her chagrin, she found that she could not. Scowling did not seem to help, so she gave it up with resignation and glared instead.

Lord Santana looked upon the woman who had haunted his every dream and smiled. Every *bit* as willful as he remembered, despite the subdued garb and the obvious accoutrements of a lady born. A puzzle, then, for he could have *sworn* she was a Romanie lass that night. Still, her accents had always been mystifyingly English. . . . He closed his eyes. Perhaps the very strength of his wishes was enough to allow a miracle such as this to come to pass. He answered her question.

"Comme il faut? Hardly *that,* you little witch, and you *know* it!"

Melinda, for once, was bereft of words. She opened her mouth to remonstrate, but her pretty little tongue seemed singularly uncooperative. She gaped at the gentleman before her.

Lord Guy Santana schooled his features so as not to reveal the ready light of laughter that threatened to creep across his lips and quite overset him. He was exultant at this small but obvious triumph. He had—he could see— the power to silence her.

All but her breathing, which was so quick and intense that it caused delicate mounds of creamy flesh to rise and fall in the most provocative of ways. He held himself tightly in check. The little vixen had her *own* powers. He must not forget that! His spirits soared at this chance meeting with the one woman who had moulded his desires for a twelve month at least.

And talking of desires . . . his body *ached* from them. He cursed under his breath and prayed, in a rather ungentlemanly manner, that the lady was suffering from the same discomforts. He suspected she was, for her morning dress, though delightful, seemed strangely tight across the front and the pulses in her neck were decidedly quickening. He grinned engagingly.

An answering gleam reluctantly sparkled in her eyes, though she closed her mouth firmly. She might have been mistaken for prim had the earl not had an intense, deep, and instinctive feel for the passions that lay very close to the surface with her.

He stretched out his hand and lightly caressed her neck. She did not move. A hoyden, a widgeon perhaps, but undeniably a lady. An adorable, utterly *unutterably* beautiful lady. The one decreed by destiny to be his. He remembered the words uttered dreamily on that cold, distant night. *"I, my lord, am your destiny."* Had she felt it, too, then? To look at her trembling lips now, he supposed she had. He looked again. They were so soft, so undeniably pliant and sweet. . . .

He moved toward her and found them parting, almost in readiness for the inevitable. In spite of his better, more chivalrous intentions, he found himself drawn to them, tasting, testing, *loving* again. They were wet with innocence, provocative beyond imagination. They held him captive in their thrall and he was a willing prisoner. Melinda felt the storm again, the lightning, the flashes of light, the burning, burning from her depths. . . . The horses were restive, but neither party to this singular impropriety appeared to care.

Despite her deep annoyance at being caught at such a disadvantage, Miss St. Jardine felt her arms creeping around that of the overbearing, dreadfully autocratic, and *devastatingly* attractive rogue of the first stare. Not just creeping, but actively pulling, wantonly clinging. He appeared not to mind this circumstance, for his *own* hands crept around her tiny waist as he applied himself with passion to the fruits of her rosy lips.

For several moments the third Earl of Camden and the gypsy Melinda remained oblivious to their public surroundings. Neither noticed a solitary black cat leap from my lord's saddle and perch in the beech tree. If they had, they would have been startled to note the gleam of triumph that sparked from shadowy emerald eyes. Neither noticed footsteps upon the path or the cheeky calls of two sweepers privy to their embrace.

Only the distinct clearing of a throat forced them to finally, reluctantly, take stock. A man in sensible brogues and an expensive, if unstylish, greatcoat of dark serge looked both embarrassed and intrigued to find his employer thus engaged. The earl grinned impishly at the man on horseback, who'd evidently entered the park at a sedate pace and come by Lord Santana purely as a matter of chance.

"Daniel! I had no idea you were fond of exercise!"

Mr. Pelliat cast an appreciative glance at the maiden, then frowned a little at his employer.

"I find town life can lead to a deal of lethargy, sir! I like to exercise Clarence at least once a week."

There was an uncomfortable pause as the earl remembered he could not introduce the lady. Since he had not the pleasure of her name, the exercise would be fatuous—not to say decidedly embarrassing—in the extreme. He noticed that she was fiddling with the bridle and wondered if she meant to make a bolt for it. Well she couldn't really, for she still needed a leg up.

Melinda was just thinking exactly those thoughts. A faint blush suffused her face as she realised the compromising position in which she had been discovered. Well, Jane had warned her and she was right. She was ruined.

The earl sensed some of these thoughts. Quietly, he helped her to mount. She could smell his scent—masculine and clean and as intoxicating as mead on a wintry day. He was smiling, though heaven knew, he had no rhyme or reason or even *right* to do so. She stared at him reproachfully, though no words were uttered.

The moment was too intense, too full of joy and sadness, hope and futility, to be translated into any commonplace verbiage. Then, as she fiddled with the restless beast's dark hidebound reins, she believed her ears were deceiving her. The delicious, masculine lips were definitely moving. She *must* be hearing him aright!

"Daniel, may I present to you my affianced bride?" Camden's words were cool and smooth. He hoped the appellation would at once save the lady's blushes and spare him the necessity of uttering her name.

In the event, it did both. Mr. Pelliat was too stunned at the revelation to inquire any further.

Melinda, it must be said, did not even *think* that the stranger was not possessed of her name or ancestry. She merely blinked in stunned disbelief. The earl grinned at her reaction. He would have to, he could see, kiss her adorable little lips shut again.

Then the world, for both of them, was shattered.

"Your lordship, this cannot be! You are aware—that is, I have explained—that is. . . . My lord, there is no getting around it. I have checked and double-checked. Ethically speaking, your lordship, you are already betrothed."

Miss Melinda St. Jardine felt ready, this time, to swoon in earnest. She teetered a little in the saddle, feeling unaccountably foolish and more than a little humiliated.

When the magnificent man she had *unthinkingly* flung her heart to did not deny the charge, she knew it to be true.

A quick look into his sardonic brown eyes confirmed the fact. Obviously, he had a short memory. She wondered what rosy beauty could proudly count him as hers. It didn't matter. All that mattered was that it was not *her.* He had trifled with her, aroused strange passions in her, and now *she,* at least, would pay the price. She remembered her own arranged betrothal and straightened up with pride.

If she could not have her heart's desire, then at least she would fulfill the terms of her grandfather's will. If it hurt the insufferable man at least a pinprick, it would be worth it. Fury overtook softer reason. She steeled her heart. The marquis would have been proud of her. She owed him *that* much, at least.

No more than a moment had elapsed, but the moment was sufficient. She straightened herself up and announced, in ringing tones that she, too, was similarly circumstanced. With a brief crack of the whip and a curt nod of the head to Pelliat, she galloped across the verdant green grass farther than even the earl's keen eyes could discern. He would have been surprised to learn that keener eyes than his followed the galloping figure long after he had turned in polite but unanimated discussion with the lawyer. Venus, it should be noted, did not blink once.

"Beg pardon?" Vivid eyes blazed in disbelief. The lawyer cleared his throat nervously. "Madam, it is monstrous but I have it on the best authority!"

"And what authority may that be, pray?" Melinda was always at her haughtiest when troubled.

"I was sent the communication through his lordship's own man at law. He is, I assure you, a most eminent colleague. I cannot think that he has not outlined the implications to his lordship."

The elegant grandfather clock chimed the hour, but Melinda hardly heard it. She was regarding her man of law with interest.

"Is he aware of the settlements?"

"I believe he is, Miss St. Jardine."

"Then the man has whistled away a fortune." Her tone was disbelieving.

"In truth he has, but I believe I may account for that, ma'am."

"How so?"

"Lord Santana is one of the wealthiest men in all En-

gland, Miss St. Jardine. He can afford to be . . ." The lawyer cleared his throat awkwardly. He had been about to
make a most miserable blunder.

Miss St. Jardine, astute beyond her years, understood at
once.

"Choosy, you mean?"

The man opened his mouth to think of some wild explanation, then gave it up as hopeless. He nodded.

Melinda stared at him thoughtfully. "May I see the letter?"

Mr. Pendleton shrugged. If the cursedly abrupt missive
would serve to convince her, so be it.

Melinda trembled as she read the note. He was a beast,
this Camden! To write so scathingly of someone he had
never met, to impute the worst of motives to someone he
knew nothing of! When it was *he* who had played for her,
he who had won her!

"Thank you, Mr. Pendleton. I believe you have done all
you can on my behalf. I appreciate your interest in this
matter, but shall now proceed as I feel fit."

The old man nodded in agreement. Better the lass make
other plans for herself than throwing her cap at windmills.
My lord, as everyone knew, was not for sale.

SIX

"I refuse to budge, Jane, until I am bathed in essences of rose oil and lavender."

"And so you shall be, Miss Melinda, so you shall be! You will be wanting to make your curtsy to the new marquis and his bride with every advantage on your side. Mind you, you might just as well bathe in pig swill, for even *then* you shall be at an advantage!"

"What an unkind thing to say, Jane!" Melinda, however, could not suppress a small chuckle at this image, despite her own woes.

"Well it be true, ma'am, and you know I don't hold for roundaboutation! Their lord- and ladyships arrived last night they did and it was not a sovereign dished out to anyone it was! There was Peggy drivin' 'erself 'alf balmy gettin' together a cold collation of Westphalian ham, roast fowl, a seasoned lamb, and a decoction of truffles and new peas, and all scoffed down it was without so much as a common thankee! My lord commented on the burgundy in unfavourable terms, and beggin' yer pardon, ma'am, you know it was only the best for yer grandfather and Cunningham not one to water down the spirits, like, so what the new lord can have agin it I cannot be sayin' and that be fact!"

"Perhaps he is accustomed to the wines of court. He has stopped a long while in Paris, I hear."

"Very likely! Poor Mrs. Darren is in a fair flutter because

she has it of Smithers that my lord intends installing some Frenchified cook in her place!" Jane's bosom heaved in indignation. "Fine thing it be when the Marquis of Fotheringham becomes frogified. I dessay his lor'ship—God rest 'is soul—will turn in 'is grave! Lord Peter was always a wastrel and a ne'er-do-well. Better thing for all of us if Lord 'Enry—your dad—was born the first."

"If he had, like as not he would not have been permitted to marry my mother, Jane! A marquis and a gypsy woman? I think not. As it *was,* the wedding was a nine day's wonder. Have done bemoaning the past. One cannot cry over spilt milk, Jane, and at least *I* have the advantage of a fortune!"

"Be careful, ma'am! I don't believe Lord Peter will let you keep it without a fight."

"He has all that was entailed to him and no choice besides. My grandfather was most specific."

"Which is why he entrusted you to Lord Santana's care. No need to glare at me, ma'am. The truth be the truth and that is all there is to it. It is as plain as a pikestaff the marquis expected some havey-cavey goings-on. As a woman alone you are easier game than as the Countess of Camden. Makes sense like."

"And what if the earl has some *other* chattel in mind for his countess?" Melinda tried to keep the bitterness from her voice, but found the effort taxing.

"Then he is bird witted and undeserving of you! Come, come, Miss Melinda! I have known you only a year but a right pleasure it has been! You have character, me love— you are not the sort to let a little setback get the worst of yer! If me lord wanted you leg shackled to Camden, no doubt 'e was in the rights of it! The man ain't married—see if you can nabble 'im then!"

"Nabble? Nabble? A little distasteful, Jane!" Melinda chewed her lip. Her options were closing in on her. It was time to set aside gypsy ways—ancient nomadic beliefs, spiritual guidance, visions of destiny. The only man she had ever dreamed of was not to be hers.

Well, she would make the man she *was* fated for take

his due. She had been lost in a game of cards—well, the player would collect his earnings. That was the unwritten law in such matters of honour, and at all costs, since her heart was already lost, she would do as Fotheringham bade. Passion for peace. Not an equal swap, perhaps, but it was the duty her birth demanded. Laura Rose demanded it, too.

Besides, the sooner she could escape Lord Peter battening on her for finances the better. Let him *have* Dewhurst Manor. She would be glad to be quit of it under a new master.

But how to change the earl's mind? If he were presented to her in society he would no doubt avoid her like the plague. She set aside the thought that even if he *were* scrupulously polite, *she* would not be able to resist giving him the crushing set down his curt note deserved.

She hardly noticed Jane withdraw from her chamber, leaving a freshly pressed sprig muslin of cornflower blue draped invitingly over the sofa. Her thoughts were elsewhere entirely. By the time she'd collected herself enough to don the gown, darkness had crept in stealthily and the long wax candles needed lighting. In the distance she heard the dinner gong sounding. The marquis and marchioness were no doubt taking up their places.

Miss St. Jardine's head spun with sudden, intoxicating excitement. It was not the rose oil and the lavender that was causing this heady sensation—nor was it the prospect of meeting with her prosy, sadly proper relatives in law. Her pulses were racing because the gypsy in her was rising to the fore.

She had a plan and it would either be her making or her total undoing. The redoubtable Miss St. Jardine would be casting off her silks for a while. Like a chameleon, she was going to slip deliciously into her alter ego, transforming herself from languid mistress to lowly maidservant. The gamble, she knew, was not without risk.

* * *

The third Earl of Camden rather uncharacteristically dropped the sauce bowl. Though a series of minions instantly rectified the matter, the reason for his folly hardly moved. Instead, she clutched convulsively at the dish she was cleaning and stared at the nobleman as if transfixed.

"It is you!" Santana said the words matter-of-factly, but it seemed to him that his entire being was shaken to the core. The serving maid turned inquiring eyes at him. They were blank and unrecognising.

Mistress Farrow laid down the tureen of soup she was preparing for the lackey's disposal upstairs. The shock of seeing his lordship grace his own kitchens was quite oversetting, particularly to one slightly past her prime. She cast a quick look at the new scullery hand and noticed that the excellent Sevres china was perilously close to being crushed against her ribs. The earl was staring at the hired help strangely. Such goings-on in her kitchen!

"Is there ought amiss my lord? The girl came with excellent fine references but if you are not satisfied . . ."

A slow smile crossed Guy Santana's face. He could not make head or tail of what was happening, but he was perfectly certain upon one point. He was satisfied. *Well* satisfied.

"Not at all, Mistress Farrow. I trust your judgment entirely. And what did you say the girl's name was?"

"Dwight, my lord."

"Dwight? Unusual name, that. Set that dish down, Dwight. I do believe it is an heirloom and I shall be very sorry to see it cracked."

The girl cast luminous, disbelieving eyes at his familiar and—yes, she admitted it to herself—beloved features. How could this be? What impossible quirk of fate caused *this* man of all others to be standing in the Earl of Camden's kitchens for all the world as though he owned them?

"I *do* own them."

The words were quietly sardonic and Melinda felt her face flushing at the impertinent, quizzical manner he had stripped bare her thoughts. That he revealed them to her was ominous. Was he challenging her? She thought so, for his eyes were twinkling lightheartedly and there was an air of triumph about him that made her certain he understood her heart, if not her motives.

She had better have a care, for this one was blessed with the gypsy sight, gentleman or no. And how did he come to cross her path in this ridiculous manner? The very man she had firmly forsworn to appear *here* in the place she least expected it. She shivered.

Was destiny a more unfathomable tie than she had given it credit for? Did it refuse to be cheated *so* strongly that the passionate man of her dreams refused to be extinguished by reason and calculated logic?

The Marquis of Fotheringham—her noble grandfather—had wished her to marry my Lord Santana. Though the notion stuck in her gullet, she'd determined to do just that. A sneak preview through the kitchens seemed like an excellent thing, for a man's reputation was often said to hinge more reliably upon what his servants thought than, indeed, upon what all of glittering society thought.

And tonight of all nights, she was to have had her first glimpse of the man who was her intended. Whether she would hold him to his obligation or slip quietly out through the servant's exit was as yet a matter of ignorance. She wanted to bide her time, be canny in her judgments, for though she raged at the brevity and insolence of the note he'd penned to her man of law, he was nevertheless held in *exceptionally* high regard by all who worked for him.

A strange enigma. Melinda licked her lips. She could be reconciled to her fate if the man was kind and generous and not *too* stuffy. She thought of his famed cat and her lips quirked. They would have something in common then, if ever they did finally meet!

"Dwight, be so good as to carry up my tea."

"Me, milor'?" Melinda slipped into her servant's role with ease. She had ever had the gift of languages, so Santana's suspicions were no more confirmed by her lowly accents than by her ugly scullery mobcap. He vowed to get rid of it at the first opportunity, for it was disastrous upon her head and entirely covered the glorious mane of wild jet hair he knew to lie beneath.

Her unedifying accents neither further enlightened him, nor did they deceive him. The shape of her eyes were too distinctive, too intoxicatingly beautiful to be mistaken. Besides, his masculine impulses were not generally aroused by his house staff. In matters of importance, his instincts were unerring. This, he knew with certainty, was a matter of *singular* importance.

One of his lazy smiles played across the length of his lips. The minx was playing May games with his heart. Well, it was *she* who had entered his domain. He might just as well amuse himself, teach her a lesson, and play a few games of his own. That she would be his bride, in the end, was not in contention. He had not burned for her seemingly forever to have his will thwarted now. Whatever she was—hoyden, angel, lady, or gypsy queen—she had a mark about her that proclaimed her his.

A pox on her origins! She would be the next Countess of Camden or there would be no other. She was gaping at him now, her jaw wide open, stupid incredulity in her eyes. He hid a grin, for the situation was more than faintly amusing, especially as Mistress Farrow was regarding him as a man not quite in full possession of his faculties.

"The footmen, my lord . . ."

"What of them?"

"*They* will take up the tray! I daresay Dwight has never seen the inside of a home as splendid as Camden Castle, my lord! She has no livery. . . ."

"Then procure her some!" My lord's tone was unusually autocratic.

Mistress Farrow blinked in bemusement, then nodded doubtfully. "I daresay I could find a few lengths of cambric. . . ."

"Velvet, Mistress Farrow! Black velvet with buttons of silver and laces of emerald green. She shall match Venus, for the shape of her eyes are exactly those of the cat. Had not you noticed?"

Melinda froze in fascinated horror as she was stared at appraisingly by the Camden staff. From the under butler to the lowliest of scrubbing hands, the scrutiny was intense and strangely devoid of amusement. If my lord was mad, his entire staff appeared to be *equally* so. No one so much as *snickered* at his lordship's strange appraisal.

Mistress Farrow, indeed, was relieved to have the resemblance so pointed out. It quite explained, in her mind, his lordship's unusual interest in the third scullery maid. She was too respectable to have anything havey-cavey going on under her roof, but one of my lord's sudden fancies—*that* was different!

If the girl was going to be used as a mascot like Venus, she only hoped she could *stand* the creature. Heaven knew, it had a *villainous* reputation for scratching and hissing. She breathed a sudden sigh. At least *she* wasn't being called upon to look after the beast anymore. Whilst it might rankle that the animal ate *far* too many of her feather-light pastries of salmon and coddled turbot, not to mention its predilection for the finest of her turtle soups, the housekeeper truly bore it no malice.

In truth, she was rather *proud* of Venus, for his lordship's reputation had increased enormously with its quirky introduction to society. The feline was inimitable, too, for when Colonel Marbridge had appeared with a *poodle* upon his lap, he had been laughed out of Lady Jennings's drawing room. A similar fate had occurred to Lady Chichester's canary and Lord Rothbart's sinister fruit-eating bat. *That* had been met with shock and active distaste, with the result that the poor man's invitations to anything other than common squeezes had declined miserably.

And now, by the gleam in her master's eye, Mistress Farrow could only imagine he was up to one of his tricks again. Well, then, *let* him have the scullery maid. Heaven knew, there was plenty *more* lining up at the servant's entrance looking for work.

"In truth, she *does* have cat's eyes, you lor'ship, though the vivid colour is nothing, I'm afeared, like our little Venus's! Still, if it be velvets you be after, I reckon we can rustle up a swatch or two. Your dear mama—"

"Mistress Farrow, I beg you, leave my dear mama out of this!" The earl sighed in resignation. His housekeeper was one of those old retainers *far* too fond of quoting his dear departed parents. Still, they adored him, so there was not much he could do beyond giving them the odd smiling set down when their prattling became tiresome. He could feel the girl's interested eyes upon him and cursed. The last thing he wished to appear to her was a little lad still in leading strings!

His tone became slightly more imperious, slightly more in keeping with the vision of him that she had cherished for a year and a day and longer still.

"You may return to your work, miss. When you are outfitted in more . . . *habitable* garb, you may attend me in the library."

He ignored the faint gasp of outrage and the flashing eyes. It appeared that Dwight had been hoisted by her own petard. If she wished to act the maid, then she'd be treated as one. With a faint nod, his lordship turned his back on her and continued a desultory—if slightly disjointed—conversation with Mistress Farrow.

Having assured himself that the accounts were in order and that the head gardener had been ordered to plant thyme as well as other assorted herbs, he ambled slowly away from the servants' quarters and up several flights. He emerged, at last, at the marble floors and mahogany balustrades that were a more fitting setting for his rank and fortune. He hardly noticed.

He took a stroll through the gallery, through his prodigious art collections, outside through his rose and topiary gardens, to his aviaries, to his stables, and finally, at length, to his library. Anywhere, in fact, except where he fervently wished himself. Back in the warm, clean, heavenly kitchens.

SEVEN

It was perhaps a day later—maybe two—his lordship had quite lost track of the interminable hours of waiting—when there was a timid knock upon the door to his private apartments. Since it was not his valet—*that* individual had long since ceased observing such niceties—he rightly imagined it was Dwight.

Venus leaped from her favourite statue and stood at attention, the hairs upon her sleek jet neck slightly erect as the priceless bracelet glimmered in the filtering afternoon sunlight.

"Careful, Venus." The words were low and warning. "You may sit upon my shoulder, but behave, I beseech you." The cat leaped across two pieces of priceless furniture before settling herself comfortably. She made no sound, not even the faintest of mews, for the moment, had anyone but known it, was one she had been born to.

"Enter!"

The maid entered and she was more beautiful, more magnificent, than anything the earl had ever dreamed of. He had seen her wet, he had seen her wild, but never, in all of his life, had he seen her subdued. Subdued she was as she made the requisite curtsy, then looked full and deep into Guy's mocking eyes. They were not mocking for long, for though her demeanour was calm, the aura emanating from her person was powerful enough to give his lordship pause.

"The velvet suits you."

Melinda clasped at one of the deep green laces and
bobbed yet again. "It should, me lor'. Cost 'alf a year's
wages, it did."

"That trumpery? Then you do not earn enough. I shall
speak to Mistress Farrow directly."

Melinda shot him a puzzled glance. She had expected . . . she knew not what. Half of her had hoped for
some rekindling of their former intimacy, but the other
half would have scorned it, branding him a deplorable
cad. This gentleness and generosity was out of keeping
with anything that had happened between them previously.

"Please, me lor'. Your wages are more than sufficient!
Do you want me to stoke up that fire?"

"Yes, Dwight. I do believe I want you to stoke my fires."
His words were alight with laughter and unashamed innu-
endo. Melinda felt herself reddening uncomfortably. The
full enormity of what she had done was only just sinking
in. Alone with this man in a private chamber, behind
closed doors, masquerading as a maidservant—she was
more than ruined. She was finished.

Something inside her simply did not care. The day's
waiting for her gown had given her ample opportunity to
reflect. By a trick of fate—or was it the inexorable, ines-
capable will of destiny?—her legal betrothed and the un-
named holder of her heart were one and the same man.
Time would tell whether this strange twist was miracle or
bane.

Heavenly hope, hellish despair. The masquerade would
continue until she knew—truly knew—the message of her
heart. If the churlish note he wrote was in keeping with
his prejudiced, toplofty character, she would return to
Laura Rose and her heritage. After him, London society
could and would not offer her anything but emptiness.

If, on the other hand . . . But Miss Melinda would not
allow herself to deal with ifs. She would observe, she would
curtsy, she would kowtow, and she would behave. Only in

this manner would she be afforded a fascinating glimpse into the soul of the man who so recklessly held her life, her desire, her very passions in the tips of his fashionably gloved hands.

"Very good, me lor', and beggin' yer pardon, sir, I am not Dwight, but *Dight*."

"A singularly unusual name. I shall endeavour to remember that, Dight! Rather mannish, I fear, but there, one does not always have the opportunity to select a name for oneself, I suppose."

Melinda looked at him suspiciously. Was he bamming her? Did he realise she'd chosen her serving girl name? How *could* he? Womanlike, she took him up on his previous point.

"It is not mannish, me lor'! It is short for Aphrodite, which, I'll 'ave you know, sir, is the—"

"Goddess of beauty and love. Are you a siren, my dear? Do you *lure* me with your sinister charms only to hurtle me brutally against the rocks? How can you *know* that the classics are one of my abiding interests, that you select such a name—such an apt and perfect name—for yourself?"

There was silence, as Aphrodite—Melinda—or whoever her soul cried out to be—stared at the earl. She wanted to drop all pretence and throw herself in his arms. But that would doom her, for she would never know whether he came willingly, or as a point of lingering honour. He had offered for her once in one persona; he had rejected her once in his other persona. The next time, there would be no turning back, no undoing, no changing destiny's inexorable choice. She would—she must—wait until both were finally certain of the crossing or uncrossing of their mutual paths. Twisting and twining, unravelling or unwinding. There could be no middle path between them, for both, she knew, were creatures of deep and abiding passion.

"Me lor', I don't know 'bout such roundaboutations, just that me name is Dight." She added, softly, as a sad afterthought, that she'd had a pet once who'd shared the unusual name.

"A cat?"

She shot him a vivid glance. He knew then! Her heart danced and she felt the pulses leaping in her throat and along her thin, waiflike wrists. She trembled a little, but acquiesced only with a tiny nod as she fiddled with the tinder box close to the grate.

The eyes of Venus were alert and followed her with silent yearning. Feeling this, she looked up, then put a hand to flushed cheeks.

"Oh!"

"Yes, unusual, is she not? Her name, peculiarly, is Venus. Since you are not tutored in such things, I shall have to explain to you that Venus was the Roman—"

"Goddess of beauty and love." She mouthed the words unthinkingly, for the shock of knowing that it was *Camden* who had purchased her kitten and Camden, too, who had so correctly, intuitively, named her made her forget her masquerade for just a moment.

It was enough. The earl's eyes lit in silent triumph, but his victory did not stop him from playing out the piece allotted to him. He could see the maid's eyes, dizzy with shock, and he allowed a faint pity to wash over his features.

"Allow me." His hands closed over hers momentarily as he deftly lit a flame and allowed it to ignite. He was kneeling now, and she could not help thinking how handsome he looked in his skintight buckskin breeches, snowy coloured and complemented by a dark claret coat of impeccable tailoring. His arm brushed hers and she knew of a certainty that the taut muscles beneath the sleeves were not padded. Nor were his shoulders, for her eyes fell to them quite naturally as she stood up, allowing him to remain kneeling at her feet. It was an awkward, heart-hammering moment.

Unthinkingly, she extended her hand to the cat, still perched upon his shoulder.

"No!" He stood up and the cat sprang to the floor.

Bewildered, Melinda stared at him, openmouthed.

"She scratches. Somehow I do not want you scratched."

"She'll come to me."

"Venus comes to no one but myself. I am her master." His voice rang with sudden, amused pride. Melinda lowered her lashes, for his words sent a strange tremor down her being—one she was not yet ready for him to notice. He could have been speaking of herself, for as surely as she was born with the gift of sight, she knew it to be true. He *was* her master, though she was a wild one and unwilling to be too easily tamed.

"She'll come to me." The voice held a peremptory challenge unbefitting a maid of her station. The earl did not care, for he felt the power of her will. Their eyes locked, but he shook his head slightly.

"She won't, you know. But if you are lonely, my little maid, I shall see about a pet for you."

"I shall have Venus, my lord, or none at all." Her lowly accents were entirely forgotten, for she could not endure the earl's patronising tone.

In a lilting, lyrical whisper, she addressed the most famed creature in all of London, possibly England, likely even the world. "Come here, my sweet, sweet Aphrodite. Come to me, my wondrous, wonderful, enchanted, enchanting creature."

Her voice developed a slight, soothing rhythm that caused the earl to look at her sharply. *Who was* this lady of the mists? There was something about her, something he was missing. . . .

The cat regarded Lord Guy Santana a little too closely. Her emerald eyes blazed at the sharp, aquiline features, the tight jaw, the masculine chin, the familiar shoulder that had been her resting place for more than a year.

Then she purred slightly, and took a flying leap into Melinda's open arms. From there, she allowed her head to be caressed ever so slightly. She regarded the earl with complacency.

"Good God!" He was shocked. "That beast has not left

my sight in all of the time I have had her. What a fickle creature she must be, for I could have sworn she loved me." His eyes were upon the maid when he uttered these words, and again, Melinda felt herself colouring quite unaccountably.

"Come here, Aphrodite."

"Dight will do."

"Pshaw! Dight is for a groom, not for a siren, a gypsy goddess, an unbearable, impossible, willful slip of a thing on a horse! Why did you ride away like that?"

"I do not know what you mean!"

"No? Then perhaps I shall have to remind you. Shut the door, Aphrodite. It is my will."

"But—"

"Do you wish to be turned off without a character? Do as I say." His eyes were once again unfathomable, hard, and unbending as flint. Melinda took several judicious paces backward and closed the heavy oak door. There was a long silence between them, as the earl surveyed that which had haunted his dreams it seemed a lifetime at least. The black cat, blazing emeralds and shimmering diamonds, nestled serenely into the soft, velvet shoulder of the square-cut gown. Black on black. Green laces matched cat's eyes, but other than the defiant sparkle in the maid's *own* eyes, the shimmer of diamonds was missing.

"The outfit is fitting for your position, Aphrodite. Call it a whim, call it a fancy, call it my will. You shall be a scullery maid no longer, for I elevate you to the position of . . . No, I shan't say vixen. I should like to say kitten, but that is too tame. Forge the position yourself, my dear, but see that your livery is complete. Come here, for I have the final trim."

His tone brooked no argument, so Melinda nodded briskly and waited. She supposed he would have a new mobcap or some such thing, though Mistress Farrow had been extremely thoughtful and sewn up the velvet one that now graced her head. Again, the glory of her locks was hidden, but this fact did not concern her. Vanity had never had much place in Miss Melinda St. Jardine's sentiments. She had always simply lived by the heart.

"Close your eyes."

She hesitated, but the tone was so peremptory, she shut them quickly. Besides, she could feel him draw closer and her breathing had quickened far too greatly to put up much rational argument. Warm hands glanced across her neck, brushing aside slight strands of silken hair. He'd taken off his gloves then, for no material marred the extreme tactile sensation that coursed through her taut, expectant nerves.

Something brushed against her shoulder, soft as a butterfly's wings. My God! Could it be? But when she turned, his hands pushed her back and she realised she must have only *imagined* his lips upon naked flesh, the velvet sleeves momentarily pushed back. It seemed like an age before the silence was broken and she felt something icy pass across her throat.

Her eyes flashed open to reveal, in the glass he'd conveniently provided for her, a choker of exquisite gems around her neck. The replica of Venus's bracelet, only with some deep amethysts embedded in the sides, crisscrossing the emeralds and complementing fully the deep sparkle of diamonds.

"Your eyes are violet. I had the amethysts set the day after our encounter in the park."

Melinda did not pretend to misunderstand him.

"You are betrothed, my lord!"

"I am not. I assure you, I dealt with the matter firmly and readily. It was a simple case of encroachment from some nobody relative of an aging nobleman. It had no significance, I assure you, for I have not even *met* the wench!"

"Perhaps you should have." It was all suddenly making sense and Melinda's heart was soaring. The curt note he'd sent was *not* the result of arrogance, a calculated slight. It was proof that his heart was engaged elsewhere, with her . . . with his gypsy queen. She could not complain or blame him, for how could he possibly guess that Miss Melinda St. Jardine was one and the same as the heathen and spirited woman he'd met damp and bedraggled that fateful night?

He had saved her reputation by offering her marriage—he would not have done that were there not some depth of feeling, some bond of intimacy. The earl—as she knew by his reputation and by the shattering letter he had written to her in that other guise—was too canny for that.

The web was unravelling swiftly, far more satisfactorily than ever she could have imagined.

"I cannot take this gift, my lord!"

"Why ever not?"

"A lady does not accept anything above trinkets from a gentleman, my lord. Even *you* must be aware of that!"

"It is fortunate then that you are no lady—just plain Dight, my servant."

The voice was a challenge, for Guy, despite his growing obsession, was hurt that the lady had still not given him the gift of her true name.

"I wish it were that simple, my lord, but life weaves strange twists and fancies. I think you know that I *am* a lady despite this disgraceful charade."

"Disgraceful? I have never been so intrigued in my life! For one glorious evening, my goddess, let us just pretend. You *are* my maid and you shall wear my bond. A garland of emeralds for my servant and my gypsy queen."

"My lord, I shall never be your servant, though if you let me, I shall be your willing slave. Destiny decrees it."

There was something powerful, prophetic, and slightly unreal in the quality of her conviction. Guy—who was longing to take her in his arms and kiss away all talk, all tears, all challenge, all mystery—was struck.

"There is more to you than I know."

She nodded, then moved hesitatingly toward him.

His embrace was crushing, not at all the tender, soft caress she had been half expecting, half dreaming of, half yearning for.

It was wild and hungry and relentless. It engulfed her, tasted her, tried her until English reason transformed, once more, to deep, fierce, unearthly Romany passion. She felt the lightning and the rain and the storm swirl about her once more. She tasted the water and the moonlight and the salt of her tears, but in truth they had not moved beyond the portals of the cosy library with its warm, flickering fire and the cool, solid oak door.

"I must stop!"

It was the third Earl of Camden who finally came to his senses. It was not an easy thing to do and it entailed an inordinate amount of cursing, convincing, temptation, resilience, and ultimate self-sacrifice, but at last it was done.

Melinda, baulked of her heart's delight, *loathed* the elegant cravat that was being neatly retied by deft, unthinking hands. She hated fingers that gently laced her bodice once more and set to rights the profusion of silver buttons that had somehow mangled themselves on her gown.

She blinked, confused, as her passions slowly abated and she transformed once more into the proper miss—though not the maid—of a few long moments before.

"I shall have to leave, my lord."

Santana nodded wistfully, but nor for long. "You shall be my bride this time if I have to drag you to the altar!"

Violet eyes regarded him steadily. "I cannot marry you until you have closed a chapter in your life, my lord."

"Which one?"

"The one in which you dismiss a young girl whom you have never so much as *met* as an adventuress and an encroacher. I expect—shall always expect—better of you, sir!"

"What do you mean?"

"Think on it, my lord, and when you do, I shall come."

"Wait!"

The earl dived for the door as soon as he divined the girl's intention. He was too late. It slammed firmly in his face, and when his bemused anger abated slightly, he nodded slowly and sighed. He was not to be trusted with her on a night like this. It was several hours later that he realised that Venus, too, was gone.

EIGHT

Dight—or Dwight, as she was still referred to in the kitchens—did not appear for service the following morning. The earl had dreaded this scenario, but half expected it, so he was able to peel an orange equably and even welcome Lord Broadhurst into his home with relative calm.

A tedious morning passed entertaining the man, who had a tiresome predilection for game hunting and would not rest until he had bagged several grouse, a pheasant, and some large, plump ducks off the earl's estate. Be that as it may, Santana was able to retain his reputation for gracious civility to his peers, though his nerves were jagged and his muscles taut from a restless, sleepless, yet nonetheless dream-filled night.

He missed the girl, he missed his cat, and he missed his composure. By the third day, he was more than a trifle out of sorts and even his loyal staff came in for some of the brunt of his moodiness. They exchanged significant glances with each other and would have been surprised to learn how close their conjecture came to the truth. The disappearance of Dight seemed causally linked to my lord's ailment. A few discreet inquiries revealed that the girl had literally disappeared into thin air. She had not taken service with any of the great households, nor were her name and references listed upon the employment registers.

Gareth, the butler, pronounced it a puzzle and Mistress

Farrow, though not quite liking to gossip with the lower servants, declared it to be a regular bumble bath.

Guy Santana, having first obtained a special licence, went over and over her words in his mind. Since he was neither dim-witted nor obtuse, her meaning finally, on the second day of his misery, became apparent. He was just penning a polite, conciliatory, and utterly pointless letter to Miss St. Jardine when he received a gilt-edged invitation from Lord Peter Fotheringham, the new marquis. Miss St. Jardine's uncle, by all that was holy! No mention was made of the lady herself, but the earl suspected strongly that her presence would be required. Further, he suspected he was once more being cunningly lured into parson's trap, but *this* danger he was able to blithely dismiss.

Miss St. Jardine could be a diamond of the first water, for all he cared. His sentiments were allied elsewhere. Accordingly, he tore up the letter he had been penning to the lady's man of law—a direct letter from himself would have been unthinkable—and sifted the invitation from the *regrets etc.* pile to the *gratefully accept* one.

Donning an elegant evening coat shot with azure silk and encrusted with several shimmering pieces his valet had decreed quite quintessential, his lordship set off for Dewhurst Manor in a delightful barouche, lightheartedly painted canary yellow and sporting a sky blue trim. He wondered whether the gypsy queen would appreciate the merry colouring and thought she would, making a mental note to acquire squabs of crimson, a bright memory of that first, storm-swept night, so very long ago.

Even as he was announced, he was scanning the ballroom for some young lady not previously introduced to his acquaintance. There were not many who fitted into that category, for any matchmaking mama worth her salt almost *instantly* introduced her daughters to his attention just as soon as they were out. There . . . in the far corner. He nodded in satisfaction.

A comely girl, not plain exactly, but with none of the enlivening vivacity of the rest of the debutantes about her.

Doomed to be a wallflower, he surmised. Well, if he had to face up to his task, then face up to it he would. He squared his shoulders, then made his way unhesitatingly toward the lady in question. "Miss St. Jardine?" She nodded mutely—unhappily, he thought.

For the first time, he experienced a stab of remorse at the callous way he had handled the whole matter. He was just wondering how to broach the topic when the waltz struck up.

"Would you care for a turn?" He smiled at her kindly.

"We are not yet introduced, sir!"

"Then I shall take an enormous liberty and tell you my name. I am Lord Santana and I believe I have wronged you, though I swear I never had that intention."

"You mistake the matter, sir!"

"Not at all! I was rude and overbearing and impossibly high in the instep. Will you forgive me?"

The lady nodded. "I did feel, when you ignored me and left me to sit out the dance that night, that you were a trifle stiff. But, sir, I assure you, that does not signify!"

"Beg pardon?" This time, Santana was confused.

"And now, my lord, I really must depart. My betrothed is fetching me a glass of orgeat, you see."

The words were so confiding that Santana could detect no guile. Nor could he fathom the meaning of the encounter that had just taken place. The young lady was evidently not repining for him, nor did it appear she knew *anything* of the arrangement that had seemed destined to unite them forever.

Whilst he was greatly relieved to find her heart whole— he would have been mortified to have inflicted unwitting pain and expectations—he nevertheless remained supremely puzzled.

The dancers twisted and swayed gracefully before him, but, as usual he demonstrated no interest. It was not until he heard tinkling laughter behind him that his lithe body moved swiftly into action. He knew that laugh anywhere, and by God, she would not slip so easily from his grasp this time!

His keen eyes searched in the shimmering half-light, for the flickering flames illuminating the manor were prodigious and sparkled like thousands of diamonds in their crystal holders. Colour upon colour, velvets and muslins and satins and organdie . . . He could not find the elusive woman who tantalised him, provoked him, teased him, then invariably disappeared.

Tonight would be different. He fingered the special license firmly. He had done his duty. He had made amends to Miss St. Jardine—though heaven knew, she apparently had no use for them—and now he would claim his prize. How right he had been to attend this evening! In his wildest imagination, he had not sought to find her here. But why not? She was a lady born—that was obvious. This was her milieu . . . or was it?

The uncomfortable notion that he was missing something crept back into his mind. Strange to see Lord Peter Fotheringham, stiff as a ramrod, greeting guests his father would never have dreamed of receiving into his home. The old man now. Santana smiled momentarily at the encounter. Cunning old soul! And he had ceded him Venus, for which he was forever indebted. The story of Laura Rose flitted into his mind. Suddenly the final piece in the puzzle fell into place.

For a quiet moment, his lordship stood stock-still in astonishment. "Then who . . ." He hardly realised he was talking aloud.

"*That* Miss St. Jardine was my cousin, my lord."

And there she was, in the finest, most figure-hugging gown he could ever have imagined, skirts damped down atrociously, laughing eyes, shining, long, lustrous hair, pert red lips adorably, entrancingly inviting and a collar of diamonds he would have recognised anywhere, for laced through the glitter were emeralds and cabochon amethysts of the finest stare. Upon her shoulder was a cat, who smirked and licked her lips and looked, for all the world, as though she had just eaten a turbot of beef—which, in fact, the spoilt little rascal probably *had*.

"You have led me a fine song and dance, Miss St. Jardine!"

"*Have* I, my lord? How terribly provoking, for truly, my dear, *dear* sir, I do not believe I can recollect ever having been introduced!"

"Can you not?" The tone was wry, but nevertheless caused the lady to blush quite delightfully and declare the evening a trifle *warm*.

"Not as warm as it is going to get, Miss St. Jardine!"

Was that a threat? She opened her eyes widely. "I repeat, my lord, that we are not yet introduced! I am a rather timid soul and insist on observing the niceties!"

"*Do* you now?" The earl chuckled. Now that he had found her, he was jolly well going to enjoy her.

"Indeed I do. If you do not this moment tell me who you are, I very much fear I shall have to return to my chaperon!"

"Chaperon?"

She made a hideous face. "The Marchioness of Fotheringham. Preserve me, by all that is holy!"

"I see that the matter constitutes an emergency, my little princess. I shall have to put you out of your misery, after all, and ensure you are properly introduced."

She grinned. "Very well, my lord! I am Miss Melinda St. Jardine."

"Melinda." The word rolled delightfully off his tongue. Still, he thought Aphrodite might, after all, be more appropriate.

"And you, my lord?" she prompted. "*Who*, if I may make so bold, are *you*?"

"I, my very dear, *impossibly* high-handed love, am something you recognised a long time ago. I, Guy Santana, third Earl of Camden, am your destiny."

There was a speaking stillness in which all the world stopped and all the dancers froze in their entrechats and quadrilles. Her lips parted, all hint of teasing erased from her expressive features.

"And why have you come?" The words were almost a whisper.

"You should know! I have come to do as I have promised." She caught the humour in his rakish features and relaxed, allowing her buoyant spirits to return. Fluttering long dark lashes more than a trifle flirtatiously, she challenged him saucily.

"Threatened, you mean?"

He nodded. "Indeed so, ma'am. Come with me and I promise you you shall either be thoroughly spanked or dragged to the altar as you deserve."

"Dragged to the altar if you please!"

"Come along then! I have a special licence burning a whole in my pocket."

"Now?"

"Now! You shall not slip from my grasp again, you little witch of the woods!"

"I shall get my muff."

"Very well. And bring Venus."

"Aphrodite."

"Venus."

They were still arguing as wedding bells pealed above their heads. It was the first time the Archbishop of Camden had performed the ceremony at such an hour, but he insisted, once he had stopped yawning and pulled the nightcap from his head, that the thing be done in style.

Thus it was that in the very early hours of St. Agnes's Eve, the countryside came alive with sound. As the last bells stopped chiming, the Earl and Countess of Camden stepped into their chaise. The dawn was crisp and frosty, quiet blankets of white enveloping the waiting countryside. Melinda wondered whether her grandfather, wherever he was, could witness the outcome of his carefully laid plans, the final payment of the wager he had lost with such cunning equanimity.

In the renewed stillness, she could almost *see* his wry

expression when he had rid himself, finally, of her cat. "The spirits work in strange ways," he'd said.

Well, perhaps, after all, he had been right. He always *had* had an instinct. And Laura Rose? She, too, had been correct. Melinda had never experienced passion as intense as she did now. She looked at Guy, all trace of mischief miraculously wiped from her lovely countenance.

He caught her mood and drew her to him. As he was lightly stroking her cheek with one gentle, ungloved finger, they noticed the lights. Endless rows of merry lanterns and the slow first strum of a lute. Then a drumroll, then a Spanish guitar, then a banjo . . . The dawn was coming alive with sound.

Melinda gasped. "Of course! It is St. Agnes's Eve!" And there, smiling brightly, was Laura Rose, grass green handkerchief in one hand, age-old castanet in the other. She drew her arm up in bright salute, but her eyes were wet with tears.

Melinda ordered the carriage stopped, but her mother frowned and waved her on. There were always *other* St. Agnes's Eves, *other* times when perhaps bonny little Melindas and tiny Lord Santanas could be brought for her to dandle.

The canary-coloured carriage with its delightful sky blue fittings drove on. A quiet peace descended on the couple, who took a long, still moment to thank the gods—and, more particularly, the goddesses.

Guy drew Melinda close up to him. She could feel his knees, encased in the most splendid of doeskins, creep up close to her own. Her dampened skirts did not save her from feeling impossibly warm as his hands crept to the figure-hugging dress and moulded suggestively to the most intimate of her curves. Melinda did not waste her breath in modest complaint. Instead, she moved forward so that my lord was permitted an even greater view of her expansive charms than he had previously been afforded. She chuckled at his sharp intake of breath, then smiled in a wanton, if slightly sleepy parody of the gypsy queen he had first encountered.

My lord would have been less than human had he not responded in an appropriate manner. Lazily but quite deliberately, he allowed the curtains of the little carriage to drop.

And Venus? She curled up snugly on a crimson squab. It is to be hoped that she then closed her eyes, for the occurrences that transpired within could *not*, sadly, be described as anything but highly delightful and dreadfully, *dreadfully* improper.

More Zebra Regency Romances